The Man Who Died Twice

The Man Who Died Twice

A Novel About Hollywood's Most Baffling Murder

by
Samuel A. Peeples

Academy
Chicago
Publishers

Published in 1984 by
Academy Chicago, Publishers
425 N. Michigan Ave.
Chicago, IL 60611

Printed and bound in the USA

Library of Congress Cataloging in Publication Data

Peeples, Samuel A. (Samuel Anthony), 1917–
        The man who died twice.

        Reprint. Originally published: New York: Putnam, 1976.

        1.   Taylor, William Desmond, 1877–1922—Fiction.
        I.   Title.
[PS3531.E286M3   1984]   813'.54   84-12498
ISBN 0-89733-121-4 (pbk.)

For
FRANK PRICE

NOTE

This novel has been written as an adventure in time. It is based entirely upon what is probably the most famous American murder mystery of all, the unsolved shooting of William Desmond Taylor in Hollywood, in 1922. The case involved many, if not most, of the famous stars and personalities of the day, who knew Taylor intimately. He was a man of mystery, and the puzzle of his death seems the only fitting way for his life to end, never resolved, and still intriguing after more than half a century has passed.

The basic facts of the story are substantiated by research that has been the author's personal hobby for more than twenty years, and some never before revealed factual incidents are included—such as the mysterious last telephone call Taylor made, which has often been considered a vital clue to the murderer by crime writers, but turns out to have actually been made to his—naturally!—female tax consultant. However, conclusions drawn are solely the long-held convictions of the writer, and not necessarily valid truths.

With only three exceptions, all the characters herein are real-life, historical personages, and they are represented exactly as they were actually known by William Desmond Taylor. The locales, buildings, automobiles, streetcars, and every minute bit of background detail, newspapers, comic strips, orchestras, and leaders—and every song mentioned, every theatrical and movie attraction concerned, are precisely as they were in Los Angeles that last week of January, 1922. It has been the author's intent to take the reader on a totally realistic step backward in time, to a yesterday that seems far better in retrospect, sometimes, than it really was.

Our memories—yes, our very lives—are made up of day-to-day trivia, of all the things that surround us, that we use, and accept as our personal reality. But, while people never change, being driven by the same passions and cares always, the everyday fabric of our existence is constantly undergoing change, and not always for the better. The contrast brought about by the changes in daily life patterns is a basic part of this story.

As for the solution to the mystery of William Desmond Taylor's murder that is postulated here—it is entirely fictional, although it represents an actual possibility.

SAMUEL A. PEEPLES

The Man Who Died Twice

I

A shadow figure moved between two buildings, and my foot lifted from the accelerator and touched the brake pedal. It was a reflex action; you pull enough night duty, and it goes with the job. Beside me, in the unmarked car, Mort Jacobs turned to look.

"See something?"

"Not sure."

But I pulled into the curb a couple of buildings farther west on Hollywood Boulevard, and shut off the lights. In the rearview mirror I watched the street. It was as empty as it ever gets, and the rain earlier still glistened in pools. Even the grubby inlaid stars in the sidewalk would look better for it in the morning. I was about ready to chalk up the shadow to nerves when I saw it again, moving fast, away from us, east on the boulevard.

There's a superstition that cops develop a sort of hunch facility that tells them when things are about to fall apart, and I suppose it's a sort of reassurance at rough moments, but the truth is, I felt nothing of the sort. Just doing the job. I've thought about it a lot, gone over and over it, and have yet to come up with anything that made sense. It was a night like a few thousand others. We'd taken our Code Seven at midnight, and I'd eaten ham and eggs, nothing to keep me awake when I finally hit the sack. I didn't even have anything much on my mind. But that was customary nowadays. My personal troubles, including money and sex, had ended with my marriage, three years before. Not my sex life, my sex troubles, since whatever May and I had had going once upon a time had soured. Since we'd split up, I'd had three or four affairs, all mutually just fun and games. Funny, but in a way I missed the problems, or maybe the serious meaning they held. I don't know. But it wasn't bothering me, at least not consciously. Sure, I'd thought about getting older, and being alone too much, but I hadn't worked myself up to doing anything much about it. You know, one of these days I'd find the right girl and pick up the pieces. One of these days. Sure.

I nodded to Jacobs, who grabbed the microphone to report our stop, and got out of the car. I could hear footsteps, running feet slapping against wet concrete, and took out after them. Not much chance of catching up with the bastard, and I wasn't sure that I wanted to catch him; but some things you don't think about, you just do, and besides, I needed the exercise. At forty-five it's too damned easy to put on a pot, and I'd been fighting it—with just moderate success—for ten years.

The air felt clean and moist, but it was cold, colder than I remembered even the tag end of January being, and my breath made white mist that whipped away as I ran. After half a block I was puffing a bit, but not badly, and that made me feel good. Ahead of me, a man's figure flickered in front of the lights of an oncoming car, then vanished. I slowed, fast, and pinned my badge on the lapel of my jacket, then pulled my .38. There was a gap between two buildings, a sort of arcade, with stores lining both sides, cheap junky places catering to the street kids as well as tourists. I poked my head around the corner of the bookstore in front and saw nothing. Two or three naked bulbs burned in the arcade, each one with a nimbus of thin mist around it. The junky storefronts were dark.

It was a cul-de-sac and the shadow I'd chased had made a mistake; there was no way out except past me. I heard brakes squeal behind me, and footsteps pounding up, and then I made the damnfool mistake of going in. I knew better; every cop does.

Following rules kept you alive, and sometimes they were all that did. Break them, and you could pay the consequences.

I walked straight in, no alarm bells clanging in my head, no premonition, nothing. I remember thinking again just how damned, miserable cold it was—then suddenly cursing myself for a damned fool. The shadowy figure moved in front of me. I started to yell *"Freeze! Police!"*—then his arm jerked up and I saw the gun in his fist. I tried to beat him to the shot. I didn't. Even then I felt nothing; this might be it for me, Ernie Carter, but I felt no violent emotion, just sudden, fast self-anger. Then blinding red flame exploded, and a jarring impact. I was slammed straight back as if I'd caught a sledgehammer in the face. Numbness, bright crimson flash, that was all. A sense of falling, of tumbling from a height; I was thinking it was taking a hell of a long time to hit the ground, then nothing.

2

My knees hit the concrete, hard, and the brightness faded. The ensuing blank darkness began to assume recognizable proportions again. Just the same, something had changed, drastically, but damned if I could figure out what. My mind wasn't working right; I could see things clearly, understand what I saw, but I felt dazed, incapable of adding it all together. So, for the moment, I took it all in, breathing a little hard, aware of the biting cold, feeling the icy hardness of the sidewalk against my knees. I felt someone brushing past me, running away, then a man yelled something behind me. He thudded up, lumbering heavily, the hurrying costing him some effort. My knees were bruised and numb, but my legs felt shaky, so I just knelt there, letting it happen. A very fat man ran past me, puffing hard, then slowed and came back toward me.

The street was darker than I remembered it. I raised my head to look around, too dazed to pick out details. Everything seemed to blur and run together. I felt my forehead; there was a lump there, and it was tender to the touch. But the skin wasn't broken. Damn, what was going on? I'd been shot—or had I? No blood, just the throbbing ache in my head, and the ugly swelling. The fat man came back and stood there. His face was round and beefy, and he was wearing a cop's uniform—one that looked damned odd, although I couldn't figure out at the moment just why. For a minute he seemed ludicrously all belly, for it bulged out grotesquely in front of him. He was carrying a long nightstick in one pudgy hand, and now let it drop to dangle from a heavy cord about his thick wrist.

"You okay, mister?" the cop asked.

I shook my head. It was clearing, but things remained blurred, a little muddled, like a TV set badly out of focus. "I—I think so," I answered, slowly. I made an effort to get up, and he gripped my elbow, helped me to my feet.

"Must've used a sap on you—you got an awful wallop on the head, looks like." His massive red features slowly came into focus. "You sure you're not hurt?"

I felt stronger; the dizziness was passing, leaving just the numbness in my mind. "All in one piece. Yell for my partner, Jacobs, will you?"

The big cop looked puzzled. He glanced around, down the empty street. I followed his look. The streetlamps burned dim and yellow, each with a faint aura of haze around it, doing little to dispel the darkness.

"Nobody around but you—and the lug that tried to roll you, mister," the cop said, slowly. "Maybe you're hurt worse than you think you are."

I forced a smile and shook my head. "I'm okay," I insisted. "That knock on the head must have confused me."

"The lousy punks, ñow they're even workin' clear out here to hell an' gone in the sticks!"

But I wasn't listening. For the moment nothing was making any sense, but it would pass, I was sure of it. Across the street, a fence fronted some building construction. A fancy façade was going up behind the fence. There was a sign lettered on the boards of the fence, only vaguely visible in the dim yellow streetlamp light. It read:

SID GRAUMAN'S EGYPTIAN . . .

I couldn't read the rest, since it was in shadow, but below it was an announcement in smaller lettering:

And that was just plain crazy. I felt suddenly dizzy, and must have swayed, for the big cop gripped my arm, hard. I shook my head to clear it, and the moment passed.

I looked away from the building theater, which must be some sort of joke, or a fancy movie-set. A line of car tracks ran down the middle of the wide street. And my guess about it being a movie location was borne out by a half-dozen old, high-backed cars parked at the curb, and they were scattered, strung along the length of the street, looking forlorn and ugly. There was no sign of Jacobs, or of the unmarked car we'd been riding in; just the fat cop and me. Far down the street a streetcar rocked along the tracks toward us, and I could hear the jangling of its bell, muffled by the haze hanging in between.

Nothing connected up. I shook my head again, trying to clear away the cobwebs that made thinking difficult. I began to feel uneasy, queasy to my stomach, and my legs started trembling again. The big cop's grip on my arm is all that kept me on my feet.

"There's a callbox down the block," he said. "I'll get you some help."

With an effort I straightened up, and felt better for making the try. "No, I'm fine," I said. "Just a little dazed, I think. Nothing serious." He looked closer into my face and suddenly grinned.

"Hell, that rotgut hooch'll do it every time," he boomed cheerfully. "Sleep it off an' you'll be okay. That bootleg stuff is lethal enough—without some stickup artist tryin' to bat your brains out, too!" He looked up the street again and shook his head. "I'll catch the bastard sooner or later. He ain't gettin' away with pullin' a heist on my beat!"

The funny thing is, I took it all in, the words, the street— everything—and nothing connected up in my head. It was no more than another part of the sense of disorientation that kept me in its grip. So I just nodded, and stood there, letting the cold night air chill me.

The streetcar came down the boulevard, swaying and rocking, beginning to slow down. Behind it a car came up, swung around, and thundered past, its yellow headlights flashing and its single round red taillight winking farewell behind it. The boxlike shape of the car made me frown. Something was damned wrong; no, *everything* was wrong. The cars, the street, even the incredibly fat cop walking a beat that hadn't been walked since . . . The thought faded. I tried to make it stay, and clarify itself, but had no luck. *Where the hell were the fancy stars set in the sidewalk?*

"You live around here, mister?" the cop asked.

"No, on Alvarado Street," I said—and then froze. I lived out in the Valley. I'd never been on Alvarado Street longer than to drive down it a block or two in my life.

"You got a car?"

"Yes. No. I mean, I don't know." My mind went blank again, receiving information but not correlating it.

"Look, mister, why don't I see you on that streetcar? It goes down Western—you can walk over to Alvarado from there. Okay?"

I didn't say anything, because I couldn't think of the words. Did you ever see a series of strobe pictures? They can show a jerky kind of continuity when flashed in succession. It was like that, now. Not a smooth flow of action like a movie film, but a series of flashes, each one recording progression. We walked down the street. The streetcar—*streetcar!* For an instant it hit me hard, and then I couldn't figure out why it had—had stopped two blocks down the street, near where Grauman's—I still think of it like that, although it's been Mann's Chinese Theater for years—should be, only it wasn't there. Just a stretch of empty, weed-grown lots, not even sidewalks or curbs there. For an instant I felt a pang of remorse, of sharp loss, then it faded. It was the end of the streetcar line, with a switchback track. The motorman was tugging down the front trolley-arm, hooking it down, as the rope rumbled into its recoil housing. I found myself staring at it as we approached. I'd never seen one up close before—what the hell was I thinking about? Of course I'd seen a streetcar before—every day! It seemed very small. Nowhere near the size of a Freeway Flyer. *A what?* Confusion made me blink and stumble, almost fall, but the big cop caught my arm again and gave me a reassuring smile.

The motorman had walked to the rear end of the little yellow and red car, and was raising the back trolley-arm, seating the flanged copper wheel at the end of it onto the overhead wire. The conductor was walking through the lighted interior, reversing the wicker-back seats. Both of the streetcarmen wore dark uniforms, and odd, small-billed caps. The cloth of their uniforms and caps was blue serge wool, shiny from wear and pressing, and the bills of their caps were of hard leather, cracked and distorted. The motorman looped the rope dangling down from the trolley-arm over a stanchion at the rear of the car, and now came up. He was tugging a small white cloth sack from his breast pocket, peeled off a flimsy brown cigarette paper, and used his teeth to open the sack. The bastard was building a stick of grass right in front of the cop! I stared at him, trying to fish up words, but he finished the cigarette, licked the edge of the paper, then used a thumbnail to ignite a huge wooden match. The smoke was clean, pungent, and just tobacco. Bull Durham—*Jesus!* Nobody smoked it, not anymore!

"Feller here got rolled," the cop said. "Drop him off at Sixth, huh? Says he lives on Alvarado. Okay?"

The motorman grinned. "Sure." He looked at me. "You all right, bub?"

"Fine," I said.

"He's totin' a full load o' bathtub gin," the cop said.

"Wouldn't mind a snort to warm me up, myself," the motorman replied. "Didja ever see it so damn cold?"

"Think what it's like back East," the cop said. He waved a hamlike hand at me and then walked away. His backside wobbled under the long skirt of his coat. He was too damned fat to be a cop, I thought—and then found myself smiling, and thinking, "Hell, all cops are fat!" I must have said it out loud, for the motorman grinned and clapped me on the shoulder.

"That's right, brother," he said. "Now climb aboard." He grinned up at the conductor. "Let him off at Sixth, Charley." The conductor reached down and gave me a helpful yank upward. The first step was high, but I made it. The motorman walked back to the front of the car. There was a farebox on a pole; I dug into a pocket, found some change, and held it out. The conductor picked out two coins, dropped them into the box, then rotated a handle, like a grinder, and the coins dropped through the brass compartment. He took them out of a hinged-flap receptacle on the bottom of the farebox and dropped them into the money changer hanging on his belt.

"Hey, I thought you guys didn't carry any cash with you anymore," I said.

The conductor gave me a funny look. "Since when?"

I had no answer, and didn't even know why I'd said what I had. The little streetcar jerked into motion, wheels screeching along the switchback to the other set of tracks. I swayed and nearly went down, but grabbed a pole and held myself up. The conductor shook his head.

"Really got yourself a snootful," he said. I found myself nodding and smiling at him; then I got the swaying rhythm of the car, and chanced moving forward to a seat. It was warmer in the car; there were heaters under the windows. I flopped into a seat. I saw myself reflected in the window. I saw *somebody* reflected in the window. Funny-looking pinched-in suit and high-buttoned vest. Round white collar—Christ, it was shiny, like it was made of celluloid. I felt it; it *was* celluloid! A fuzzy-looking, shapeless green hat, the brim turned down in front. I took it off and stared. The lean face was unfamiliar; the hair was curly, not straight—and almost white, not gray-black. It was a stranger's face. Shock hit me, then faded. I looked at my reflection and smiled. *Still a looker*, I thought, *not bad for forty-five. You're going to last a long, long time, Bill, my boy!* And then caught myself. Bill? Hell, my name was Ernie—Ernie Carter. *Who the hell is Ernie Carter? My name is Bill Taylor, for Chrissakes! What kind of booze was I lapping up, anyway?*

The sharp thoughts started slipping away. Everything got fuzzy again. I let it go. Every time I tried to put all the pieces together, they started sliding out of my grip.

3

I watched the dark streets for a while. I recognized nothing. There seemed too few buildings and too many vacant lots—bean fields? Most of the buildings were frame bungalows, fronted with yellowed lawns and scruffy, ragged palm trees. We passed a section with imposing old gingerbread-decorated mansions—on Hollywood Boulevard? I felt a faint, disturbing puzzlement. Then it started to rain again, and we made a turn, the little streetcar seeming to move in a vague universe of its own, the misted windows reflecting the row of needle-pointed bulbs burning yellowly overhead. Needle-pointed bulbs? Blurred thoughts, obscure doubts, a faint uneasiness, none of them important. I closed my eyes. Riding a streetcar was an oddly pleasant experience; the clickety-clicking wheels over the rails, the groaning of the wooden coach, the rattle of the wicker-covered seats, all blended into one coherent sound, a streetcar sound that was absolutely strange—and very familiar to me at the same time. The heaters threw out warmth, and there was a comforting musty smell that pervaded everything. At a street intersection, the motorman, hidden behind the flapping green curtain he had drawn down behind him, stamped one foot to set a bell a-clanging; yellowish automobile headlights flashed, and a Klaxon horn blared. Klaxon horn?

I must have slept, for I awoke with a start at the clutch of a hand on my shoulder. It was the conductor, shaking me.

"Sixth Street," he said loudly.

The airbrakes were hissing, and the car slowed. The front sliding door clattered open and I got up. My legs were steady beneath me, and I felt vaguely better. I made my way down the aisle and climbed down from the streetcar. I stood there, the rain wetting my face, as the little streetcar moved off, down the dark street. There was a dangling overhead streetlamp that had lost its flickering battle with the dark night. I was getting soaked, and I didn't know where the hell I was, nor where I was going. I thought: "I should've asked the conductor where—what was the name of that damned street?"

Then, suddenly, *I knew*. Just like that. I knew. I was at Sixth and Western. Alvarado was just east, not far. I'd walked it a thousand times, when I didn't have my car at the studio with me. At what studio? Blank. Every time I tried to knit it all together, nothing. To hell with it. I let myself sink away, deliberately not thinking—and almost instantly started walking, exactly as if I knew where I was going. I bent the wet brim of the fuzzy green hat down to keep the misting rain from my face, and walked east. Flicker, another strobelike jump in the time sequence; flicker—another. I'd turned left—north—on another street, which I somehow knew was Alvarado. My sense of elapsing time was erratic, passing in quick-cut little jumps. Ahead of me I saw a big apartment-court, of the type that hasn't been built in forty years, with red-tiled roofs, and red-brick walks, and even a stucco-and-Spanish-tile fountain-pool in the center. *Home.* The word came into my mind, and at the same time I knew damned well I'd never seen the place before in my life. Just the same, I found myself turning in, going up the two or three red-brick steps to the courtyard, and bearing left. Second bungalow in—on the north side of the court. The back of the two-story separate bungalows probably faced the next cross-street. The second—center—bungalow was a duplex arrangement, with two small, separate front porches and glass-fronted doors.

The styling was 1920s fake-Spanish, but the buildings—the

whole court—looked new and expensive. Most of the windows facing the courtyard were dark, lace curtains dimly gleaming behind them. Only one porchlight burned—the same oddly dull-yellowish glow that went out when frosted lightbulbs came in, back when I was a little kid—and I walked toward it. I went up the steps, and the tiled porch-roof afforded scant shelter from the rain. What the hell do I do now? But even as I wondered, I'd pulled a chain from a pocket, attached to the end of which was a ring of keys. Without giving it a thought, I selected one key, turned it in the lock, and opened the door.

A silk-fringed table lamp burned in the hall, but the heavy, embroidered shade didn't let much light through. The walls were papered, some floral design, but not too garish; even the fancy old silk lampshade, and pottery lamp, and the dark, heavy table it sat on, along with the high-backed, carved-wood manorial chair beside it, reflected good taste—old-fashioned but acceptable. I closed the door behind me; I was tired, wet, and cold. My mind was still numb, blanketed with confusion, making coherent thought more than difficult. Just the same, I felt better; I was home. By now I'd learned to go along with my strangely dichotomous state of mind, accepting the mixture of total familiarity and absolute strangeness; to resist it, to try to arrange it in some sort of order, brought the strobelike jumps of elapsing time, and deeper befuddlement. So I stood there, trying to let things sift themselves out, dripping on the expensive-looking Oriental rug, chilled to the bone, fighting against spasms of shivering—and not just from cold. The fine edge of fear, even hidden beneath the surface, still cuts deeply.

A door thudded down the dark hall, spilling light across the paneled corridor, and a man hurried toward me, tying a cord around a rumpled Navajo-blanket patterned bathrobe. Shapeless slippers shushed along the carpet. He was black, and without thinking about it, I knew his name was Henry Peavey, and he was my houseman. Houseman? What the hell was a houseman?

"Yo' ah later than yo' said yo'd be, Mistuh Taylor," Peavey said, smiling, then stifling a yawn. "An' yo' ah soaked to the hide! Yo'll be catchin' yo' death an' damnation!"

"I'll be all right, Peavey," I said. It just came out. "Go on back to bed."

"Lucky yo' ain't got no studio call in the mo'nin', Mistuh

Taylor," Peavey said. He sounded just like a 1930s Movie Negro; people just didn't talk that way anymore—and I couldn't remember when they ever did. "Le 'me fix yo' a toddy—an' get them wet clo'es off!"

Peavey's manner was genuinely solicitous and his soft-toned voice ingratiating. Deliberately so? He could have used it to pitch used cars on TV . . . *TV?* I sensed a sudden strange feeling of disorientation, and for an instant I couldn't think what the hell TV meant. Everything started to flicker, so I pushed it out of my mind. There was a living room off to the left, and a light burned over a desk; a green-glass-shaded Tiffany student desk lamp. I knew what it was, because I'd paid forty dollars for it, in New York on my last visit—half what the grapeleaf design glass-shaded library table lamp had set me back in the same store. What the hell kind of a memory was that? I'd never bought a dingbat lamp from Tiffany's in my life. I didn't even know they made them. In fact, why would a jeweler make electric lamps? Damn, my thoughts were not only muddled, they were plain stupid! The room, everything blurred around the edges, and I stopped worrying it in my mind.

"Yo' feelin' all right, Mistuh Taylor?" Peavey asked, his expression troubled. He came and helped me out of the wet coat, even unbuttoned my vest with practiced fingers. I sank down into a comfortable deeply upholstered chair, and Peavey knelt and unbuttoned my shoes. Unbuttoned them! The fact didn't shock me; there is a limit to a man's reactions to strangeness. Peavey slipped a pair of elastic-insert, high-topped leather slippers on my feet. *Romeos* . . . Somehow I knew the name for them, but I no longer gave a damn. Still, I'd have to start sorting all this out, pretty soon— Strobe-jump, blurring. I stopped the thought.

"Drink this, Mistuh Taylor," Peavey said, holding out a tall yellow glass with an impressed design. It was steaming. I could smell whiskey and lemons. I took the glass and sipped the drink. My God, I remembered my grandmother giving me a hot toddy when I was a kid—not as strong as this one, but the taste was the same. The steamy vapor smelled great. The toddy burned all the way down and made a pleasant warmth in my stomach. Damn, a couple of these and I wouldn't care what the hell had happened to me or how mixed-up things became. . . .

"Let me help yo' up to bed, suh," Peavey went on, when I'd

finished the toddy. His strong hand half-lifted me out of the deep chair.

"Thanks, Peavey," I said. And stood there, confused. I didn't know where my bedroom was. *Upstairs, you stupid bastard*. The thought was angry, forcing its way into my numbed mind. The stairs were in the hall; I'd seen them when I came in. I started out, and Peavey walked close beside me, but I shook off his helping hand.

"Go back to bed," I ordered. Peavey looked at me, then grinned. He had two huge gold teeth set in the front of his mouth, glittering yellowly, but I just accepted it. Enough was enough.

I made it up the stairs, letting myself sink back into nothingness, and found myself moving toward the front bedroom. A lamp burned beside the bed, a big, carved-wood affair. It was a man's bedroom, one I wouldn't have minded owning, myself, with good hunting prints framed on the paneled wall, a couple of rifles, and several handguns, massive-looking and impressive, in a glass-fronted case. I wanted to look them over—but later! There was a dressing table with a silver-mounted comb-and-brush set, and beside the big tilted-slightly-up mirror, several framed photographs of women in old-fashioned clothes and hairdo—beautiful women, just the same, by any time's standards!—each inscribed. I tried to read the inscriptions, but they blurred. I was too far gone to do much more than glance at the rest of the room. There were thick lace curtains and heavy velvet drapes at the windows. A stack of mimeographed pamphlets—*movie scenarios, damn it!* This last just popped into my mind. Scenarios? They were neatly piled on the shelf under the bedside table on which the opal-glass-shaded lamp burned. A couple of big movie magazines were on top of it, the light shining from their bright covers. The colors were garish, like an old lithograph, and they were portraits of old-fashioned film stars. I didn't recognize either of them. *Not recognize Dorothy Dalton and May McAvoy . . . !*

I shook off the startled, probing thought, and sat down on the bed. There was a heavy velvet coverlet, which along with the covers had been turned back. The bed smelled faintly of perfume—expensive perfume to hang on so long. I started to unbutton my shirt. The stiff collar gave me trouble—then suddenly came off in my hand. The damned thing really was celluloid! It had been held on by a gold—something . . . *collar button!* What in God's name was a . . . ? Never mind! Forget it! The world was blurring again. Forget the whole damned mess!

I was too tired, too shaken, too cold, to think. I fell back onto the soft pillows that seemed to melt away beneath my weary head. Down-filled, and not the foam rubber that I was used to. *Foam rubber—in pillows?* It came from somewhere deep inside my mind, startled, shocked—I could sense that. Stop it! Don't worry about it. Not now. Flicker—strobe jump-jump-jump. I closed my eyes to stop it. I welcomed sleep. It came swiftly. And when it came—instantly—I was fighting for my life, for my very existence!

4

Get out! The command came compellingly, urgently, backed by fear and stress. It was directed at me, Ernie Carter. *Get out—go back where you came from! You don't belong here!*

I didn't ask for this!

Then get out! Now! Fear and something very close to frenzy.

I wish to hell I could!

Try!

It's no good. I'm here. To hell with it. To hell with you, too, Bill Taylor—or whoever you were.

What in hell do you mean, "were"? I'm here! I'm me!

Okay, okay—and so am I! I don't like it any better than you do.

I was lying back, the covers drawn over me against the cold of the room. It was dark. Peavey must have followed me up, removed the rest of my clothes, and tucked me in, and I was too zonked to know it. But now I was comfortable and warm, resting, at ease, not really asleep, now, but edging back to it.

Goddamn you! Despair and fear were in the thought, and it annoyed me.

I can shut you out, completely!

I did; I thought about my condominium in the Valley, about the shadowy goon I'd chased on Hollywood Boulevard, about my partner Jacobs, and the crazy red flare of a gun muzzle in my face. . . .

Please! Pleading. *Don't!*

Okay, Mr. Tanner.

Shock and dismay. *Goddamn you! How do you know?*

Know what? Oh, your real name. I'm not sure; I just know. Let's see, it's William Cunningham Deane-Tanner, that right? Not even a citizen. English. Me, I was born in LA—lived here my whole life. So did my folks. They came from Iowa back in the twenties. Everything plain and simple, that's me—but damned if I can say the same thing about you, Billy Boy. Kinky bastard, aren't you?

That's insane—stop it! You have no right—no, I don't mean that—you can't help . . . God, what's happening to me?

To us, you mean! And if He knows, He isn't telling. Take it easy. Go with it. Don't fight it. There've got to be some answers . . .

Flicker—blurring—strobe-jump.

Damn it, stop!

My turn to be shaken.

Are you doing that?

Doing what?

That. Bump. Jump. Flicker. Whatever the hell it is.

No. You are. When you—I don't know. It happens when you try to orient your thoughts. You slide—I can't think of a better word . . .

That'll do. Does it happen to you, too?

Yes. Afraid. I've heard fear before, and it was suddenly strong. *Will it change? Go back the way it—we—were?*

How the hell would I know? I don't even know what it is, what's happened to me—us. But I'm here. And dominant. I'm boss. You understand that? I don't mean to be tough about it, but somebody has to call the shots—and it seems like I'm elected!

Oh, God, dear God, help me! Let me wake up from this nightmare!

Amen, But until He does, we'd better reach an understanding. You agree?

What choice do I have? Bitterness. *Goddamn it, I hate this—I hate you!*

I'd rather be watching prime time, myself.

Make sense! I don't understand you!

Okay. We make the best of it, somehow. Muddle through. Which means, we cooperate, stop fighting each other.

Damn it, why should I go along with you? I don't want you here! You're not part of me—of my life! I won't have it!

All you're doing is making it tough for both of us, but if that's the way you want it . . .

I stretched out. The bed felt warm and soft, and I was tired. Too tired to continue this madman's self-dialogue. Everybody has nightmares, but wow, this I'd remember . . . !

No! I want you out! You can't stay! Dear God Almighty, help me to rid myself of this—this—

The thoughts were strong, terrifying in their strength, in their alienness, in the fact I could not control them. For an instant I felt the blurring, nauseating disorientation, as Taylor struggled to force me out. Then, deliberately, I started thinking about myself, Ernie Carter, my job as a cop in LAPD, my partner, Jacobs, my next vacation, when I planned on taking my camper-rig down to Baja for ten days. . . .

I felt Taylor's presence fading, his struggles weakening.

Please—don't shut me out! Please! I won't fight you!

Okay, then. No more bellyaching. We'll figure this all out when we can. Until then we make the best of it. Understood?

Reluctantly: *Yes.* Despairingly: *You don't know what it's like—letting you take over, letting you be me. . . . I've never let anyone—*

I know. You're a secretive bastard. I've seen the type. Always wondered what made guys like you tick, never letting your left hand know—

Bitterly: *Now you'll find out!*

I sensed Taylor's admission of defeat, and then the fading away—withdrawal—of his personality, and I let myself drift back into sleep. No squawks from Taylor, no trying to shove me out, to destroy me—or the me that was in this body that belonged to someone else—to somewhere—somewhen?—else. . . . I slept again, a troubled sleep. I kept dreaming, bits and pieces, over and over—mingled with odd, strange things that were never a part of my memories, or my life. But these faded, slowly, into nothingness, leaving sharper impressions. The little old-fashioned streetcar, swaying and clanging down the tracks that didn't exist in my L.A.; old mansions serenely facing Hollywood Boulevard, solid and real, and impossible; funny-looking big-wheeled high-bodied cars with dim yellow headlights; the grossly fat cop; the structure being built where Grauman's Egyptian Theater should be standing; and only a bean field where the Chinese should be, no forecourt, no paving with the footprints of old-time movie stars. . . . Bits and pieces of nightmare. That fence in front of where the Egyptian should have been, what was that sign? GRAUMAN'S EGYPTIAN THEATER—OPENING— 1922 . . .

1922.

More than half a century ago.

I tried to stop thinking, and just sleep, but a cop's mind doesn't work that way. I'd spent too many years trying to sort out pieces of other puzzles, some of which didn't make much better sense than this. And the pattern of it was consistent—that bothered me. There should be no logic in nightmares.

Fat cops, I'd seen them in old movies—and for real in old pictures still hanging on police station walls. Streetcars were for real, too, once, long ago. Did they used to run along Hollywood Boulevard? Hell, who could remember that far back? I *did* remember the Pacific Electric, when I was a little kid, the Big Red Cars—I'd ridden them out to Venice with my mother— Venice at the beach, long-gone, just a fading memory, too. I hadn't thought about them in years. Why should I? They didn't exist; the Pacific Electric tracks had been ripped out years ago, and Venice Pier demolished. And I hadn't the faintest idea when red and yellow streetcars last ran on Los Angeles streets. . . .

It had to be a crazy dream. I'd wake up and everything would be back to normal. Just open my eyes, and I could watch the Johnny Carson Show on TV. But I didn't want to open them; I *knew* I'd see only the strange dark-wood-paneled bedroom belonging to a man I'd never known in my life.

1922. Funny to pinpoint one particular year in a dream. Why that year? Why 1922? Why not 1926, or 1935, or, hell, 1866? I didn't know anything about any of them. One was no different than any other pre-Ernie Carter year. . . . No, wait a minute. 1922. Funny. 1922. I did know something about that year. It meant something to me. I was suddenly sure of it. 1922—if I could just bring it into focus, what there was—what had happened then. . . .

Flicker. Strobe-jump. Blurring dizziness.

Stop it! You goddamned fool! Stop it! Urgent, frightened.

It scared me, too.

Okay, Bill Taylor-Tanner, or what-the-hell, crawl back into your hole in my mind. We'll sleep it off. Good-bye to you, to 1922, to Toonerville Trolleys, to this whole, stupid, crazy nightmare!

I stretched out. The bed was warm. I felt good. This time I slept without dreaming.

5

The tapping sound was insistent, and I woke up. I felt like hell. I had a throbbing headache, and I could feel the lump on my forehead, as tender as a boil. I was in a strange bed, wearing strange pajamas, soft and sleek, and when I turned over, I damned near slid out of bed. Opening my eyes was a painful ordeal, but I forced them to stay open, looking at a fancy plaster ceiling with an ornate molded border and an elaborate crystal light fixture in the center. There was a cluster of clear-glass electric bulbs in it—but also two glass-shaded gas jets. Gas jets? The nightmare was still with me, proven when the bedroom door opened and Henry Peavey came in. He was wearing an alpaca jacket and a checkered vest, the very image of a right proper 1920s valet.

"Yo' all right, Mistuh Taylor? Yo' never sleep this late—I mean, unless—" His big gold front teeth shone in a broad grin. "Less'n yo' got yo'self some company!"

I had no choice but to go along with it, at least for the time being. Damn! Still, sooner or later, I'd have to wake up. Or would I? The thought was more disturbing than my headache.

"Just fine, Peavey, except for a headache."

"A bromo will fix yo' up, suh! Yo' want yo' tray up heah?"

"My what? Oh. No, I'll come down. Got some coffee?"

Peavey raised his thin eyebrows a full notch. "Yo' mean *yo'* wants *coffee* this morning?"

"Jesus, doesn't everybody?"

Peavey blinked and shook his head. "Yessuh, Mistuh Taylor, whatever yo' says." Everything but a foot shuffle, I thought. Peavey had missed his calling. A grown man really acting the way Stepin Fetchit, and Sleep'n'Eat—what was his name? Willie Best?—used to do in old movies? I didn't believe it. He couldn't be for real.

"Hey, man, do you always work that jive?" I asked.

Peavey stared at me, mouth open, eyes wide; then he grinned and chuckled a nice Clarence Muse chuckle. "Yo'ah sure the one, Mistuh Taylor! Coffee in the mornin, an' a-talkin' like a downtown nigguh!"

He was still chuckling as he went out, closing the door behind him.

I sat up in bed, and then clutched at my head. The blinding pains diminished after a moment, but I was careful not to move too fast. The thick velvet drapes half-covered the heavily curtained windows. It looked like a gray day. No sunlight filtered in. The room wasn't cold, but I shivered anyway. A pair of soft-soled slippers with embroidered silk uppers were at the side of the bed, and a white silk dressing gown was laid out over the back of a chair.

I got up and slipped my feet into the slippers. I crossed to the full-length mirror backing the dressing table I'd noticed the night before. It wasn't me—Ernie Carter—in the mirror. I was about the same height, but thinner, not as wide in the chest or shoulders, and weighed thirty pounds less. Lean and wiry, I would call it. The face was lean, too. Handsome, I suppose. I could be objective about it, as it sure as hell wasn't *my* face that looked back at me. At least this body had no incipient potbelly. The white silk Russian-style pajamas, high-collared and tight-cuffed, six buttons on each sleeve, and a red sash around the trim middle, looked great, and I wished I owned a pair myself. My—Taylor's—hair was almost white, and thick-wavy, without the thinning spots that had been troubling me the last few years. I ran my fingers through it, then used a comb, made a face at myself—this other self—in the mirror. Okay, Bill Taylor, you unlucky bastard, we'll play this hand out the way it's dealt—from the bottom of the deck for both of us. . . . There was no response from Taylor's ego. I was on my own, at least for now.

I heard a muted telephone bell. I looked around for the phone, automatically responding to it. Pavlov had it right, about conditioning animals. I saw the telephone, sitting on a table to one side. It was a black upright model, the kind with a separate receiver—they've made a big comeback with the kooks who go in for the nostalgia kick. I lifted the receiver and heard Peavey talking.

". . . when he comes in, Mistuh Sands."

"You're lying, you black son of a bitch! I know he's there, and I want to talk to him—you hear me?"

"I heah yo'," Peavey replied, unruffled. There was both firmness and dislike in his voice—the latter scarcely veiled by his polite words. "But Mistuh Taylor ain't heah, now. When he gets back, I'll be shoah to tell him that yo' called."

"Goddamnit anyway! The bastard's never around when you want him! Off skirt-chasing, no doubt. Who is it this time?"

"I said I'd *tell* him, Mistuh Sands."

"Be sure you do, Peavey, or I'll bend your fat black ass for you!" The voice was hard, rasping, and had a thick British overcast accent. It was familiar, and at the same time I knew damned well I'd never heard it before in my life. I hung the receiver gently back on its forked prong rest, replaced the telephone on the table, then looked around for the john, saw a door, and opened it. It was a deep closet, with a dangling overhead light, a brass chain hanging down. The next door was a better guess; it was the bathroom. White tile. Built-in tub that stood on fancy clawed feet, with a ring shower above it. Funny-looking affair, but not hard to figure out. The toilet was white porcelain, with a varnished wood seat, and the watertank high above it, next to the ceiling, with a brass pull-chain and hardwood knob to flush it with. A hell of an arrangement, but it worked just fine.

After showering I dried off on enormous white towels, softer and thicker than any I'd ever seen before. Each one had an embroidered monogram, WDT, all entwined. The swelling on my forehead had gone down, but still looked inflamed, with a darkening bruise, yellow-brown, around it. I studied Taylor's face in the medicine-cabinet mirror, but it remained that of a stranger. The toothbrush had been used—but, hell, used by the body I was now occupying. So I used it, and not finding a tube of toothpaste, sprinkled on some dental powder from a can labeled "Dr. Lyons." What won't they think of next? The stranger's face watched me as I brushed, so I winked at it.

You son of a bitch, get out! Taylor was back.

Ah-ah! We made a deal, remember? I didn't ask to be here—to be you.

Taylor drew back, but remained present. I could sense him being there, with me. I found a straight razor and a brush stuck in a china mug that had a gold-lettered name on it: WILLIAM D. TAYLOR. Bang! Something registered. That name . . . I knew it!

Flicker—jump-cut.

Don't! Stop it! You promised, too! Panic.

Okay, okay, Billy Boy, but sooner or later we've got to sit down and knit the pieces together. . . .

I opened the closet again and tugged on the light-chain. It was loaded with clothes. I counted a dozen hats, most of them odd-shaped, or at least odd to me. An equal number of suits, all of them pretty damned sedate, nothing bright or gaudy; not one damned piece you could call normal—by Ernie Carter's standards, anyway. But in a tall chest of drawers I did find some shirts with collars attached, softer than any synthetic fabric you ever touched; raw silk, hand woven, and when I tried one on, it fit like no store-bought goods ever did. But even it was a bit odd; the body wasn't tapered at all, and it would bulge out over the top of any pants I wore, while the tails hung down almost to my knees. It was obvious that in Bill Taylor's day they weren't worried about saving material—not even hand-woven raw silk. The labels on the shirts and ties were good ones, even in my time, for you can't buy much better than A. Sulka. However, no matter what their label, and no matter what kind of fancy material they were cut from, their ties were too damned narrow, and too long.

I settled for a gray suit—there wasn't a single sportcoat on the racks, and apart from some white flannels, no casual slacks. Well, when stuck in Rome. . . . I picked a pair of lace oxfords—there were no slip-ons—socks that matched the solid-color knit silk tie, and got dressed. The necktie gave me a problem, but I remembered the old narrow knot after a couple of tries. A leather box on top of the dressing table held jewelry—a lot of it, and all good stuff. I know; I worked Burglary Detail for three years. There was even a perfect blue-white diamond ring I wouldn't mind owning myself—hell, the way it was, I *did* own it.

You lousy thief.

Look, chum, keep this up and you'll make me feel unwanted.

I did my best to ignore the snarling thoughts just below my direct level of consciousness, and admired myself—my new self—in the mirror. The shirtsleeves were too long—if they had been made for Taylor, like the rest of his clothes, his arms must have shrunk.

Armbands, you lout!

I found them in a drawer. Narrow and soft, it was plain they weren't the fancy ladies' garters I'd seen on bartenders in cowboy movies, but actually made for the purpose of holding up a man's shirtsleeves. Functional, but to what purpose I couldn't guess. But I tried them; they worked, shortening the sleeves to just a bit longer than the sleeves of my suitcoat. I also found a platinum watch, and a chain and fob to match, all bearing the initials *WDT*. I dropped the watch into a pocket, draped the chain across the plain vest, and again admired the result.

Fashions change, but this wasn't bad. Not bad at all, especially since vested suits had made such a big comeback this past year. Or the past year when I came from. These lapels were narrower, and the waist pinched in a bit, but otherwise I looked pretty sharp, even if I did say so myself. And I'll let you figure out what's wrong with *that* thought!

Feeling a bit more chipper, even though my head felt like it was flying off at every step, I went downstairs, and Peavey was in the dining room, setting out some chafing dishes. From the number of them, Taylor ate a hell of a breakfast, nothing at all like my six prunes and Sucaryl-sweetened coffee. But then his waistline didn't bulge, either, the lucky bastard!

Dried fish and mucky-looking scrambled eggs, and some half-burned sausages that smelled a bit ripe; I lifted the silver covers and decided I'd stick with the coffee. It was black and had an odd taste—chicory? Packaging laws were different back then. Then? Now. A folded newspaper lay on the table. I opened it, braced myself. The Los Angeles *Times*, Wednesday morning, January 25, 1922.

All the things that had happened, everything I'd seen, the reality that was evident, should have prepared me. I think, really, that I *knew*—but seeing it in print, in prosaic type, on an obviously brand-new newspaper, the pulp paper pristinely white, drove it home, like a blow to the pit of the stomach. For an instant the room went dark, and my hands shook, then everything settled back into place. I wasn't me, Ernie Carter, but Bill Taylor, and this *was* 1922, like it or not. Accepting the finality of that reasoning made it possible to breathe again.

I picked up the paper that had fallen from my hands, and forced myself to study it. It was thinner, the headlines not of the banner type. The typeface wasn't noticeably old-fashioned, just quieter, if you know what I mean. There was nothing earthshaking on the front page, except for one column devoted to:

EARTH SLIPS OFF CENTER
MANY SHOCKS FOLLOW

Shifting of a Few Million Tons of
Rock "Somewhere in Pacific"
Jars Seismographs

(By A. P. Night Wire)

New York, Jan. 24. — The earth, in its whirl through space, got off center a few moments today and shifted its poles, or axis, to fit the center of rotation.

Then, that it might not be traveling on a "flat wheel," so to speak, a few million tons of solid rock, somewhere off the West Coast of the United States, in the bed of the Pacific Ocean slipped a hundred feet or so to even things up. . . .

Every time the San Andreas Fault acted up, there were a half-dozen (usually more) scientific theories as to what had happened, what caused the shake, and how we would soon be able to predict the next one. But this was a new one on me—and damned if it didn't make a sort of half-assed sense.

The big headline, across the top of the front page, read:

SLAYING STIRS HUB CITY
Policeman Killed
By Negro; Three
Others Wounded

Boston. — Renzy Murray, 62-year-old Negro, who stood off fifty policemen for more than an hour early today in a gun battle centered around his home, spent tonight in jail, charged with the murder of Patrolman Daniel McShane. . . .

In the center of the front page was a picture, sharp and clear, of what was left of a moving picture theater after its roof collapsed. I could tell it was a movie house, as the little, round-cornered black-bordered screen was visible amid the rubble on the stage. The picture itself rated as a lead:

PHOTO SENT BY WIRE OF CATASTROPHE IN WASHINGTON
Picture Coded and Decoded by
Means of Duplicate Telephoto-
gravers, a Device for Sending
Pictures by Wire.

Snow had collapsed the roof of the theater during a performance, and ninety-seven people had died. Whatever else my cohabitant might be, he had his own sense of humor: *Now there was a movie that brought down the house!*

What a creep!

Your influence, no doubt. Biting sarcasm, but no frenzy. I wasn't the only one accepting the situation for the moment.

To shake him up, I started thinking about the last jetplane to New York I'd taken—to bring back one of Charles Manson's murderous family on a still-standing charge.

No, please!

I stopped it and concentrated on the paper again. The coffee cup was empty, and when I looked around for the pot, Peavey had it and was pouring more. I nodded my thanks. The next headline—and on the front page of the Los Angeles *Times*, I swear it!—read:

Chicago. — A flapper is a girl who parades the campus bareheaded, wearing a huge fur coat and unbuckled galoshes. Her favorite occupations are dancing and counting classes. In most respects she is 1923 model, built on campus lines, with streamlined body and a sporty carriage, sixty miles an hour guaranteed. . . .

I still don't know who "Bath-house John" is—or was—or why his name was supposed to mean something to *Times* readers. *A bootlegger or a politician, no doubt.* Thanks a lot. *You're welcome.* Just stay that helpful, chum, and we'll get along. *I'm not your bloody damned chum!* Temper!

FIVE I.W.W.
PRISONERS
FREE AGAIN

Convicted Under Syndicalism Act, Paroled Recently From San Quentin

Sacramento. — Five convicted I.W.W. leaders recently were paroled from San Quentin Prison according to George H. Hudson, formerly an Operative of the Department of Justice. He declared the parole of the radicals is a blow to the breaking up of radical organizations in California. . . .

Even though they had been operating long before my time, I knew what IWW stood for—Industrial Workers of the World. But damned if I'd ever heard of what they had been convicted. *Stupid oaf!* I ignored Taylor's mental jibe.

"Peavey, is there a dictionary around here?"

"On youah desk suh," Peavey said, looking a little surprised. "Ah'll fetch it fo' yo'."

At least he didn't shuffle as he walked. That would have been too much. He came back with a leather-bound desk dictionary, well-used, showing wear. I looked the word up. It said that Syndicalism was both a strategy for revolution and a plan for social reorganization. Syndicalists were dedicated to the destruction of the state, and government by trade union, inspired by P. J. Proudhon and Georges Sorel, who the hell ever they might be. But the IWW had raised hell for a brief time, especially in the Pacific Northwest, and Congress had passed a law against them and their form of political activity. I wondered if that law was still on the books, and thought I'd have to look it up, when—

When you go back to where you came from?

That's right. And I am going back—you'd better believe it! *The sooner the better, as far as I'm concerned.*

The newspaper had a squib about a trial over the publication of some sensational memoirs or diaries by Margot Asquith. It sounded pretty spicy. Then my attention was grabbed by a real winner:

SMOKING GIRL GETS WAGES

Ought They Be Allowed to
Puff Cigarettes at Work?

Question Raised

London. (By Cable — Exclusive Dispatch) — Ought girls be allowed to smoke during office hours? This question was raised today in a republican court in Dublin by Miss Smith, a young bookkeeper, who claimed a week's wages in lieu of notice from her employers by whom she has been dismissed for smoking a cigarette during working hours. She said all the men workers smoked. Her claim to a week's wages was granted by the Court. . . .

Hurrah for Women's Lib! Who the hell said you've come a long way, baby? *You're an imbecile.*

I turned the pages. And I was thinking, absorbing, trying to get the feel of things. I must have been on the right track, because there were no strobe-jumps, now, no blurring of the scene. I paused at the sports page, which featured a picture of a wrestler, dressed in what looked like black long johns with leather patches on knees and elbows. In a box, the lead story took my eye:

BIG BOUT WON'T BE
IN GOTHAM

———

Dempsey and Brennan
Will Have to Pull Their
Little Party Elsewhere

Dempsey I recognized—hell he was still alive. *Still?* That's right—where—when—I come from, he's alive and kicking—getting up there in years, but doing okay. For that matter, so is Gene Tunney.

Gene Tunney? Puzzlement for a moment. *Wait, I know of him. The AEF Light Heavyweight Champion—what is he called? The Fighting Marine, that's it! But what has he to do with Jack Dempsey? They haven't fought and probably won't. Harry Wills will get the next shot at Dempsey's title—if Dempsey doesn't draw the color line. . . .*

Color line? It was my turn to draw a blank. There was a dim recollection of criticism directed at Dempsey, but, hell, the first World's Heavyweight Champion I really remembered was Joe Louis, the Brown Bomber—God, how long ago that seemed! But not so long ago as *now*—the thought was chilling, and I suddenly shivered, involuntarily.

Tunney will fight Dempsey twice—and lick him both times, although there's always been a hassle about the long count he took on a knockdown.

You're crazy! Tunney can't beat Dempsey!

Don't bet on it.

I felt the worry, the disturbed acceptance, experienced by Taylor. *Where do you come from?*

"Where" was the wrong question. *When* . . . More than fifty years when. Half a century. My God, most of the people I saw *here* would be dead then, including Peavey, and Bill Taylor would be pushing a hundred if he were still alive. But he wasn't. I *knew*, suddenly, absolutely, and with a cold feeling that bit deep.

Flicker—strobe-jump. Stop it, quick! Read the damned paper. Accept it. Don't think. This is *now*. This is what counts.

WILLIE HOPPE OUT TO REGAIN LOST LAURELS

Another name I knew. Anybody who ever shot pool knew who Willie Hoppe was. He was billiard champion for so many—
No! Read this! Urgent, demanding. *Back on page 6!*

ARBUCKLE DEFENSE ENDS

San Francisco. — The taking of testimony in the second trial of a manslaughter charge against Roscoe C. Arbuckle closed today. The final arguments are scheduled to begin before noon tomorrow. . . .

Fatty—poor damned soul! They'll crucify him more than they already have.

Friend of yours? Fatty Arbuckle? Hell, I know about him. He killed some broad by shoving a jagged piece of ice up her—

That's a lie! Not Fatty! He's a kid who never grew up—out for all the fun there is in the world—but he'd never hurt anybody.

Okay, okay, knock it off! I've got to think.

Something was churning in my mind, seething, between icy coldness and the sickening strobe-blurring.

What the hell do I care about some fat-assed comic who's been dead for forty years?

Dead? Fatty, dead? Shock, bewilderment.

And fear, so strong I could taste it. Inside me. Not Taylor's ego—*me!*

Fatty Arbuckle was dead—had died back in the early 1930s. And I knew it. I'd never seen one of his pictures, knew nothing about him, except the Virginia Rappe case. Virginia Rappe! Her name wasn't even mentioned in the news story I'd just read. I read it again to be sure. But I knew—and not from the dim, latent memory cells of Bill Taylor. I knew it because, like most young cops who make the detective grade, I'd read up on every famous California murder case. Every damned one.

But it wasn't the Fatty Arbuckle affair that frightened me, froze me to the chair, unable to move. It was another memory that it had triggered—another one of my own. You've seen the camera-magic stunt on TV where all the oddball pieces suddenly fly together and make up a single picture? It was like that. The pieces came together and hit me right in the face with all the impact of a brick.

The Arbuckle case wasn't the most famous Hollywood murder case, far from it. There was another one, still marked UNSOLVED, still kept in the active file at police headquarters, for there is no statute of limitations on murder. A case that every goddamned rookie detective for fifty years had taken a crack at solving. The cold-blooded murder of one of the best-known directors in Hollywood films.

A guy named William Desmond Taylor.
Me.

6

Shock has various ways of expressing itself. With me, there is a cold numbness that sometimes persists until I can emotionally adjust to the problem, rationalize if not solve it. But there is a faster way. If something happens that is plainly unfair, a real shitheeler, I get mad. And I was getting mad, now.

I'd been handed a genuine grade-A bummer. I hadn't asked for what had happened to me, didn't understand it, and hadn't done a damned thing to deserve it. Dirty tricks are a part of life, sure, but not this goddamned dirty! Thrown to hell and back to a time I knew nothing about, as alien to me as another planet, and worse luck, not even as myself, but as some poor bastard who wound up a file number in the LAPD backlog of unsolved murders. A victim society had never avenged, to put it in Taylor-Tanner's stuffy terms. In his day the death penalty was not only customary and legal, it was practically certain in a first-degree murder rap. And no gas chamber for painless euthanasia, either—it was a hemp necktie and a drop long enough to break your neck, if you were lucky and it was done right. Otherwise you kicked futilely as you slowly strangled to death—which could take ten or twelve minutes. At that moment, I felt even hanging would be too good for the son of a bitch who had murdered William Desmond Taylor—and me along with him?—back in 1922.

Me, Ernie Carter. Sure, like everybody else, when I did a long stretch of the same old routine, and started feeling sorry for myself, I'd think my life was an empty waste. But that is just emotional overreaction. Sure, one door had slammed when May had walked out on me, and I hadn't yet found the key to unlock another and better one. But some guys take longer to get over things, and that was me. My life hadn't become an empty shadow, hell, no, it hadn't! I still liked the tang of beer on a San Fernando Valley summer day when the temperature climbed above a hundred degrees. I still recharged my batteries by climbing into my RV and heading for some isolated river or lake, like Panguitch up in Southern Utah. And my dog, Kirby, the little bugger filled up most of the emptiness, all by himself, the way only a good dog can. I hoped to hell that Jacobs was taking care of him, now.

And my work—it had never palled on me. I'd garnered enough semester credits in the past few years to earn a degree, which damned near made my promotion to lieutenant a sure bet next exams.

Maybe it isn't your life, or even your idea of personal fulfillment, but I knew in that moment it suited me—and meant a hell of lot more than I might usually admit. A cop is expected to have a visible hard shell, but that doesn't necessarily change what's inside him. Ernie Carter might not be a book-type hero, but he was exactly what I wanted to be. And that didn't include dying as somebody else eight years before I was born.

The cold hard knot in my stomach held firm. This had to be the most miserable damned nightmare anybody ever had! It couldn't be real, none of it. Sharing the body of a man dead more than fifty years, reliving events that had happened in 1922. For Christ's sake, it was just a stupid dream. It *had* to be!

But it wasn't. There were too many things to prove it. I hadn't awakened back in my own condominium in the San Fernando Valley, with my dog jumping onto my chest to be let out at the first crack of dawn. I'd gone to sleep in 1922, and it was still here. I was as awake as I'd ever be. The winter sun was trying to fight through the gray overcast, as real as the heavy lace curtains at the windows, the dark wood paneling on the walls, the old over-stuffed furniture, the newspaper on the table in front of me, or Henry Peavey humming to himself out in the kitchen. Even the clothes I wore—the silk socks with the embroidered clocks up the sides, and the Paris garters that held them up. . . . No, it all added up, beyond any doubt, reasonable or otherwise.

As a trained, professional investigator, accustomed to working with facts and using them to arrive at a logical, doubtfree conclusion, I had no hope that this was a dream, or even some weirdly realistic hallucination. It was for real. For goddamned real!

But if it hit me hard, it knocked Bill Taylor to hell and gone. Not a peep out of the back of my mind, not even a murmur of protest. I stopped thinking about myself, about Ernie Carter and the problem he faced, and tried to let my mind settle down.

Come on, Taylor! How about it? Did you read me? You're going to be murdered. A classic mystery. One for the books—and believe me, books will be written about it. Who killed you, Taylor? No, you're—I'm—still alive. Who is going to kill you? Who hates you so much they are going to put a bullet in you? If you've got the answer, you'd better come up with it, fast!

Nothing. Silence. Not even the feeling of dismay or fear.

I picked up the coffee cup, and my hand didn't shake. The coldness was gone. I was just plain damned angry. Okay, okay, play the hand out. But I'm no wide-eyed Britisher, born before the turn of the century; I'm Ernie Carter, born in 1930, and both tough and smart. Twenty-five years a cop, and I've done it all twice. Maybe I was wearing William Desmond Taylor's body and his clothes, and living his life, but I'd brought my own rules with me. And some know-how to go with it. If I couldn't outsmart a killer—1922 style—I'd hand in my badge.

Or my chips.

The stakes were high. William Desmond Taylor—William Cunningham Deane-Tanner—had been a mystery man, I remembered. The case was fuzzy in my mind. I hadn't read the file in twenty years. But it stuck with me, to some extent, and there'd been mention of it in books and magazines and newspaper articles I'd read. It would have been nice to have total recall, but my memory wasn't all that bad. It sometimes took a little while for things to come back to me, but trying to force it had never worked. Just let it muddle through in its own way, bit by bit. . . .

But I did remember the basic facts. It happened early in the year—1922, I was certain of that, which meant I didn't have much time to waste. Today—this today—was Wednesday, January 25, 1922. It was on or about the first day of the month that Taylor had been shot. *February*. That was it. Memory clicked into place. February 1, 1922. I had a week. One lousy week to find a way back, or out. A week's a long time. Long enough. Bear down a little.

William Desmond Taylor was shot. Funny thing there, too. The bullet hole in his body didn't line up with those in his clothes. The angle was odd, too—*up?* He had been shot from low down, probably while his arms were raised over his head. But it hadn't been a stickup, for nothing was missing, according to Henry Peavey, his houseman. And Taylor had been carrying a wad of cash—over two hundred bucks, and a platinum watch—the same one in my vest pocket, right now!—worth five times as much, and a diamond ring, and none of it touched. And the killer hadn't been disturbed. He just hadn't been after the loot. Not the negotiable kind, anyway. He had been after something else, most likely, even if the joint hadn't been ransacked. A crime of passion, maybe. Taylor had been in Hollywood for nearly ten years, first as an actor—extra, probably—and then as a director. He'd been either good at it, or lucky, for he soon had a longterm deal with the biggest studio around in those days—Famous Players–Lasky, with trade names like Realart, Artcraft, and Paramount.

Hey, that was pretty good remembering! Or not so good, for that's damned near all. There had been confessions—it seemed like confessing to famous crimes was popular back then—it still is. Christ, how many phony confessions had we checked out on the recent—future recent—Skid Row Slasher killings? Now there was a thought! Not one of the winos cut up by the slasher had been fifty years old, and the slasher himself was barely thirty when we finally caught him—none of them even born yet, here in 1922! Yet I remembered the case as closed, ancient criminal history, like the Tate-La Bianca murders of Charles Manson's mad family, and the shooting of Robert Kennedy—and no one involved in those cases had been born yet, either.

I found myself laughing, maybe a bit harshly, but laughing; it was just too blasted ridiculous! Circles within circles, without rhyme or reason.

Peavey was suddenly there, looking oddly at me.

"Laughing at the funnies," I said.

"That *Kernel Cootie* makes me laugh, too, suh," Peavey said, still looking faintly puzzled.

There was no funny page in the paper, but there were several cartoon strips scattered on various pages. Only one of them rang any memories with me, *The Gumps*, and I didn't remember seeing it since I was a kid. Me, I grew up with *Tarzan*, *Flash Gordon*, *Terry and the Pirates*, and *Prince Valiant*, and there was nothing remotely like an adventure strip back in 1922, except for an oddball strip just being introduced to *Times* readers, called *Minute Movies*. It was just what the title implied, a cartoon version, not a little satirical, of the regular silent picture programs playing currently at the nation's Bijous. It featured a regular cast of "actors" who in turn played the various type-cast roles. I don't know how long it lasted, but I can't remember ever having seen it before.

I thought about the old-timer strips I'd enjoyed most of my life, and I knew that *Bringing Up Father*, with Maggie and Jiggs, went back that far—even decades earlier, for that matter—but I didn't see it in the *Times*. Maybe I was reading the wrong paper. The *Times* was obviously trying hard for the New York namesake's dignified image.

"What about the *Examiner*?" I asked Peavey.

"Suh? Ah have it out in the kitchen. You nevah read it, suh."

Trust stuffed-shirt Taylor!

"Are Maggie and Jiggs in the *Examiner*?"

A wide grin was my reply.

"What other papers do we take? Besides the *Examiner* in the afternoon?"

Again Peavey's bland face was marked with a puzzled frown. "The *Examinuh*'s a mo'ning paper, suh, like the *Times*." I remembered then; it had been a morning daily when I was growing up. "We gets them all. The *Express, Herald*—an' the *News.*"

TV had killed off most of them, and crippled the rest, except for the *Times*, which had become of the biggest of all publishing empires in my day. But from *now*, in 1922, the papers still had a quarter of a century to go before the advent of the electronic media.

"Have I got a radio?"

Bright grin. "Put watuh in the batteries this mo'nin'—same as usual, suh!"

"What stations do we get?"

"Come a good night, we do pretty good—I tuned in San Francisco last night while I waitin' fo' yo' to get in, suh. Loud an' plain!"

"I meant locally."

"Los Angeles? Three of 'em on every night, an' another s'posed to start soon. KNX, KFI, an' KHJ already doin' fine!"

They'd still be doin' fine a half century later, which somehow made me feel better, sort of diminished the feeling of isolation that had gripped me every time I relaxed.

"All of them carry a newscast?"

"A which, suh?"

Mistake. The second one in minutes. I'd better watch it. But I wondered if they broadcast news back in 1922. Maybe, but come to think about it, pretty doubtful. The newspapers had it all—and they owned the new radio stations. "Thought I read somewhere about a news program being broadcast . . ."

"Yessuh." Peavey gave me a doubtful look as he poured me more coffee. "Yo' ought to eat yo' breakfast, suh."

"I'll make up for it at lunch."

"Yo' remembuh yo' got yo' self a date fo' lunch, suh?"

Hell, no, I didn't remember. "Must've slipped my mind, Peavey."

"Yo' really did lap up a snootful last night, ah reckon!" Again the rich, Clarence Muse chuckle. "Youah eatin' with Miss Betty, suh—Paulais', same as always."

"That's right, of course," I said. Miss Betty *who?* A thought struck me. "I was wondering, about last night—did I have the car? I mean—"

48

Peavey just grinned. "No, suh. Mistuh Howard had the cah, suh. He asked me if yo' got home all right, after he dropped you off at Brandstatter's fo' dinnuh."

Mister Howard? Who the hell was Mister Howard, and just how the hell could I go about asking Peavey questions, the answers to which I was supposed to know better than he did?

"You told him?"

"Yessuh, just like you told me to, that he could have the night off, an' yo'd catch yo'self a cab home."

"Just like I told you. . . ."

"That's right, suh. Comin' back to yo', now? Usually do! Maybe if you took a hair of the pooch that bit yo' . . ."

"Not right now. Bootleg booze doesn't seem to set well with me."

"None o' that cheap hooch evuh does! But yo' got yo' own private stock—took off the boat with yo' own hands! Yo' still got most o' that case o' gin Mistuh Ince sent yo', an' Mistuh Lasky give yo' some bottles o' that scotch yo' admired at his place." He grinned, his big front gold teeth glinting. "Miss Mabel give yo' a case o' champagne, an' Mistuh Fairbanks—"

My vague impression that Prohibition meant doing without the good stuff suffered a setback, but money always could buy anything in Hollywood, and still would, for that matter. It was—and is—a part of the Hollywood charisma. Not that things were and are much different anyplace else. Just that I—Ernie Carter—grew up in this cockeyed town, and understood some of the topsy-turvy rules. The Haves really *have* . . .

"Reminds me, Peavey," I said, thinking like a cop again. "I'd like an inventory—you know, a list of everything we've got around this place—all the stuff I own." He looked surprised. "Need it for insurance."

He grinned. "Reckon that's somethin' yo' should'a had when Mistuh Sands was still heah." He shook his head. "An' speakin' o' the devil himself—Mistuh Sands called yo' this mo'nin'. Ah told him yo' wasn't heah. Yo' a fool if yo' evuh talk to that man again—except through prison bars!" His glinting gold teeth took away any animosity his words might have generated. Peavey's sincerity was as real as his movie-Negro manners.

"What did he want?"

"He nevuh says, but it ain't hard to guess what Mistuh Sands wants!" Peavey's total lack of regard for Sands—whoever he might be—was most evident. " 'Tain't none o' my business, suh, but if yo' don't turn that man ovuh to the police—well, yo'ah out of yo' mind!"

"You may be right, Peavey," I said.

"Yo' got a warrant out right this minute fo' his arrest fo' robbin' yo' blind—and then he's got the gumption to telephone yo' every day! Some nerve that man's got, if yo' ask me!"

"A warrant for his arrest?"

"Now yo' can't have fo'gotten that, suh!"

"No, of course not, Peavey." I smiled. "But, I mean, after all, how serious—"

"Fo'gin' yo' name to checks, hockin' everything he could get his mitts on! Yo' told me yo'self he cost yo' bettuh than ten thousand dollahs while yo' was gone t' Europe last year." Peavey shook his head. "I nevuh did take to that man! The way he was always a-sassin' yo' back, like he figgered he was as good as you was, or that he had somethin' on yo'."

"Maybe he has, Peavey," I said, slowly, thinking hard. Damn it, where was Bill Taylor's ka when I needed it? He could give me answers to a hell of a lot of things, and I would need them, if I was going to keep him—me!—alive for longer than the next week.

The door knocker clattered and Peavey hurried off. He was back in a minute with a handful of mail. He placed it on a silver salver, laid a fancy-handled letter opener beside it, and put the whole thing on the table beside my morning paper.

"Mo'nin' mail, suh," he said.

The carmine stamps—2¢!—caught my eye on the envelopes. Not a piece of junk mail in the lot—who says everything has changed for the better? Mail was delivered twice a day in 1922—morning and afternoon, delivered overnight between San Francisco and L.A., and next-day from any part of Southern California to any other part. The last time I got a letter at home in the San Fernando Valley from downtown L.A., it took three days. But I felt a sudden sharp pang. Knock it, I might, but I wanted back where I belonged, now. I shut my eyes, kept them shut. Let me wake up—let this all be a lousy dream. Nothing had changed when I opened them, and somehow I felt empty, lost. A telephone bell was jangling—funny thing, the sound was strange, and yet unmistakable.

Peavey came in, frowning. "Mrs. Denker—wants to speak to yo', suh."

The day of phone outlets in every room hadn't arrived yet. I got up and went out into the entry hall. The receiver was off the hook, standing by itself to one side. I picked up the stand and mouthpiece in my right hand, the receiver in my left, as naturally as if I'd been doing it all my life. For the first time I noticed there was no dial on the base of the phone. How the hell did you get a number? I remembered the old song, "Hello, Central, Give Me a Line." What would happen if I asked her for my San Fernando Valley condominium number? If it rang in the empty house, my little dog, Kirby, would dance around, barking at it. . . . The thought almost hit too hard, and I forced it away.

"You dirty son of a bitch! How many times have I told you to stay away from her?" The voice was strident, screeching with anger. "You're goddamned well old enough to be her father! You ought to be ashamed of yourself!"

"Hey, now, cool it, Mrs. Denker—"

"Don't you Mrs. Denker me, you filthy bastard!" The voice from the receiver rose sharply in pitch, as grating as a fingernail across slate. "You stay away from my baby or I'll see you dead, you—you child fucker!"

The receiver slammed up hard on the other end of the line. I noticed that when the connection was broken there was no dial tone, just a faint electrical humming sound. I hung the receiver on the hook upside down, because Peavey lifted it off, reversed it, and hung it back in place.

"How many more people are there standing in line to hate my guts, Peavey?" I asked.

"Suh?" Peavey managed a puzzled look, but I didn't buy it; Henry Peavey might be loyal and sincere, but he was a hell of a lot sharper than he pretended to be. Maybe Peavey was in that growing line, too, with an ax of his own to grind—and sink in Taylor's thick skull?

One thing was damned sure: Mr. William Desmond Taylor,

AKA William Cunningham Deane-Tanner, had his enemies. In just one week from now, one of them was going to shoot him dead, dead, dead.

7

I needed some air and a chance to think. I told Peavey I'd be back and went out through the lace-curtained french doors of the dining room. I found myself in the areaway between the big two-storied bungalows of the court. One of the small yellow-and-red streetcars went clattering down the middle of the street beyond. It was moving fast, and I learned later that was because there were seldom any passengers at the corner of Alvarado Street for it to pick up or let off—a fact that would later figure in the police investigation into Taylor's murder. The street directly behind Taylor's bungalow was Maryland Avenue, and it was largely residential, with small, frame California cottages set back behind postage-stamp lawns, yellowed by winter. There were tattered palm trees scattered haphazardly down the street.

The sun had finally won a temporary victory over the overcast, and it was brighter, the sky an incredible deep blue I couldn't remember ever seeing before—and I've spent my whole life in the L.A. Basin. There weren't more than a half-dozen automobiles parked the whole length of Maryland I could see, which probably explained the color of the sky. A bulging-sided bus, the motor-hood sticking out in front, with a massive radiator, and black lettering that read PEERLESS STAGE COACH CO. rumbled past the intersection, going north on Alvarado. A uniformed man sat facing backward beside the driver, a fiberboard megaphone to his mouth, obviously addressing the passengers, who were gawking out of the windows as they went by. Tourists? I felt surprised.

What the hell else would they be?

So you're back. Welcome home, Bill Taylor—where the hell were you when I needed you?

You kept me—blocked out. . . . Couldn't get through.

He was being evasive for some reason of his own. To hell with him!

Why the tourists? I mean—

I know what you mean. I'm a famous man. Name above the title, now. A touch of pomposity.

You and C. B. De Mille.

That's right. Pause. *You know C. B.?*

I met him once, when I was assigned to Robbery. Somebody had grabbed some souvenirs from his office while he was in Egypt shooting his last sex-and-sand epic. He's been dead several years, now, but—

You're insane! I saw him last week—talked to him. . . . He was screening his new picture, Saturday night, *and had Jeanie Macpherson and Leatrice Joy with him . . .*

A different last week—one I'd never known. What about *next* week? Would I be back where I belonged—or lying dead here in 1922, with some bastard's bullet in my heart? It was funny, but I *knew*—with absolute certainty—that I had to see this absurd melodrama all the way through, and I felt a growing conviction that when Taylor bought it, the same slug would write finis to Ernie Carter, too. . . .

Finis? Where the hell did I pick up that word? I knew; from Taylor. It was part of the deal, little memories that were just there, ready to mind, without thinking about them. Part of Taylor that didn't go into limbo when the rest of him did.

Taylor? Damn it—

If you'd stop shutting me out, maybe we'd get someplace.

Okay, okay, I'll try. How much of what I know has percolated through to you?

All of it—most of it, at least. . . . Somber, worried thoughts. *But it's preposterous—nobody really wants to kill me.*

Somebody does—and damned well *will*, too. Unless they're stopped.

But—how? What can I—we—do? There's no one—I mean, I know of no one who would want to actually see me dead. Everything is fine. There are problems, naturally. Every man has enemies—people who dislike him, envy him, perhaps even some he has—unintentionally, of course!—harmed, but—

Come on, Taylor—you can do better than that!

I must have spoken out loud, for a kid in knickers, lugging a canvas bag lettered COLLIER'S—THE NATIONAL WEEKLY, filled with magazines, gave me a look and hurried past. I was at the corner of Alvarado, now. I studied the street. There was some traffic, but not much. Another streetcar went by on Maryland, jangling its bell as it crossed the intersection, this one westbound. I turned back, walking east on Maryland, slowly, letting my thought sink into my brain. Taylor was there again.

I'm telling you—

No, you're not—and that's the trouble. I remember the case. You were involved with broads—a lot of broads, famous ones, too. And there was a drug angle. If you want to go on living, Mr. Taylor-Tanner, then spill it.

There is a limit to how much I can take from you.

Not if you want to live longer than another week, Charlie Brown.

You don't make sense. Who is Charlie Brown?

Never mind. Figure of speech. Look, you've got to help—it's the only chance—for both of us. If you're as with me as you say, sharing my thoughts, you're got to know that I'm leveling with you. I'm a cop—and a good one. Maybe I can bust this case before—

Before I'm murdered?

You've got it. But I'm floundering. I don't know enough. For instance, who the hell is Howard?

My chauffeur, Howard Fellows.

That's more like it. See, we can get someplace if we try. Now, Mrs. Denker. She called me a—

I know! Hastily, but I sensed his underlying amusement. *Did it shock you, Carter? I can assure you that I am not a—a molester of children.*

Try assuring Mrs. Denker. Who is she, and why—

If you must know, she is Betty Blayne's mother. Miss Blayne and I have—we have had a deep personal relationship.

Two in one. That also explained the Miss Betty I was supposed to have lunch with. I felt Taylor's confirmation of the fact.

Guys have been shot for laying somebody's daughter before now. . . . Tell me, Taylor, how many other dames do you have these deep personal relationships with?

Indignation. *I refuse—*

It beats getting wasted, chum. And remember, I *am* you!

Pause. *I've been—close with Mabel Normand, recently, but—*

Anybody jealous enough of that closeness to put a bullet in you?

Of course not!

No ex-boyfriends with a mean look in their eyes?

There's Mack—but of course that's ridiculous!

Mack who?

Sennett. His real name is Sinott, I believe. He owns a studio, and—

Okay. The Keystone Kops, I know who he is. That's two, so far. Any other deep personal relationships?

Well, naturally—a man in my position—living alone. . . . I can assure you that I—

Don't bother. There have been others. A lot of them.

Now, see here—

Let it drop. Every mention of the case I've ever read called you a mystery man—not using your real name, running away from your wife and family back East, somewhere. . . .

The change of names means nothing! More than half the people in Hollywood change their names—the public expects it! Gladys Smith became Mary Pickford, Douglas Elton Ulman became Doug Fairbanks—real names don't matter. Don't you see?

Sure, I see, but in your case—

I've never committed a crime in my life! I've nothing to hide, really.

What about the wife and family you abandoned?

Do you have to—

You're damned right we do.

Very well, then. My wife and daughter. I left them in New York—for—for personal reasons. . . .

That again. You ran out—why?

Silence. Thinking about it bothered Taylor. Conscience? After all those years?

It's very difficult for me to say. Or for someone else to understand. But have you ever felt boxed-in, I mean absolutely, with no way to turn, and digging yourself deeper, every day? Things smothering you, blinding you—making your life a sheer hell of nothingness. . . . No way to strike back, to smash your way out, to live your own life, do the things that make life worthwhile for a man—a man like me. . . . It was in 1908—fourteen years ago. I'd been married several years. My wife was—was a good woman, a good wife and mother—damn it to hell, why am I subjecting myself to this? Pause. I waited him out. I could feel his deep agitation and overwhelming embarrassment. *Too good— too goddamn almighty good! Do you understand that? Too good for me! I couldn't stand another minute of it—smothering me—her goodness. . . . And I didn't desert them—leave them destitute—I left plenty of money, and the antique business was worth a small fortune. I'd built it up from nothing, until the last year I cleared more than twenty-five thousand dollars just for myself. . . . All I took was five hundred dollars from my own checking account, I even left most of my clothes behind—and just —vanished. . . .*

A longer pause. *She's remarried—well . . . she's happy. Happier than she ever was with me, a man more her type. . . . And I've been—free. Happy for the longest period of my life, doing what I want to do, making the kind of life that I enjoy. . . . I've hurt no one—not seriously, not even my wife and daughter. They are far better off without me. I know that!*

Okay—and what happened—to you—afterward? After 1908?

Wry amusement, but the memories were obviously not unpleasant. *Everything—good and bad! I went hungry, almost died—and loved every damned minute of it. I prospected in Canada—almost froze my bloody ass off. Three years of it,*

Alaska—you would have a hard time naming where I haven't been, what I haven't done.

And Hollywood? How did you get started here?

It was just one of those things—a matter of chance. I'd drifted south, out of the cold winters, and came across a company shooting in the redwoods, in Northern California. I got in a few days work, as an extra. It was a whole new, exciting, make-believe world—and the people in it were like marvelous children, playing games, twenty-four hours a day. . . . It was what I'd been looking for—escape from reality, if you like—I don't care! It's a far better world than the one I'd always loathed. Perhaps it's that I—fit in better. I don't know.

At least you were good at your job.

Do you mind not referring to me in the past tense? It's damned unsettling.

Yeah. I can see how it would be. Now, tell me, how did you make it big in Hollywood?

Sounds so simple, so easy—but it wasn't. It was hard work, and took a long time. I became a hanger-on in films, taking any job I was offered, no matter what it was. Extra work, back lot laborer—name it and I've done it. At first I thought it would prove to be an acting career I was best suited for, but it turned out differently. All I accomplished was to betray myself to those I'd—left behind. . . . My sister-in-law saw some film I'd had an atmospheric bit in and recognized me. Not that it really mattered very much, it was far too late for that. . . . By chance, I was in the right place at the right time—when they needed an expert on British South Africa for a serial that North American Film Company was making, and my British accent and background served me well. I wound up codirecting the chapter play— something called Diamond from the Sky. *That was in 1915, and I thought I'd made it—but I was wrong. Nothing big happened. I kept on, doing everything I was offered—finally got billing as an actor in* Captain Alvarez, *a Vitagraph six-reeler. I was good in it, too, but that was the end of my acting career. The usual Hollywood switch—I was given a chance to direct again. I made good. Every picture I've done has made money.*

Okay, so far, good enough. What about the drug angle?

Nothing. I'm not personally involved. I've never touched the rotten stuff! In fact, I've worked with the United States District Attorney's office, trying to stop the open sale of drugs in Hollywood.

An informer?

Certainly not! I told you, I've never been personally involved, but some of my—my friends. . . . I can't stand by and watch them being destroyed by these vicious bastards! Taylor's thoughts were hard and angry—too much so.

Damn it, Taylor, you can't lie to me—I can tell there's more to it than that—you've got a personal stake in it.

Sudden, intense emotion, blanking me out, keeping me from Taylor's mind.

Take it easy, Taylor.

Too late. He was gone again, faded away. My fault—or his? I couldn't be sure. But I had a jumbled mindful of thoughts. Jesus, if I ever saw a guy earmarked for murder, and strung up tight about it, it was W.D.T. And the cold, hollow feeling dug into my bowels again. Sure, I was a homicide cop, and pretty good at it, by the record, but that was *then*—fifty years after tomorrow, not here and now. I suddenly felt helpless, floundering in a morass with no bottom to it.

I'd stopped walking, and was just standing there, lost in my—and Taylor's—jumbled thoughts, seeing nothing. Then, slowly, sounds penetrated, an automobile rattled past—was every single damned car in 1922 painted dull black? Everything came back into focus, including the steady throbbing of the swollen, bruised spot on my forehead. Peavey came from between the two big bungalows, looking for me.

"Yo' won't want to be late fo' yoah luncheon date, Mistuh Taylor."

I looked at my left wrist, found my watch missing, started to ask Peavey the time, then caught myself. I even managed a bit of a gesture as I pulled the platinum ticker from the watch pocket of my vest. It was pushing noon, but the only thought that seemed important was that I had that much less time left. Peavey was holding a furry-looking cocoa-colored hat, a topcoat, and—so help me!—a silver-headed cane. It wasn't cold enough for the coat, and I hadn't worn a hat—until last night, as Taylor—in years. Hell, I didn't even own one, come to think of it. As for the cane—Jesus, did men actually carry them, even in 1922? They did. And it's a funny thing, there's something special about a well-balanced cane. You half-swing it as you walk, like you're pointing out the next place you'll step, and it's an enjoyable experience. My God, now I'm talking like a street child on the Strip! Just the same, I made a little note that when—if?—I got back where I belonged, I would buy me a cane—a walking stick—and use it, too.

"Mistuh Howard's workin' on the sedan, suh," Peavey said. "Ah tol' him yo'd be takin' the roadster. Is that all right?"

"Sure. I mean, fine, Peavey, just fine." There was a row of small, narrow, door-closed garages farther down Maryland. One double door stood open. It slid on an overhead track-wheel, over the second door of the double garage. Trying not to act too self-conscious—and not fall over the damned cane—I made my way to the garage. Peavey went back through the narrow areaway between the bungalows.

Howard Fellows, in shirtsleeves rolled to his elbows, was hand-grinding the valves of a lumbersome Packard sedan. It was big and square and ugly, but in its pristine, almost-new condition, would have made an old-car buff whinny with delight. There was no collar on Fellows' shirt, and he was wearing gray britches and black leather puttees. A matching gray uniform coat and a black-leather-billed chauffeur's cap hung on hooks to one side. He was a short, slim man, somewhere above thirty, with a roundish, pleasant face, and evasive eyes that couldn't quite focus on me as I walked in. He straightened, smiled without meaning, and touched his forelock of hair with a fingertip.

"I'm getting her done, Mr. Taylor," he said. He shared an obsequious voice-tone with Peavey. Maybe it went with their domestic kind of jobs—which in my time were few and far between. The only chauffeurs I'd ever seen worked for one of the limousine services or were on the city payroll for officials afflicted with bigshotitis. His eyes remained expressionless, remote and aloof, no matter what his voice implied. I found myself studying him for a moment, and wondering if he was one more possibility for the role of Taylor's killer. But I decided my nerves were acting up; everybody couldn't be out for Taylor's blood. Just the same I'd keep him in mind. "Will you be needing the sedan tonight, sir?"

"Don't worry about it. If you're not finished, I'll use the roadster." I had been wrong about all the 1922 models being painted basic black. I gave the Pierce-Arrow roadster the once-over and fell in love at first sight. The body was painted a light canary-yellow, while the gracefully arched fenders and running boards (with a fancy chromed stepping-plate) were a glossy black. It was low-slung, with clean, sharp lines that were ageless. The two seats were upholstered in roughed-out light-brown leather, and the keys dangled in the ignition in the center of the walnut-burl dashboard. There was a hooded lamp over the little cluster of instruments, an odometer, speedometer, amp-indicator, and fuel gauge. A tachometer was directly in front of the big polished-wood steering wheel, which was nearly twice the diameter of the one on my Chevelle. It had a self-starter, for which I was grateful, as such "novel luxuries" were far from standard equipment on most cars in 1922. From the solid round steel bar of the front bumper, to the two spare tires with covers striped in the same yellow as the body mounted on the trunk-compartment lid continental-style, it was a dreamboat, as unaging as any perfect work of art. I found out later that the roadster had a built-in jacking system and electrically driven air-pump, for fixing flats, and the hand-built six-cylinder dual-valve engine could turn up enough revs to top 110 mph.

I climbed in and sat there for an instant, trying to get the feel of the car. It had the new-car smell unlike anything else in the world. But the spark and throttle controls on the steering wheel threw me a curve. Trusting to luck, I switched on, and stepped on the starter button set in the floorboards to the right of the brake pedal, after carefully shifting into what I hoped was neutral, and holding the clutch pedal down with my left foot. The engine turned over—and over—and over.

"Advance your spark, Mr. Taylor," Howard Fellows called. I'd made another goof—but how the hell could I know how to start a car nearly ten years older than I was? *Was.* Past tense? The coldness slid into my stomach again and churned, slowly. I felt embarrassed. Up or down—and which one of the two levers was the spark control? I moved one, and ground away at the starter again. Nothing happened. Fellows came over, moved both levers easily, and smiled—a bit superciliously? "Try her now, Mr. Taylor."

"Not one of my better days, Howard," I said, and saw the surprise on his face. Of course, damn it, stuffed-shirt Taylor wouldn't call a manservant by his first name. Not done, old boy, no doubt. Chalk up another mistake. To hell with it. I jabbed my toe on the starter and the big engine caught instantly. It thundered noisily for a moment, then Fellows reached in and readjusted the two levers. He waved a hand and returned to the Packard, but he gave me one hard, direct, calculating glance as he did so. It was out of character, somehow. I made a note not to cross him off my list of suspects. Or did servants back then play the subservient game as a part of their life, constantly aware of any mood change in their status? The thought was somehow a little depressing.

All I needed to really make Fellows give me a look would be to shift into the wrong gear. I tried to draw a mental picture of where each gear was, and drew a blank. Then I forced myself to relax, to think of something else, of Mrs. Denker and the name she had called me—Taylor. Automatically I shifted into reverse and backed out into the street, smooth as glass; I found low gear, too, and started east on Maryland.

I got the feel of the Pierce-Arrow roadster after a few minutes, and my first-sight infatuation grew quickly into true love. It had power to spare, and handled like a dream; no power accessories, no electric windows (no side windows at all, for that matter), no power brakes or steering, not even an electric cigarette-lighter. The power driving-assists it didn't need; it turned as quickly, easily, and sharper than my late-model compact Chevrolet, despite its greater wheelbase and overall length. And, sitting higher, I had a superb view of the street. That long, lean hood thrusting out in front gave a macho feeling to driving it. I found myself thinking that if I ever managed to get back to my own time, I'd like nothing better than to take that car with me.

Going through Taylor's papers, later, I learned that it was a special-order custom job from Pierce-Arrow, and that it had set him back a little over seven thousand 1922 dollars. And, no matter how much those dollars were worth preinflation, it was a steal!

Downtown L.A. was a pleasant surprise. The sun was bright and warm, and the canvas top being tucked away in its compartment behind the seat made it perfect. The air was clean, and the old saw about it sparkling wasn't too far off. There was no smog at all—even the word hadn't been invented yet. I know, the newspapers of my day constantly quote self-appointed authorities who insist pedantically that Los Angeles has always had smog, and old-timers' memories of hazeless skies and invigorating air to breathe are faulty. But let me tell you, as one who has been there, we've lost a hell of a lot—and fouled up what's left.

The streets were busy, even crowded, and I felt a growing sense of strangeness, of disorientation. It wasn't just the oddly dressed pedestrians, the women with their too-full dresses and skirts, and the men with their bulky coats, stiff shirt-collars, and too-tight pants; the day of the flappers was at hand, and there were enough glimpses of silk-stockinged legs to satisfy even me—and I'm a leg man, myself. Which brings me to the thought of nylons versus pure silk stockings—no, wait a minute, I'll get around to that later. . . .

The streetcars rattled and jangled along their tracks, in assorted sizes, almost all of them, except for the huge all-red Pacific Electric interurbans, painted yellow and red. There were no motorbuses, except for a couple of Peerless Stage Coaches, and one funny-looking, bathtub-shaped Gray Lines sightseeing bus. I was so busy gawking, trying to take it all in, to adjust to it, that I almost ran down a cop who was standing in the center of an intersection, waving his arms. I jammed on the brakes, and the Pierce-Arrow stopped like the thoroughbred it was, and I suddenly knew what had been bothering me so much—there were no traffic signals, not even a stop sign, all the way downtown!

The cop, who stood in the middle of the street, was directing traffic from a little wooden kiosk. He gave me a glare as I screeched the tires of the Pierce-Arrow, but I gave him a friendly smile, and he nodded. He turned on the kiosk, halting the flow of traffic in one direction, and motioned me through the intersection. As I passed him, he said: "Take it easy, buddy!" It was said in a pleasant, easygoing manner, and I had the sudden conviction that police-public relations hadn't improved at all in the next fifty years.

Paulais' Restaurant and Candy Shoppe—Shoppe!—was at 741 South Broadway. I'd stopped at a corner drugstore to look it up in the phonebook, which was already a good-sized affair, although the Yellow Pages were included in the back of it. I drove past and around the block, looking for a parking lot, but didn't find one; there weren't any, nor any need for them, it seemed. I parked around the corner from Paulais'—there were plenty of empty parking spaces along the curb—and walked back.

There were a lot of autos on the street, and their horns squealed more often then their brakes. Another thing that struck home to me was the people I passed—no bums, no weird wayouts, no surly faces or angry scowls; smiles and nods were commonplace from people I didn't know, and who didn't know me. This was a different world; perhaps slower paced, but perceptibly cleaner, and certainly friendlier.

Paulais' had gilded planter-boxes in front, a purple awning over the sidewalk, and potted ferns obscuring the big front windows with their wrought-iron grillwork. A doorman in a gold-braided uniform opened the door, touched his cap, and said, "Good afternoon, Mr. Taylor."

"Same to you, Stanley," I found myself saying automatically. A maître d' appeared magically, and although there were several people waiting, held back by a red-velvet-covered rope, unhooked it for me and escorted me to the cloakroom counter, where a girl took my hat, topcoat, and stick, but didn't offer me a claim check for them. It was obvious that Taylor was too well known to need one. The maître d' led me to the almost-hidden little gilded wrought-iron elevator cage. I glimpsed the main salon, a huge room, with potted plants thriving everywhere, and snowy-white linen-covered tables discreetly placed among them, affording pleasant, gardenlike privacy—a neat little touch I'd never seen before.

The little elevator slid silently upward. I unlatched the door and stepped out onto the balcony. It had a matching gilded wrought-iron railing—and still more potted plants, mostly ferns. A trim young black-satin-clad woman smiled and pointed to a gilt-covered door. I nodded to her, opened the door, and went in.

A naked twelve-year-old girl was waiting for me.

8

Betty Blayne's petite size and tiny figure, as perfect as an art deco nude, along with the golden curls to either side of her pixie's face, made the illusion of childhood complete. But it didn't last long. Twelve-year-olds don't act that way—or at least none I've ever met have. She smiled, impishly, her small, firm breasts slightly upward tilted, then flew into my arms. The impression of holding a naked child in my arms lasted only an instant. This was a woman, and she left no doubt in my mind. She kissed me softly, then harder, her tongue darting provocatively between my lips. Then she tugged me toward a silk-covered divan.

Some women accept love, others give love, but only a few *are* love—if by love you mean sex. It was a vital part of Betty Blayne. She needed love—sex—the way she needed food. She was vibrant, alive, lustful, if that's the right word. It was a natural physical need with her, enhanced, beyond doubt, by the fact she had to play a too-youthful role most of her waking hours. But when there was opportunity to be herself, her own age, she made up for restrictions she resented so much. And I think there was a side to her that took delight in shocking others—especially men—who might have accepted her at face value, unaware of her true self beneath the little-girl frills. If she had any sexual inhibitions, I was never made aware of them. Her hands were knowingly busy, her mouth warmly seeking to arouse a man's passion, displaying an expertise partly natural, but more the end product of experience. Any thoughts of her being childlike were quickly dissipated. Along with me. I've never been a great one for sex in the afternoon, but I must say it's a hell of a way to work up an appetite for lunch. . . .

Her responses grew in duration and intensity, and her slimly youthful body demanded fulfillment. But when it was over, there was no languor on her part, for she instantly vanished through a gilded door, and when she came back, she was flushed, laughing—and dressed. The innocent child image, if a bit breathless, was restored. Her dress was designed for a twelve-year-old, all flounces and frills, and she wore white stockings, little white Mary Jane shoes with buttoned straps, and even had a big blue bow-ribbon nesting atop her golden curls. She wore little makeup—she didn't need it—just a touch of red on her soft, pouting-look lips, to match the natural pinkish flush of her creamy cheeks.

"How was that for a surprise, Billy-love?" she demanded pertly. Her voice didn't match her young appearance, for it was a woman's full, throaty voice.

"Do you greet all your luncheon partners that way?"

"Only the boys, darling!" She came across and kissed me, quite sedately. Her skin was fresh and lovely, and unbelievably youthful.

"Just how the hell old are you?" I blurted.

She made a face at me. "Old enough, wouldn't you say?" Then she laughed her husky laugh again. "The studio says I'm sixteen, my mother says I'm just a little girl—and I was born in 1895, if you *must* know!"

"I don't believe it!" I said. "But even if it's true, that still makes me old enough to be your father."

"Then you must have lost your virginity very young, Billy-love!" She laughed again, affectedly, a trilly ripple of sound, perfectly suited to the little-girl image; so perfect, in fact, it had to have been developed carefully for a long, long time.

"I'm starved! Sex always makes me hungry—how about you?"

"I'll get the waitress," I said.

"I've already ordered—push the bell and they'll serve it!"

I found the gilt-covered bell-push and punched it. The trim young woman in black satin came in, smiling and pushing a little cart that held a tall china teapot and dainty little cups. She removed the lid of the teapot and lifted out an ice-frosted cocktail shaker. She poured the liquid into cups and backed out. Betty Blayne handed me a cup, took the other, smiled at me over the brim of it. Her eyes weren't twelve years old, and neither was their message.

"To sex, Billy-love!"

We drank.

"Your mother phoned me this morning."

"What did the old bitch want?"

"My hide—if I don't stay away from you." I liked the bite of the cocktail. It was mostly gin, with lemon and orange juice in it. Good gin. "She called me a very dirty name and said she'd kill me."

"I wouldn't put it past her, the old whore!" Again the carefully studied childlike laugh. "Did she scare you, Billy-love?"

"Yes."

"Then why are you here?"

"Maybe because I thought it was worth dying for."

She set her cup down, took mine, and moved into my lap. She kissed me again and guided my hand up under her frilly little girl's dress. She wasn't wearing anything under it. I must have jerked my hand back, because she laughed again, this time full-throatedly, and hugged me hard.

"I love you, Billy-mine!" she said. "You're so damned old-fashioned proper under that man-of-the-world image you project. All the girls' bottoms you've felt—and you're still easy to shock."

"Not that many girls—or bottoms—and none that looked as young as you do."

She jumped up, frowning, and moved to a gilded-frame rococo mirror on the wall, studied her face and figure, made a face at her little-girl image, backed away, turned and flipped her frilly dress up over her naked backside, in derision. She straightened, slowly, frowning hard at me.

"That's what I think of how I look!" She turned back to glare fiercely at her reflection. "How would you like to spend your whole goddamned life being a twelve-year-old kid? 'Think about your image, Betty. Don't show your legs, Betty. Flatten down your tits, Betty. . . . God, how sick I am of it!"

For that brief instant she was a grown young woman, not a vestige of child-elf left, her pretty face sternly older, and mature. It made her human, made me understand what drove her, why sex was so important to her. It forced the child-image away, if even only for a brief while. If I'd ever thought of the image-making, of old Hollywood, it wasn't something real. In my time, actors and actresses were totally human, foibles and all—sometimes just too damned human, flaunting every detail of their cesspool private lives to their public. But in the old days, those silver screen images weren't real people, with human needs and desires; they didn't have bellyaches, and break wind, and go to the toilet, and fornicate. They were bright dream-shadows, unreal—and kept that way by lollipop fan magazine publicity. No wonder the scandals that occurred from time to time hit the public so hard, and destroyed so many screen careers—and lives.

Betty Blayne's way of living with her pure-white little-girl screen-shadow was to indulge her sexual appetites as often and as fully as she could—and drink. She refilled our cups, lifted hers in a mock toast.

"To my mother's itty bitty baby girl!"

We drank, and then there was a discreet knock on the door, and the waitress brought in another cart, this time loaded with food. She laid out lunch on the table in the center of the room, and moved up the too-small woven-wicker—gilded, too!—chairs. The gin had loosened me and I felt ravenous. The food was good, a big salad with an oil-and-vinegar dressing that had a faint fish taste to it, but no garlic or onions. Lamb chops in fancy paper panties, and green mint jelly. Little squares of buttered toast with cinnamon and sugar. A fruit compote to top it off, along with a silver pot of coffee.

Betty Blayne opened a white leather shoulder-strap purse, removed frilly silk bloomers—bloomers!—I'd never seen a pair before—and pulled them on. The little-girl illusion was not total. It also meant an end to the sex for that meeting. I was surprised to realize that I was still interested: Taylor had better recuperative powers sexually than Ernie Carter did. I had the feeling that the thought made Taylor feel smugly self-satisfied, wherever he was

She stood on tiptoe to give me a little-girl kiss, warm and moist, but hardly passionate, and then was gone. The check was for thirty dollars, which I didn't think was very much, considering everything that went with lunch. I opened the bulky billfold tucked into an inner pocket of my suitcoat, and got another surprise. Funny money—or what looked like it. The bills were not only the size of pancakes, they were yellow on one side. For an instant I panicked, then I realized they were legal tender— yellowbacks, payable in gold at the nearest bank. Gold—hell, it had just become legal to own it again, back in my own time. Which made me plunge a hand into my pants pocket; I came up with a fistful of change—all solid silver, not a single cheap base-metal sandwich coin in the lot. Not only that, gold glinted pleasantly among the other pieces—two heavy twenty-dollar coins, three smaller ten-dollar eagles, and even two or three five-buck pieces, about the size of a nickel. Now I intended not only taking the Pierce-Arrow back with me, I'd stick a few nice gold pieces into the leather glovebox under the polished hardwood dashboard. . . .

I left thirty-five bucks on the table. "What, no credit cards?" I asked the waitress, who of course looked blank. "Just kidding you along, honey," I found myself saying. Next I'd be telling somebody to twenty-three skidoo—which I never did understand. *It means a quick exit offstage, you cheapskate!*

Hey, Taylor! Stick around.

There was no response. Taylor was gone again. I wondered if he had vicariously shared my recent love-session with Baby Betty Blayne. *You bloody bastard.* He had.

The waitress looked disappointed, and I understood Taylor's "cheapskate" crack. I picked up the five and replaced it with a ten, and she smiled, broadly, and gave me the eye. Then Betty Blayne was back, frowning hard, and kicking the gilded door shut behind her, hard, as the waitress hurried out.

"Damn! Damn! Damn!" she said. "Now what will we do?"

"I don't know—what did you have in mind?"

"Don't be funny." She glared at me. "Do you know who's sitting downstairs, big as life? Mary Miles Minter and her mother, that's damned well who! And Mrs. Shelby won't waste much time phoning my mother all about our tête-à-tête—and all hell really will boil over!"

Taylor? Damn it, I need you!

Smugness, again. *Of course you do. Pay attention, now.*

Taylor's thoughts made sense. I smiled and kissed the agitated little girl's face. "Take it easy, baby," I said. "Let Papa handle it."

She gave me an angry look. "Don't 'baby' me!" Then she abruptly laughed, her full-throated woman's laugh. "I'm sorry, Billy-love—what should we do?"

"You wait here. I'll send the maître d' up to smuggle you out while I cover for you."

I kissed her again, and went out. The maître d' was hovering near the little wrought-iron lift, and bowed with a Continental flourish.

"The service was all right, sir?" he asked.

I gave him a grin. "I've never been better serviced in my life. But you can do me a favor, please?"

I peeled off a yellowback double sawbuck from Taylor's roll, as I told him the problem. He smiled, and the bill vanished into his hand.

"Of course, sir, no problem at all."

He hurried into the lift, and it rose silently. Sixty bucks shot—but it was worth it. I've never been a heavy spender but this didn't seem like my money. As a matter of fact, it didn't seem like real money at all, so parting with it didn't bother me. Since it didn't seem to bother Taylor, either—no cracks from him—I gathered he wasn't the frugal type.

I glanced at the main salon, and suddenly realized I wouldn't know either Mary Miles Minter or her mother. But I didn't have to worry. Taylor was enjoying himself, and I tried to pull back, to let him take over. They were sitting at a tiny table near the entrance—and no wonder Betty Blayne had panicked when she saw them. There was no way of avoiding seeing them—or them seeing her. I found myself bowing, slightly, from the waist, then smiling as I apprached their table. Mrs. Shelby registered no expression, but blondly beautiful young Mary Miles Minter smiled, and I—Taylor—took her hand, in warm greeting. They talked for a moment—how long it had been—how much they had enjoyed working together in all those pictures. Taylor supplied the data from his latent memories: *Anne of Green Gables*, late in 1919, and three more, *Judy of Rogue's Harbour*, *Jenny Be Good*, and *Nurse Marjorie* in 1920. But none last year, in 1921. It was about time that they made another film together. . . .

Their dessert came, and I took my leave. The big front windows were darkening, and light were being turned on. The maître d' was at the front door, smiling at me. One eye flickered slightly in a hidden wink. "We will be having *dansants* beginning next week, Mr. Taylor, with a small orchestra, if it interests you? Private rooms for more . . . intimate luncheons, of course."

"Right on, brother," I said, and went out.

The street was almost dark; there was still a minor touch of glowing color in the sky, and also a darker, threatening buildup of clouds over the distant Hollywood Hills. It was cool enough to make the topcoat comfortable, and I swung the cane jauntily. I could get to liking this kind of life, I thought. What there was left of it! The darker thought rushed in. Just one more week, unless I came up with some pretty damned good answers. And dying in 1922 didn't grab me at all—no way!

I rounded the corner, heading for the Pierce-Arrow, where I'd parked it, and ran into a brick wall, or what seemed like one. It was a man. Taylor was no midget, standing six feet, at a guess—an inch taller than I did—but this bird topped him by inches. He was wide, and thick, and his face matched his body, broken nose, bent ear, and all. A gold tooth shone in his scarred-lipped mouth, and he grabbed my coatfront with hamlike hands, and swung me against the wall of the building—hard enough to knock my wind out. He balanced and then drove a piledriver fist into my gut. But I'd had time to move with the punch; for a pug, he had the deadly fault of telegraphing his punch. I dropped the cane, heard it clatter on the sidewalk—then caught him with a backhanded karate chop across his windpipe. It surprised the hell out of him, and he staggered back.

Up to that point it was bad enough, but it quickly got worse. He had a friend, a dark, slim type, who moved like a dancer—and carried a switchblade in his fist. It ripped a hole in Mr. Taylor's two-hundred-dollar London-tailored topcoat. I caught the little man's arm, before he could draw back for a second try, jerked him toward me, and the brick wall of the building behind me snapped off the blade of his knife. He leaped back, but I came at him, kicking. The first one caught him high, on the hip—sent him sprawling back over a car hood.

The big man had recovered enough to grab me. He held me, spun me, and slammed a fist into my face. It hurt. My knees buckled. Then I backed away. He made the serious mistake of coming after me. I fell back, using arms, hands, and feet, and tossed him, using his own momentum, a good ten feet. He hit the pavement hard and stayed there. The smaller man scrambled around the car, saw the carnage, and took off. It was getting darker. He was gone in an instant, without even the sound of running feet.

Breathing a little hard—but not as hard as I might have been in my own body, damn it!—I walked down to the big jaybird. He was trying to sit up. I knelt, grabbed a fistful of thick, greasy hair, and jerked him to his feet. I slammed him back against the building and rammed his head against the bricks.

"Talk!" I ordered. "Before I beat your brains out!"

He glared at me, so I made sure that he understood that I meant it, and slammed his head a couple of more times. There was blood on the bricks. He glowered at me and tried to bring up his fists. I jammed my knee into his groin. The fight left him, and he slumped, groaning, his battered face agonized.

"You heard me!" I insisted.

"What d'ya want to know?"

"Who sent you—why are you after me?"

"Nobody—just a heist—hey!"

This last as I banged his head against the wall again.

"Okay, okay, okay!" he said, harshly. "Not that it'll do yer any damned good, see? You talk too fuckin' much, an' the mad dog says shut yer up . . ."

That was all I got. I heard the car peeling rubber around the corner. Instinct took over. I dropped flat to the pavement, trying to dig myself into it. I heard the ripping explosions of the shots—twenty or thirty of them. A tommy gun, by God! I looked up and saw the bullets chewing into the bricks, viciously—and across the wide, thick chest of my erstwhile assailant. He lunged erect, smashed against the wall. I twisted, to see the car. It was a big, dark touring car, with side curtains up. I thought I recognized the smaller of the two men who had attacked me, behind the gun that poked its short, ugly snout through the curtains, then the car flashed past, down the street, and was gone, leaving me prone on the sidewalk, with a dying man slowly crumpling down on top of me. I got up, fast, and caught the big man, eased him down. He stared up at me.

"Corbo—that son of a bitch," he said, and died.

Far away, I heard a police whistle screeching, then an odd rapping that carried through the cement of the sidewalk. I'd almost forgotten, but cops on the beat pounded their nightsticks on the sidewalk in an emergency, in the old days. Then feet slapped, and a cop in uniform came running up, a gun in his fist. He eyed me, decided I wasn't a menace, and knelt beside the dead man.

"What the hell happened?"

"A car—came around that corner—on two wheels—I heard a machine gun firing and dropped to the sidewalk. He didn't." I nodded at the sprawled-out body. It sounded reasonable.

"Are you okay?"

"Fine," I said. "They weren't after me."

The cop bought it. He nodded.

"Goddamn hooligans—shooting each other in the streets— that's what Prohibition's brought us to." He shook his head. "Heard about them newfangled machine guns—typewriters, the bastards call 'em. Tommy guns on the streets of L.A., for Christ's sake!"

I wondered what he would have made of the Watts Riot, and the average of more than five hundred murders a year in his nice little L.A. The most famous of which, even after fifty years, I was likely to be a party to.

Two more foot patrolmen hurried onto the scene; they confabbed with the first one and then one hotfooted it to the corner callbox. The first one was the youngest and probably the brightest; he produced a notebook and pencil—not the omnipresent ball-point of my time, which wouldn't even be invented for a hell of a long time to come, but a stubby yellow-painted piece of lead pencil—and started asking questions. My name, what I was doing there, did I know the victim or his assailants, how many men were in the getaway car, and what year, make, and model was it. I hadn't the faintest idea, because all these high-assed models looked alike to me, except for standouts like my snazzy little Pierce-Arrow. I was thankful it was parked far enough up the block not to have been damaged by any stray .45 tommy gun slugs. The second cop hiked up the street to it, then came back and nodded to my younger questioner, and something passed between them, for they both acted a bit more respectful. Obviously Taylor and his car had impressed them. An L.A. cop in my day wouldn't have acted that respectful to God Almighty, Himself—a Murder One inquiry was a good time to showboat it, to exercise the authority they didn't really have anymore.

In minutes, two unmarked touring cars pulled up; one had a windshield-mounted spotlight—it was actually set in rubber, *through* the glass, with a pistol grip and trigger, and easily swiveled by the driver of the car. I'd never seen anything like it before, and found myself wondering how many other once-popular gadgets had vanished over the years. The spotlight was trained on the dead man and the wall behind him. The straight line of the slugs hadn't been interupted by his body; they had gone through it and chunked out pieces from the bricks like the rest. A half-dozen men got out, two in uniform had been driving the cars, the others in plainclothes—detectives, I gathered.

One of them was plainly in charge. He eyed the scene, taking his time, before turning his attention to me. Sergeant Dan Cahill was a pleasant-faced man, a bit rotund, but hard-muscled. His eyes were bright Irish blue, and his reddish face was freckled. He always looked as if he'd been in the sun a bit too long. He had a slightly twisted upper lip in one corner of his mouth, which made him seem to be smiling all the time. But his eyes were sharply intelligent, and his voice was pleasantly cultivated. It didn't take much to figure out that Cahill was no dummy.

He talked to the cops on the beat, knelt beside the dead man, inspected the bullet-pocked wall, then walked over to me. I had recovered my silver-headed cane and my dignity. I kept my arm down close to my left side, covering the knife rip in my coat—but I'll be damned if I can explain why, or why I had lied to the beat cop who first questioned me. It was not a matter of just not wanting to be involved; Taylor had an obvious stake in the matter and was desperately trying to control my reactions and play it close to his vest.

Cahill studied me for a moment, then introduced himself by name and rank. "Dan Cahill, detective sergeant, Homicide Detail, Central Division," he said, perpetually half-smiling. "You saw the shooting?"

"I damned near *was* the shooting, Sergeant," I replied, smiling back.

"But you ducked in time?"

"That's right. I was coming from Paulais', walking to my car—I'd parked it up the street, here—and as I turned the corner I bumped into the—dead man, there. We both sidestepped— you know how confused a simple thing like that can get— somehow each of us making the wrong move for an instant or two." He nodded. "Suddenly, I heard tires screeching behind me—a car racing around the corner, I think—and then the sound of gunfire."

Cahill's smile didn't soften his face a bit. "You were so certain it was gunfire—and not an auto backfiring—that you dropped to the sidewalk?"

I kept my smile friendly. "After two years in France, Sergeant, I know the difference. I've been strafed before." *Strafed?* Taylor's words came easily, now; I didn't even have to think about them. But why the hell was I covering up the fact the two bastards had been after me? Whatever Taylor's reasons he kept them to himself, and I couldn't get an inkling.

Cahill nodded. "You told the officer that you didn't know this man?"

"Never saw him before in my life." I hesitated. "I say, Sergeant, I am a bit shaken. Would it be all right if I went to my car? I need a drink."

Cahill's permanent smile widened a trifle. "Sure thing. Only a couple of more questions. I'll ask them as we walk along."

At the Pierce-Arrow roadster, Cahill admired it, walked past to look at the imposing front end, came back. I took a silver flask from a door pocket, uncapped it, drank a swig of damned good brandy. I eyed Cahill, questioningly, and he looked regretful.

"I'll have to take a raincheck, Mr. Taylor." He asked three or four more questions, my home address, where I could be reached, then smiled wider again. "That should do it. Sorry a thing like this had to happen to you."

"Me, too, Sergeant." He walked back to the others. A high, narrow-bodied ambulance had arrived. No red lights, no sirens. The body was loaded onto a canvas litter, lifted into the ambulance. It drove past. I got into the Pierce-Arrow and started the engine. My hands were trembling a little. I looked back. Sergeant Dan Cahill was looking at the bloody smear high on the brick wall where I'd banged the hoodlum's head so hard, then he turned to look toward me. I waved a friendly hand at him and drove off.

9

The streets seemed much darker than I was used to, and the electric lights seemed dimmer. The sparsely scattered street-lamps didn't help much, and only the more powerful headlamps of the Pierce-Arrow lit up the sidewalks. Oddly enough, I'd seen photographs of old Pierce-Arrows before, and their most unusual feature was the headlamps flowing out of the fenders; but it was a feature my yellow baby didn't share. Its headlamps were round and massive, and set on chromed bars between the fender and the radiator shell.

Fog—not smog, but whitish, wispy fog—was moving in, already a fuzzy gray-white blanket overhead, and making a blurry nimbus around every light. There was some traffic, but it wasn't even moderately heavy; the passing streetcars were reasonably full, but not jammed, and their soft-lighted interiors gave a warm feeling. The bottoms and tops of the big streetcar windows were beginning to steam over, leaving ragged holes in the center of each glass pane, so it was beginning to get colder. With the open roadster letting the cold wind whip around me, I appreciated the topcoat, especially since the unnatural body-heat generated by the fight had worn off.

Back in my own time the freeways would be jammed, bumper to bumper, tail-enders raising tempers, and even with the windows rolled up and the new soundproofing on cars, the roar of the city's traffic was a constant threnody. Here and now, it was quiet; the purring of the big Pierce-Arrow engine and the humming of its thinner, harder tires—balloon tires weren't around in 1922, and tubeless tires wouldn't be manufactured for another quarter-century, while nylon cord, steel belts, and radial designs weren't even inventor's dreams, yet—were gently reassuring, like the firm, positive feel of the huge wooden steering wheel.

How did you do that? Taylor was back with me. *You almost killed those two men. Jujitsu?*

They—or at least that little jerk in the car—tried to return the favor with that chopper. And it was karate, not jujitsu—although they have something in common.

Were—are you a professional fighter?

Hell, I told you—I'm a cop, detective sergeant.

Like that man—Cahill?

That's right. Which brings me to the payoff question. What in hell is the idea of lying to him? If I ever saw a guy who could use a little help from the police—

No!

Yes. You're up to your eyebrows in potential killers. These boys tonight were holding up your number for grabs.

You don't know that! If you hadn't fought them—

We'd be bleeding all over that street, either dead or crippled. They were playing for keeps, Taylor.

Pause. Sharper. *You really believe that my life—that I'm in danger from—someone?*

What does it take to convince you, Taylor? God damn it, your murder is famous—it's been unsolved for fifty years.

You're just trying to frighten me.

Damned right I am—because it scares the hell out of me too! Remember, I'm *you*—as alive as you are, and I'm not looking forward to getting shot to death with you a damned bit. You're not stupid, Taylor. You're as aware of things as I am—and you know a hell of a lot more about why it's happening. Now open up!

Silence. But Taylor hadn't gone to—wherever he went. Limbo? Jesus, what was happening to *me*—to Ernie Carter—while I was stuck back here in 1922? The thought suddenly pressed in upon me with all the weight of those years to come. I was more alone, more frightened, than I'd ever been before in my life—and more helpless. I wanted *out*, back to where I belonged, to crowded freeways, and smelly smog, and McDonald's hamburgers, and compact cars, and nylon-stockinged legs. . . . Flicker—strobe-jump! Everything blurring, sickeningly.

For Christ's sake, don't do that!

Okay, okay, Taylor. But believe me, I'm scared. I don't want to die—and neither do you.

Of course not . . . . Taylor was agitated, worrried. *But what can we do about it?*

I don't know. I haven't any glib answers. But you know things that I don't—things that might keep us both alive.

Again there was stubborn silence.

Suddenly I found myself doubting the whole thing. It was unreal—it *had* to be unreal. I was William Desmond Taylor—once William Cunningham Deane-Tanner—Irish-English-American, a runaway, a family deserter, a wanderer who struck it rich in the new Babylon called Hollywood. Nobody else. No lost wanderer in Time, just Bill Taylor, and I had made it good, and all this split-personality bunk—what I needed was a long talk with an alienist. Psychiatrist. They don't call them alienists anymore, not for many, too many years, and split personality went out with Jekyll and Hyde—"schizophrenia" is the word. *What's wrong with me? Why are my thoughts mixed up, crazy, like this?*

Get back, damn it! I'm Ernest Carter, and I'm a cop, living in the not-so-hot 1970s, not some forgotten yahoo who was murdered before I was born! *Like hell you are!*

Flicker, blurring everything, closing in, strobe-jump, again and again.

I came back just in time to avoid wrapping the long nose of the Pierce-Arrow around a stubby cement lightpost. There were still a few of them left, scattered around in the older sections of L.A., but here they were the latest thing, installed this past year, replacing the older gas-filament streetlamps. I got the roadster back on the street with a jerk of the wheel. The fog was thickening, swirling across the street in the headlights. The oncoming headlamps hardly burned through it; they would be suddenly there, and just as suddenly gone. The fog had a muffling effect on the noises of the night traffic. A streetcar had halted at one end-of-track intersection, and I could hear the thud-thudding of its compressors as I passed. At least the streets hadn't been changed—not in this part of town, anyway—so I knew where I was. I turned onto Vermont and headed north, driving slowly.

I knew one thing for certain; I had to stop—*we* had to stop—doubting the situation. It didn't change anything, and it sure as hell didn't help. *Agreed.* Taylor understood, at least as well as I did—which wasn't much. But it was something. The situation we shared, regardless of our personal reactions to it, was real, period. And accepting that fact made it all the more vital to do something about Taylor's coming murder. *What?*

Level with me, to start with. Those two goons who jumped me—why? What the hell kind of business are you mixed up in to get them set after you? The drug business you're so damned secretive about? Did Betty Blayne's mother hire them?

That's ridiculous. Mrs. Denker couldn't possibly have anything to do with men of their sort. I could sense evasiveness again, hidden, but there.

Then who do you know would? Who's the "mad dog"?

I'm sure I wouldn't know. They could have been hired, I suppose, by almost anyone with a fancied grudge against me. . . .

That's a crock. Nobody can just casually go out and hire a couple of killers. Putting out a contract isn't that simple. And those guys were pros. Remember, Taylor, two of them are still alive—still willing to waste you at the first chance they get.

Taylor remained silent. Thinking it over in his own hidden little corner of my mind, no doubt. I drove on, giving him time to work on it.

The drug angle, remember? Pushers play for keeps. Isn't it more likely?

I don't know! I've never seen those two men before in my life—not that I remember. He was hedging again, but I couldn't do anything about it.

God damn it, Taylor, our lives may depend on my knowing who the hell has reason to kill you—and why. Even a cop has to have something to work on.

Then find out for yourself. Defiant, stubborn.

But I was increasingly certain that there was more than one force at work against Taylor. How many different forces I didn't yet know. The drug business, for one, and Betty Blayne's mother's insane resentment of Taylor's affair with her daughter, for another. And what about this guy Sands? Henry Peavey had more than indicated he might be another angle. I tried to remember the Taylor case. Sands was almost as much of a mystery figure as Taylor himself. He disappeared before the murder took place, and although he was hunted for years, he never turned up.

Interest, hesitant, but plainly evident: *Sands wouldn't kill . . . me.* I caught the slightest hesitation.

What makes you sure?

It's just that—I know, damn it! Sands forged my name to a few checks, and stole some money and things from me while I was abroad last year. I've sworn out a warrant for his arrest on the charge of theft. That's all there is to it—hardly reason for him to want to kill me. It wouldn't do him any good, nor would it change anything.

You wouldn't be around to press the charges.

I know the man, after all! I tell you, it's absurd to even consider the possibility. You're just wasting time. He believed it; I could tell.

Then tell me why, if it's that cut and dried, he's still calling you on the phone?

I'm sure I haven't the vaguest notion why, unless he's hopeful I'll withdraw the charges. Even as I received the thoughts, I knew that Taylor was lying, for reasons I couldn't understand. Keeping things to himself had become an ingrained part of his psyche. No wonder the secretive bastard was murdered—half of L.A. could have had a motive, for all I knew. But I did know that it was useless to try to force him; he would only vanish again into silence, and I desperately needed whatever scraps of help he was willing to give. However vague they might be. But it was evident that I was going to have to find out most things for myself.

Communication with Taylor wasn't as simple and easy and direct as this makes it seem. But I don't know any other way of setting it down to make sense. It wasn't actually dialogue, questions and answers, or even direct discussion. A lot of it was gut-level stuff. And his thoughts—and mine, for that matter—weren't usually put into individual words. Minds—at least mine—don't work that way. It's something simpler, more direct, more basic, faster than talking, more honest than words that don't always mean what you want them to. But, just the same, Taylor was never open and outgoing with me; I never really felt what he felt, except on a very basic level—and when he wanted me to. He—his psyche, presence, call it what you want to—was evasive, secretive, a man who had devoted his entire adult life to living a deception; I think he even had himself fooled. He was part play actor, part dilettante, and all liar. But good at it.

I turned east on Maryland and drove down to the garage I had taken the Pierce-Arrow from earlier that day. The doors were closed, and there was no sign of Howard Fellows. I put the nose of the roadster close to the door, got out, tugged out a ring of keys at the end of the golden chain that clipped into my narrow belt, and let Taylor's instincts pick out the right one. The door slid aside easily on the well-oiled overhead rollers. I drove in, switched off the lights, got out, patted the Pierce-Arrow after closing the driver's door, affectionately.

"There's got to be a way of taking you back with me," I said.

You remind me of my—of my ex-valet, Sands.

Thanks a lot.

I noticed the funny hesitation in the thought, though, even if I could make nothing out of it. I closed and locked the garage door behind me and started for the areaway beside the bungalow. As I reached it, a man stepped out, confronting me. I stopped, and brought my hands up to the defense position, then lowered them, slowly, as the man laughed. Just my hands, not my guard. It was a harsh, grating laugh, and an unpleasant voice that I had heard before. The English accent was more noticeable than it had been on the phone that morning.

"Jumpy, Mr. *Taylor?*" Sands asked. He was almost as tall as

I—Taylor—slimly built, too thinly featured to be called good-looking, and with a habit of nervously licking at his lips. A habit I'd seen before—on junkies. He was wearing a thick wool shawl-collared sweater, tweed knickers, and heavy wool socks that came to his knees. A tweed cap was pulled low over his eyes, shadowing them. Knickers! My God!

"What do you want, Sands?"

" 'Sands' is it, eh, Billy?" He laughed again, without humor, a dry, rasping sound. "It's blood I ought to be after, you stinkin' bastard. Swearin' out a warrant for my arrest. Mine!" He half-screeched this last, almost indignantly, it struck me. And Sands' manner and tone didn't match that of a man facing his legitimate accuser. There was more between Taylor and Sands than I was aware of—a hell of a lot more. Mr. Edward F. Sands promptly rose to the top spot on my growing list of murder-to-be suspects.

"You're a thief, Sands."

"And what are you, Mr. *Taylor?*" Again the peculiar emphasis on the name. It wasn't hard to guess that Sands was aware of Taylor's masquerade, probably even his true identity. Maybe that explained Sands' cocksure arrogance of manner. And maybe it didn't.

"Get out of my life," I found myself saying coldly, "or I'll put you out." I held myself apart, letting Taylor handle this. "You've more to lose than I have, Sands."

"What about the charges you've made against me? I ain't spending the rest of my life on the dodge from the coppers. Not half, I ain't."

"If you leave now, they'll soon be forgotten. I won't press them."

"And how the bloody hell do you expect me to do that?" Sands glared at me. "Using what for money? Look, Billy, for old times' sake—for the way it used to be—it doesn't have to be very much—just enough for a real stake, a chance to start over again . . . ?"

"You've had all the chances you'll get from me. I'll give you no more money—you've stolen enough. God knows!"

"And what if I talk—tell all your fancy Hollywood friends

just what kind of man you really are, Mr. Deane-Tanner?"

"Two can play that game, remember," I found myself saying firmly. Taylor had the whip hand and knew it. Sands wouldn't ever admit it, but he knew it, too. I could tell. "I won't spend the next twenty years behind bars—and you will, Sands!"

"You son of a bitch—you'd do that—to *me?*"

"That's right, I would." Hard, mean. The hatred between these two was something you could taste.

"All right, all right—but I've got to get a stake together." Sands' voice had thinned into a strident whine. "Not much, Billy—and I won't come asking for any more—not ever again."

"No. You've had everything you're going to get from me— except trouble. I never want to see or hear from you again— understand that! Be certain that I mean it."

For a moment Sands held there, facing me, his thin face twisted away from his prominent teeth. "We'll see! We'll see!" The words were almost snarled.

A cheery whistle sounded, feet thumped heavily, and a huge uniformed cop swung around the corner from Alvarado Street. Sands backed, quickly, then turned and ran, his feet making very little noise. The cop came up, hurrying his steps, looking after Sands.

"Everything all right, sir?"

"Fine, officer," I said. "Just fine."

"Oh, it's you, Mr. Taylor—thought I recognized you. Been keeping an eye out, ever since you reported bein' robbed."

"Thank you, officer."

"Marley—Jeff Marley. Just doin' my duty, sir."

"I appreciate it, Officer Marley. If you care to stop by—any time—my man Peavey always has something to refresh you."

"Thanky kindly, sir." Looking off. "That feller was in a mighty big hurry to get away."

"Panhandler," Taylor replied glibly. "I think you must have frightened him off."

"I run 'em in whenever I catch 'em at it," Marley declared righteously. "I don't allow none o' that on my beat."

"It's good to know a man like you is on the job, Officer Marley." Pure, undiluted bull that would have got a laugh in my time, and the big cop accepted it as his gospel due, touched the bill of his cap, and sauntered on down the street. Officer Marley on his beat, and all's well with the world. . . .

Peavey was putting on an overcoat when I entered the bungalow. His gold teeth sparkled in the yellowish glow of the silk-shaded lamps. "Just gettin' ready to leave, suh," he said. "Wednesday. My night off."

"Of course, Peavey," I said. "Have fun."

"Ah'll do mah best, suh!" His professional movie-darky chuckle still grated on my ears, but it was part of the man's makeup, which made me wonder if the civil rights people in my own day didn't actually play down the subservient-Negro role of the past. What bothered me most was the fact that even to Peavey it wasn't anything important or unusual, just the matter-of-fact acceptance of things as they were, without criticism or even awareness of just how demeaning and inhuman they really were. "Miss Mabel will pick yo' up at seven, suh. Did yo' want me to lay out yo' clothes, suh?"

"I'll find something, Peavey," I replied. I remembered my platinum pocket watch before I looked at my naked wrist, this time. It was just after six.

"Say, now, what happened to yo' coat, suh?" Peavey had helped me out of my topcoat, and now was holding it up, looking at the ugly rip under the left arm.

"Caught it on something, Peavey," I lied. "I don't think it can be repaired."

"No, suh," Peavey said, shaking his head, then looking at me. "Whatever it was you caught it on, it was sharp! It ain't ripped—it's cut."

"Throw it away, Peavey. I'll have to get another one." What the hell, Taylor could afford it.

"Yessuh." Peavey shook his head again. "If I can patch it up, can I have it, suh? Rip an' all, it's bettuh than what I'm wearin' now."

"Of course. Good night, Peavey."

"Yessuh. Uh, Mistuh Taylor—I thought I saw that no-good Sands hangin' around this afternoon. I tol' the policeman on the beat, an' he said he'd keep an eye out—just in case, yuh know?"

"Thanks, Peavey," I said slowly. "But we won't be bothered with Sands anymore." It was Taylor speaking, without any prompting from me. But I had the feeling he was kidding himself. Sands would be back.

With a .38 in his fist?

10

I came out of the bathroom wearing the peculiar union suit underwear that Taylor seemed to prefer—and that one-piece coverall effect with the hatch in the back took some getting used to, believe me—to find Charlie Chaplin, the Little Tramp, just entering my upstairs bedroom. For a second I could just stand there, in my knee-length undies, staring. Chaplin, I thought, was a hell of a lot smaller than I remembered him, even as an octogenarian returning to Hollywood to pick up the special Oscar voted him in an attempt to make up for a long lifetime of sins of omission. But it *was* Charlie, the Little Tramp, every movement, gesture, facial expression. He smirked at me, jumped his black-painted eyebrows up and down suggestively, wiggled his black-painted little square mustache from side to side, then did a funny little turn-around step, flexing his ridiculous little bamboo cane. Then he hopped into the room and kissed me full on the lips.

Then abruptly he bounced away, stared up at me, rocking back on his worn-down heels, balancing on that silly cane, and smirked lasciviously at me again—then broke out into peals of the most delicious feminine laughter I've ever heard. My mind refused to function for a moment. I remained rooted to the rug. And Charlie bent double with gales of laughter. It was natural, beautiful, and I would never forget it.

"If—if you could only—have seen your face!" Mabel Normand said, and choked up with laughter.

"Mabel—you little devil!" Taylor took over, smiling and reaching for the Little Tramp.

Mabel Normand backed away, beyond my—Taylor's—reach, then lifted the battered old derby hat, did a one-footed turn and hop, and headed for the bathroom, still laughing. In a moment the trappings of the Little Tramp flew out, to scatter themselves across the bedroom rug. Then, her beautiful imp's face, dripping water and soap, and running with black makeup which was smearing a white hand towel beyond redemption, wearing wispy black step-ins and frilly black satin garters supporting the sleekest pair of opera-length black silk hose I've ever seen, Mabel Normand came back into the bedroom.

"I was doing the impersonation on the set today at Goldwyn's, and I just had to show it to you!" She was not bubbling, but glowing, more alive than any woman I've ever met. Her dark eyes burned brightly, and her face was constantly animated. In repose—which never lasted for more than seconds—she was beautiful, but when her face reflected her constant change of mood, her incessant vibrancy, she was more than that. I've seen some of her pictures—all I could find—but they captured no major part of the magic that was Mabel Normand. She was quicksilver, all flowing, changing brightness, and impossible to catch, even on film. And, if that sounds like the prattle of a man in love, I won't deny it. No one who ever knew Mabel Normand failed to love her. Period. All it took was one mocking facial expression, pouting lips, or a devastating wink from one huge, luminous almost-black eye. I know. I saw it work, again and again.

"It's perfect," I said, slowly. "Almost uncanny. You *are* the Little Tramp! Even Chaplin isn't better."

She laughed, and looked wistful. "Thanks. I should be good at it—I worked with Charlie long enough—we made up a lot of it together, when we were doing those old movies together. Charlie gives me too much credit, but I did help him with the Little Fellow." She eyed me in my one-piece union suit and giggled a little. "If Mack could only see us now, I do believe he'd shoot you dead."

"The line forms on the left," I said.

Mabel blinked, her face going blank. She shook her head, slowly. "Sometimes I think you're as loony as I am—and they call *me* a madcap!"

"Sorry," Taylor managed to say, ahead of me. "If we're going somewhere—"

"The Winter Garden, snooks," Mabel said. She grinned, widely, and stood close beside me, to look at our image in the big dressing-table mirror. "What a sensation we'd be if we walked in like this—the Fisk Tire 'Time To Retire' Twins—got a couple of candles?"

I drew a blank, but Taylor was amused. "Not quite—we should be wearing Dr. Dentons," he said.

Mabel's peals of laughter rang out, and she threw her arms around me and kissed me again. Her kiss tasted of fresh mint—it always did. She often chewed on a twig of it, but that wasn't the whole explanation. It was part of her, of her natural magic, that I would remember, not some fancy, high-priced perfume—although she often wore that, too—but the clean, fresh smell and taste of mint. Mabel, dear, dear Mabel. . . .

The black silk chemise—she referred to them as teddies—or step-ins—was sheer to the point of lewdness, and clung to her perfect figure. There wasn't a bulge or even the shadow of a curve in the wrong place. But take a look at her in those crazy old woolen bathing suits of her day, in any of the many books about Mack Sennett and his comedies, and see for yourself. My hands moved, possessively, and she backed away, pretending shock.

"Why, Mr. Taylor! I'm surprised at you—and here I've always trusted you like my own dear uncle—and he was always copping a feel, too." Beautiful, remembered laughter. Fresh mint, and gales of youthful laughter. Mabel . . .

But instantly she was animated again. "Get dressed. We'll be late—and I've ordered a Chinese dinner during the show. It's the Frivolities of 1922—and everyone says it's just great—and you've got to put your pants on, and go down and get my clothes out of the car—I told Davis to bring them to the front door—and I suppose you know that Douglas MacLean and his wife are scandalized at the way women keep running in and out of your place at all hours of the day and night." She giggled, archly. "But the Little Fellow will confuse 'em! What with Charlie keeping his favorite honeybun in the bungalow next door. . . . How is she, Willie?"

"Do you mean Miss Edna Purviance?" Trust stiff-britches Taylor to make it sound stuffy.

"I don't mean Teddy, the Keystone pooch."

"But I hardly know her—I mean, not to—to—"

"You mean you haven't short-timed her, Willie? Maybe you're missing something—Charlie sure thinks she's hot stuff." More laughter.

Taylor's dignity was bruised, I could sense. Despite the man's shortcomings—and there were no end to those—he had an inner self-pride that was easily injured. But at the moment my interest in William Desmond Taylor was minimal. It was funny, but I didn't want him around, sharing this moment. Crazy, I know, but that's the way it was.

"I like your stuff better," I said. Not Taylor. Me.

Maybe something different in my voice caught her, for she suddenly looked very closely, very intently at me, studying my face, her pert little head cocked to one side, her lips pursed slightly. "Whatever happened to my oh, so teddibly, teddibly proper Englishman?"

"To hell with him," I said, and took her into my arms and kissed her. She responded, totally, enjoying the physical contact as much as I did. I'd never felt like that with a woman before, not just aroused, but aware of an intimate mutual glow, and I was pretty damned certain I never would again. Chemistry, magic, sexual attraction, call it any name you like, but it was there, between us, shared, every time we touched. I didn't have the faintest idea if Taylor was in love with Mabel Normand or not, but it was a cinch bet I was.

The sheer silk chemise was under my hands. I've held women in nylon in my arms—who hasn't? But scientific progress in the next fifty years wasn't going to match the utterly soft, clinging warmth of cobweb silk. No way, man! For sex appeal, synthetics are just not in it.

I let her go after a moment, holding her out at arm's length, just to look into her oddly surprised little face. Her eyebrows were raised slightly, her enormous eyes round as marbles. "Willie, you're a bundle of surprises tonight! Stop it, or we'll never make it to the Winter Garden."

I stopped it, but held onto her a moment longer, letting her image burn forever into my mind. Mabel. She was twenty-eight years old in 1922, and she would be destroyed by her association with William Desmond Taylor's murder, at least her career would be suddenly headed for oblivion. She would live another eight years and die in a sanitarium. I remembered that much about her from studying the Taylor case, and it held in my thoughts. There was no possible future for us, together; she would die the same year I was born, 1930. . . .

Something in my eyes made her draw back, grip her arms and shudder, as if from cold. "Don't look at me that way, Willie," she said softly, the laughter gone from her voice. "It frightens me, and I don't know why. There's something"—she paused, staring at me—"I'm not sure I like you this way, Willie. You scare me."

"Nothing in this world can scare you, Mabel," I heard Taylor say gently. "Not so long as you can laugh."

But Mabel Normand wouldn't have that much longer to live and laugh, and her whole world would be lost before she died. It would come tumbling down around her beautiful little ears, in big, ugly chunks. Unless I could find a way to keep the future from happening. . . .

"Please get my clothes, William," Mabel said. Not "Willie" this time. She had moved away, her eyes still on my face.

"Things on my mind," I said, smiling. "Forgive me?"

She moved in again and kissed me, softly. "That's my problem, Willie—I'm not the forgiving type. I find it hard to do." I gathered she was thinking of someone else. The Taylor case reports had mentioned her on-again, off-again romance with Mack Sennett. I felt a sudden surge of jealousy.

I opened the closet, tugged on the light, picked out a dark suit, climbed into the pants. The fly buttons gave me a problem; the zipper was a hell of an improvement! I opened a drawer, found a shirt—no collar on it. I opened a small upper drawer, automatically; Taylor's built-in responses, again. It was filled with white collars, all by themselves. He also opened a little drawer on a tiny wooden chest atop the chiffonier—chiffonier? I'd never heard the word before. Hell, they called them chests of drawers, now—or would when *now*—my now—got here. There were a lot of tiny gold studs in the drawer. I picked one up, held the detached collar in my left hand, around my neck, and started inserting the gold button at the back of the shirt-neck, to fasten the two together. I promptly dropped the gold collar button.

Mabel laughed, and stooped, picked it up. "I never saw a man so clumsy—you act like you'd never seen a collar button before in your life! What do you do when there's nobody here to help you?" She gave me a studied look. "Or do you always have *somebody* here?"

"Not always," Taylor replied, and laughed. "Just usually." I believed the bastard!

Mabel adroitly fixed the collar, and even picked out a narrow tie, tied it for me. She had had practice at doing both. I found myself wondering—jealously—who the lucky guy had been.

Davis, her chauffeur, was standing on the little front porch, a tiny valise in his hand. He was dressed in a gray double-breasted uniform, black leather puttees, and matched black-billed driver's cap. He was slim, and darkly handsome, too darkly handsome for his name to be Davis. He handed me the valise, snapped around, and strode off—back to his waiting car. His manner was stiffly formal, but his eyes gave him away; they didn't like me one damn bit. Chalk up one more for Taylor. But remembering my own reaction to Mabel Normand, it wasn't hard to understand. Davis loved her. Hell, like the confidential police report that cleared her from suspicion in the William Desmond Taylor murder case said, *everybody* loved Mabel Normand.

Only not enough to forgive her for being involved in the case at all.

Mabel took the tiny case, opened it atop the bed, and took out a black dress. I never saw her wearing any other color, except in front of a movie camera, although she often wore brightly colored neckerchiefs. She twisted around and hiked up her dress to straighten her seams—another lost art! Her long, sheer black hose set off her perfect, slim legs. No hosiery model ever had better ones.

"You like?" she asked.

"We can go to the Winter Garden another night."

She laughed, and kissed me—lightly—again. Fresh mint. And French perfume. I'd never forget it.

"I already have the tickets—and ordered the dinner, too." My disappointment showed, and she laughed, and patted my cheek affectionately. "Next time—I promise."

I made a mental note to make sure there was a next time—soon.

Davis snapped to attention as we came out, and held open the back door of the big sedan. I didn't recognize the make, but saw the name "Leach" on the radiator shell. Leach? I'd never heard of it, but I've since found out there were thousands of different makes of automobiles between 1900 and 1950. Thousands! Mabel's limousine-sedan was a big, heavy car, comfortable enough to ride in, but sluggish, and not in a class with my Pierce-Arrow roadster. *Yours?* Taylor was still with me when he chose to be.

There was a glass partition behind the driver's seat, and it was closed. Davis got in and pulled away from the curb. He drove a little awkwardly, but maybe it was the car, not the driver. I decided that the Leach sure as hell wouldn't win any road races. Neither would Davis, for my money.

Halfway downtown, Mabel saw something and grabbed the horn-shaped communicator. "Go around the block, Davis," she ordered. Davis made the turn by jamming on the big mechanical brakes, which squealed mightily. He came back around to Vermont again and pulled into the curb near a small corner grocery store. The front windows were steamed over, the interior lights glowing behind them. A big canvas awning overhung the sidewalk, and in its shelter were fruit stands. A dangling clear-glass bulb lighted them, swinging in the soft gusts of wind. A peanut roaster whistled in the doorway—I remembered them at the zoo, when I was a little kid—the sound cheerful. "Buy me some peanuts!" Mabel commanded, and Taylor jumped to obey, climbing out quickly, and banging his head in the process. I'd hit the bruised place on my forehead, and for an instant lights pinwheeled and skyrockets lit up the scene, then they faded, but my head throbbed painfully. Damn! The trick of it, I found, was getting up from the seat first, then stepping out. The lost art of limousine-climbing-out-of had long since joined that of stocking-seam-straightening . . .

The smells from the warm interior of the grocery store welled out, half delicatessen, and half dry-goods, and I enjoyed them. They brought back memories—old memories, long since forgotten in the growing-up and grown-up years. A man in a greasy white apron came out and waved a hand in recognition at Mabel. Everyone recognized her and everybody loved her. Only, why hadn't they stuck by her when she needed them, the bastards?

A striped paperbag was jammed with peanuts in the shell, still hot. I carried them back to the car, and Davis drove off. Mabel went hungrily after the peanuts. Taylor shook his head when offered some—the snob! But Mabel just smiled, and broke the shells, ate the hot nuts with her bright, white teeth, and scattered the empties over the floor of the Leach sedan. The floor was thick with them in a few minutes. She didn't even notice. That was Mabel Normand, too. Only the desire of the moment—and its indulgence—really mattered. But I found myself in favor of living for now. There just might not be anything more. And I had the feeling that although I was experiencing this emotion for the first time, Mabel Normand had lived with it for a long, long time.

The old Winter Garden was on Spring Street, just across from the Alexandria Hotel. The old hostelry, still standing in my time, looked great; it was still comparatively youthful, just sweet sixteen, in 1922, and yet to fall upon the bad times that, along with newer and fancier competition, would keep it closed for years. Davis pulled up at the curb, hopped out, and opened the streetside back door for us. Down the block there was a line of big limousines and boxy taxicabs waiting for their owners and fares.

There was a table waiting for us—the best in the place. What else for Mabel Normand? A small dance orchestra was playing, and several couples were shuffling slowly around the floor.

People dancing in each other's arms, instead of standing a foot apart and simulating some demi-obscene African mating jig. Mabel excused herself to go to the ladies' room—and I was suddenly aware of how quiet she had become in the last few minutes. Like a clock running down, ticking slower and slower. But she came back in a few minutes, as animated as ever, and I decided it must have been my imagination. I just wish to God it had been.

The Winter Garden was garishly trying to be stylish, and succeeding only in being tawdry. The decorations were dusty and tarnished, drooping awry in places. The show wasn't much, a lot of bare skin and sleazy long-feathered headdresses, but the chorus line kept in step, and although the strange falsetto-tenor voice of the hair-dyed singer in the brassy-looking, too-tight tuxedo grated, I rather enjoyed it.

A waiter came up, looked around, and bent low to whisper, "No hooch tonight, folks. The Prohis've been snooping around. Sorry."

Mabel shook her head and gave me an arch look. "Got your flask on your hip, Willie?"

I remembered seeing the big full-pint sterling silver flask on my dressing table, and shook my head. "Forgot it," I said. "I had other things on my mind."

"In that case I'll forgive you." She laughed again. "But there's got to be someplace better than this!" She frowned, then brightened, and stood up in one swift little movement. "I know! Come on!"

The other people nearby looked at us, but Mabel made a face at them and dragged me away. She hurried ahead of me while I reclaimed our coats and overpaid the bill, and had the car door open when I hit the sidewalk. Davis blared the Klaxon at me impatiently. It was getting cold again. Mabel jumped into the Leach and jerked me in after her. The car was moving before I'd slammed the door shut.

"Hey, what's the hurry?"

"We've got to be there before ten—and it's a long way off!" she answered, breathlessly, then picked up the speaker horn. "Hurry, Davis!"

I saw his becapped head bob, and the Leach lumbered to pick up speed. I noticed the pile of peanut shells at the curb as I got in; Davis had swept them out of the interior of the car. But a crunch under me proved he hadn't gotten them all out of the seat. I heisted up and swept my hand over the seat. Mabel caught my hand, pulled it into her lap, then leaned against me to be kissed. I lost all interest in peanut shells, and even in where we were going; I just hoped we wouldn't get there too quickly.

11

I recognized some of the streets. Davis drove steadily. We were heading east, toward Pasadena, but that was about all that I was sure of. The back of the big Leach sedan was in darkness, but the passing streetlights and cars gave Davis a pretty good notion of what was going on in the back seat. The notion of an audience bothered me a lot more than it did Taylor, I think. Either way, I cooled it. Mabel Normand was relaxed, half-smiling, almost dreamily, returning my lovemaking, but only to a degree. Perhaps it was all of herself that she could give; the thought still bothers me.

We drove for nearly an hour; but without freeways and their flashing speeds, I couldn't be sure how far we had come. Abruptly we stopped. It was dark. I could see the loom of mountains, unmarked by lights, against the sky. A trolley car was waiting, only three or four passengers aboard. Mabel sat up, grinned at me, then hopped out.

"We made it!" she cried, happily, like a child finding the park was still open, and headed for the trolley car at a skipping run. I tried the better way of limousine-exiting and found it worked fine. Maybe just the thought of banging it was the reason, but my head was throbbing again. The trolley car wasn't painted the yellow-red scheme of the streetcars; it was a solid, deep red, and across the side of it was lettered in gold: PACIFIC ELECTRIC. But it was far too small, and too close-coupled to be a Big Red Car—the interurban system that Southern Californians had dumped like the mass of idiots they were and are. A lighted box at the front end of the car had a glowing sign that read MOUNT LOWE. It meant nothing to me. I'd never heard of the place. Probably like other old-time districts, such as Edendale, it had vanished into the sprawling conglomerate that was Los Angeles in my time.

The seats in the trolley car were polished wood and hard as hell. The conductor was wearing a heavy dark-blue coat, somewhat like a Navy peajacket, with leather collar and cuffs, and his hands were covered with wool-palm, leather-back mittens. Gloves I could have accepted without notice, but mittens—in L.A.? I paid our fares. Mabel was in a window seat, nose pressed against the cold glass like a kid, trying to see out into the darkness beyond. I could feel her excitement.

"Where are we going?" I asked.

She turned to grin at me. "Up!" She looked out again, her breath steaming up the window glass. This close to the mountains it was cold. "I'm glad I remembered they were running specials up this week—the Republican thing in town, you know."

I didn't, but I nodded anyway. At the back of the car the conductor jerked a bellcord, and a musical clanging rang out. Then the car started forward with a lurch. It was the beginning of a trolley-car ride I'd never forget.

Mabel jittered on the edge of her hard wooden seat, and used her hand to wipe away the mist from the window. She kept looking out, like she was watching for something. The trolley car rumbled up a good grade, the reduction gears maintaining a steady growling vibration through the wooden body of the car. The heaters under the windows were popping and gurgling, but losing the fight against the cold wind that found many entrances into the little rattling car. I buttoned up my topcoat—a dark-gray model that Peavey had dug out for me—and I was grateful for the heavy velvet insert of the collar, which I turned up against my neck. Taylor's wardrobe might have lacked imagination and color, but it was plentiful. I even found a pair of lightweight, dark-gray suede gloves tucked into one of the big side pockets, and pulled them on over my numbing fingers. It was cold, and getting more so, rapidly, as the trolley kept climbing steadily higher and higher into the chilly night.

The streetlights, and window lights from houses we passed, soon ended, and the night seemed solid black. The trolley slowed for a sharp curve, but never altered its steady upward slant. It felt like we were following switchback tracks going right up the mountainside—and that was exactly what it was. The ride up Mount Lowe used to be advertised as the most thrilling trolley-car ride in the world, and apart from the Alps, I don't doubt it a damned bit. But the car seemed well-powered by its overhead wire, and made good time on the way up. It would make even better time coming down.

There were a number of shallow-grade straightaways, ending in switchback curves that made the steel wheels scream against the rails. The motorman timed them perfectly, taking them as fast as he could, and the little trolley car swayed dangerously more than once. I found myself almost grateful that I couldn't see out. Then Mabel laughed and clapped her hands together. She gripped my arm and tugged me closer to the window to look out. Through the thinning mist I could see lights—far away and far down. We were still climbing, and I could see dull-gray-white shadows in the dim yellow headlamp glow as we made another sharp curve.

"See!" Mabel exclaimed. "Look!"

"At what?"

"Snow, ninny! See it? We're way up high!" Her eyes were shining, and twin red spots glowed on her cheeks. I forced myself to look through the window.

The gray-white masses evolved into melting snowbanks. And the mist was suddenly gone, and it was colder than hell in the car. The conductor went past, swinging his arms against his chest and stamping his feet. He grinned at Mabel, sharing her brightness for a moment.

"Still plenty of snow up on top," he said cheerfully.

A final steep grade, and the air brakes hissed, and the little electric car slowed abruptly. Mabel jumped up and hurried me down the aisle, to the front door, ahead of the other passengers. There were two men, together, and a young couple; they were all bundled up in heavy wool sweaters against the cold. And they needed the warm clothes! A sharp icy wind whistled around the trolley car, and snow streaked the steep hillside, covered some of the higher slopes and ridges.

There was a little roofed shed stationhouse, here at the end of the trolley line, and beyond it, four incredibly steep tracks shone brightly, pointing almost straight up the mountain. A cable hummed noisily over its big revolving drum, and far up the tracks I could see a flickering little yellow battery-operated headlamp, coming down. The funny little slanted car that arrived at the bottom of the sharp incline reminded me of the old Angel's Flight of my youth, but this cable car climbed a high mountain peak. Far below I could see clear patches through the ground mist, and the twinkling lights of Pasadena, spread out like unset jewels on a black velvet cloth. Then the cable car rumbled and banged to a stop, and Mabel hurried me toward it. She wanted the very top row of seats, and we stumbled over the steps to get to them. She slid in, across the wooden seat. The cable car had a roof, but was otherwise open—and there was no heater. The hard wooden benchseat felt like a chunk of ice, and I shivered with the freezing cold.

The cable car started upward with a jerk, then smoothly made the ascent. We were far above the fog and mist, now, and the sky was bright with stars, and the patches of snow were still unmelted and serenely white against the barren hillside. The farther peaks of the mountain range were all white and icy. The wind grew stronger, and it had the numbing bite of snow in it. Mabel snuggled into my arms, burrowing up against me. She was warm, and she chattered happily.

"I love it up here—nothing can touch you—and everything is so nice—so clean . . ." She stopped talking, and just hugged up against me. I kissed her, and her lips were softly warm, and I could still taste fresh mint—and roasted peanuts!

The incline was almost vertical, but the cable hummed powerfully, smoothly drawing us upward. Then the car bumped into an open snowshed, and stopped, and we climbed back down the steps to get out onto the upper platform. A big, log-sided, chalet-styled building stood to one side. Below it was the steep mountain peak, snow-streaked, angling sharply downward to the distant lights of the city. The overhang was still spotty, and through clear patches, far off, we could see other, more distant sections of the City of the Angels, sparkling like Christmastree lights strung out across a dark floor.

We stood at the log barrier, looking down, until the freezing chill of the wind sent us running toward the lights of the chalet. I was surprised at how many people were there. It was called the Alpine Inn, and the dining room had big windows looking down on the L.A. Basin, so far below. The tables were covered with spotless linen cloths, and dark-clad waiters moved cheerfully. Mabel's smile got us a window table, and special attention; they knew her, of course, and of course they loved her at first sight! It showed, and oddly enough, it was real, not a put-on.

The Prohis—Federal Prohibition Agents—must have been allergic to the cold, for we were presently sipping the inevitable orange juice and gin from a china teapot. The menu was good, and the food better. I had a steak—a T-bone, which seemed to be *the* cut of meat, usually smothered in onions. I never saw a New York cut, a top sirloin, or porterhouse steak in 1922; and no baked potatoes, with or without sour cream and chives. Usually thick-cut french fries, and often spaghetti. Like everything else in the world of 1922, change would occur in food and restaurant menus. For the better? Yes—and for worse, too.

But while a part of me noted the differences that were all about, registering surprise, and often dismay and puzzlement, the rest accepted it as perfectly normal. The Taylor part of me, no doubt.

Mabel toyed with her food, but I was hungry. The cold and the orange juice and gin cocktail gave me an appetite. I ate my steak, and half of hers—and suddenly felt a pang of guilt, of sharp loss. My dog, little Kirby, of course—I always brought him a part of my steak in a doggie bag—something which didn't exist in my present here-and-now. Damn! Kirby! My own world never seemed better— or farther away—than in that moment.

Mabel seemed unaware of my mood change. She was looking

pensively out the window with her big, wide eyes, and sighed, again and again. The constant animation, the vivacity, was dying inside her, visibly. She was like a clockwork doll, slowly running down. It bothered me, strangely, driving my own worries out of my mind. This was a part of her I couldn't reach, couldn't cope with. Abruptly she stood up and excused herself, hurried off to the ladies' room.

Taylor—not me—raised a hand, and a waiter hurried up. "Cigars?" The waiter bobbed his head, returned with a box of perfectos—made in Havana by H. Uppman, which indicated either superior taste or cheaper import prices in 1922. Taylor lit up after warming the big, thick cigar in the match flame for a moment. Not being a smoker—me, Ernie Carter—I choked.

Damn it, the Surgeon General says smoking is bad for your health!

If you're correct about my being murdered—who's worrying?

I couldn't argue with that, and relaxed, and let Taylor enjoy his after-dinner smoke. The inn was warm, and I was comfortable. I hated the notion of that long, cold ride back down the mountain; but the gin would fortify my spirits. I drank some more.

The Alpine Inn crowd thinned out. After a while some of the room lights were lowered, and the view outside became clearer. Mabel was gone a long time, and then she was back, bright and merry-eyed. I'd finished the cigar and the teapot of gin and orange juice. The place was empty except for a couple of cleaning ladies and the tired-looking waiter. The little string trio had called it a night, and the alcove where they had played was dark and empty. The waiter was giving me the eye.

Mabel hugged herself, looking out the window with her big, darkly luminous eyes. "Isn't it *just great* up here?" She was back to her normal self, sparkling, alive and beautiful. But I felt a growing aching coldness in the pit of my stomach. Something was goddamned wrong—but I wouldn't let the thought take shape in my mind.

The waiter came up. "Sorry, sir—Miss Normand—but the last cable car will be going down in a few minutes."

Mabel made a face, but stood up. I overpaid the check— getting used to spending Taylor's money with a liberal hand—and we went out. The cable car was down with the last load of passengers. The cable was humming over its drums, the connectors rattling, as it brought the empty car back up the mountain incline. The fog was closing in down below us as we stood at the log railing. Ice sparkled; the black sky's stars spangled back. It was colder, but the wind had died away. Mabel snuggled under one of my arms, pressing her body against mine.

"I hate going back down there . . . to everything," she said. "I hate it!"

"People always have to go back."

"I know." She was quiet for a moment. "But wouldn't it be just great if we didn't have to? Just going on to something new, always, never the same things—or places—twice!"

"I'm not sure I'd like that. I like familiar things—and people."

"People." Mabel's voice was solemn. "Why do we have to be the way we are? Always so much sadness, and unhappiness. . . . Does it have to be that way?" She sighed. "I suppose it does. But when I was a little girl it didn't seem like that. Why did it have to change? Huh, Willie? Everything was so—so simple—so nice. . . ."

Like 1922, for me . . . except . . .

The little string of colored lights across the front—upper—end of the rising cable car slowly winked clear of the fog covering the lower shoulders of Mount Lowe and swept smoothly up toward us. It was empty. The operation of the cable cars was almost entirely automatic; when one reached the bottom, the other was at the top, in a sort of counterbalance system. The cable car swung up to the platform and stopped. Almost reluctantly Mabel straightened, out of my sheltering arms, and moved toward it. She slid into the first seat, at the lower end of the car, and we huddled together against the cold. A man came from the Alpine Inn, opened a little metal box, punched a button, then hurried back to the warmth indoors. The car jerked, then started its slow, smooth descent. After a minute or two we sank into the thickening mist. It closed in on us, damping out all outside sounds. We were alone, just the two of us, the world shut out for the moment, and I wished that moment could last forever. But it ended abruptly, as the mist thinned out, and we sank down toward the lighted wooden arch at the bottom of the incline railway, and the glowing windows of the waiting trolley car.

We transferred to the trolley, and the meager warmth inside it was welcome after the penetrating cold of the open cable car. The conductor closed the doors quickly behind us, and the trolley lurched into motion. We chose a seat in the middle of the car; we had our choice, as we were the only passengers on this final run. The conductor flopped onto a bench on the rear platform, and the motorman was hidden behind his flapping green curtain at the front. The little car swayed and rattled, gaining momentum in its rush downhill, and this time Mabel just sat quietly beside me, hunkered down into her fur-collared coat, not wiping the steamy window clear, preoccupied with her thoughts. I hugged her and smiled down into her face. She smiled back, still a little withdrawn and sad.

We hit the first switchback fast; I heard the hiss of airbrakes—then a sudden, loud, explosive sound and a blast of compressed air escaping. The car lurched, steel screamed against steel, and we hit the next curve of the switchback tracks too fast. I grabbed the back of the seat in front of us and had to use all my strength to keep us both from being catapulted into the aisle of the crazily rocking car. Behind us I heard a yell, and twisted in the seat to see the conductor hurled across the rear platform, where the centrifugal force must have been extreme. He crashed into the metal upright beside the closed wooden doors; glass crashed down about him, and I knew he was badly hurt.

The motorman lunged off his little stool, the end of which dropped into a socket in the wooden floor of the platform, and the green curtain behind him shot up on its roller, to bang against the wooden slats of the ceiling. He was frantically working the airbrake lever back and forth—with no effect at all. He shouted something and grabbed for the emergency mechanical brake wheel, but the car lurched wildly, sending him sprawling to one side.

"Hang on!" I shouted at Mabel, and got to my feet. I plunged into the aisle, banged into the seats opposite, got my precarious balance, and moved forward, grabbing each seat back to pull myself along. The motorman was on his knees and hands, scrambling for the emergency-brake wheel. I got to it at the same time he did, but the damned thing wouldn't turn. Out the front windows I could see the next switchback curve coming up fast, as the trolley car rocketed down the tracks. The icy snowbanks and black rock beside the track raced past in the yellow glow of the headlamp, which jumped back and forth to the swaying of the car. The speed was building up steadily, and the wheel flanges wouldn't keep the trolley car on the tracks much longer.

I strained at the wheel, to no avail. Then the motorman got to his feet, kicked at the restraining gear on the floor, and slowly we began to turn the braking wheel.

"Easy!" the motorman shouted. There was a smear of blood across his forehead, and his ruddy face was drained of color. He was plainly damned frightened—and so was I! But the car seemed to slow a trifle as we held the wheel, bringing the brakeshoes against the madly spinning steel wheels. "Not too hard or we'll burn through the brakes!"

I nodded, then felt a presence beside me and turned to see Mabel, standing on the front platform of the insanely speeding trolley car, staring out the big front windows. Her pixie face was entranced, her eyes huge, and she was laughing. Excitement gripped her, and she loved it, every dangerous moment of it. I think she almost wished we would crash, as a final, supreme thrill. The thought was crazy, but I could not deny it.

We hit the switchback curve, fast, and for an instant I thought we were going over—and it was one hell of a long drop below us! The trolley car swayed, started to flip, then slowly, reluctantly, settled back down, rocking, as the steel wheel flanges held. If the track didn't go, we would make it. It didn't, but we sure as hell loosened a few spikes! I held onto the braking wheel, and the car seemed to be slowing a little. The motorman stared at me.

"This one won't stop her! I've got to get to the back brake-wheel!"

I nodded. "I'll hold this one."

Beside me, Mabel stood transfixed, swaying to the wild movements of the car, both hands gripping the handrail across the front end of the platform, staring out at the mountainside rushing past us in the flickering light of the headlamp. The motorman turned, climbing against the downward tilt of the car, and headed for the back. The car had slowed, but not enough; we took the next curve hard enough to make the wooden sides of the car groan in protest and the steel wheels screech insanely. I heard the motorman yell and curse as he banged into a seat back, but I kept watching Mabel's face, fascinated by how alive it had become in that moment of danger.

We must have been nearing the bottom of the hill, and the car still didn't show any signs of stopping. I hit the wheel harder, shoving my weight against it. I heard the motorman yelling something behind me, but I paid him no attention; if we didn't slow down—and damned fast—that dinky trolley car was going to fly off the bottom of Mount Lowe like a rocket heading for orbit. The scream of steel resounded, and smoke from the wooden brake-chocks poured up through the floorboards. But I felt the car suddenly slow, then slow again. I could see the mist-auraed glow of a streetlamp ahead—and it marked the end of the track.

I grabbed Mabel, jerked her down, and fell on top of her on the rough, splintery floorboards. The car was still slowing, but not enough. It hit the end of track, jolted as it dug into macadam, then crunched through a cement curb. It upended, crashed back down, then slewed around and fell on its side, digging up a fair stretch of paved street. But it stopped. The glass windows were gone, leaving jagged splinters, and the upper part of the trolley car was torn from its chassis and wheels. The metal front end plates of the car held us, and apart from my badly bruised shoulder, neither of us was hurt. The front door slid open, crazily, banging back, and we climbed out.

The trolley car was a complete disaster. The wooden brake-chocks were burning, and the wooden body beginning to smoke and smolder. Mabel was staring at the car—and smiling. I left her and made my way to the rear. The motorman had fared as well as we had, and was all in one piece. Together we got the injured conductor out of a splintered mass of seat wreckage. He was cut about the face from glass, and I couldn't tell how seriously hurt he was. At least he was still breathing.

A man came running up. It was Davis, Mabel's driver. His handsome face expressed no emotion, no surprise. "Get to a phone—call a doctor—an ambulance!" I yelled.

Davis gave me a look, glanced at Mabel, then moved away. He

wasn't breaking any records to comply. I went back to Mabel. She was still looking at the totaled-out trolley car. She looked at me and gripped my arm, hard.

"Wasn't that *something!*" No fear, no shock, just an overwhelming excitement. She had loved every desperate minute of it. She kissed me, suddenly, fiercely. "Take me home, Willie—I want to go to bed with you, *now!*" The need was clear in her expression, urgent, compelling, overpowering.

12

Impressions, fleeting and indelible, sharp and in soft focus, limn my memories of the next few hours, contrasting and yet blending into each other. Of the wreck, and the time we spent there, waiting for an ambulance, and for the arrival of the police, and work crews, I have only vague flashes. It was cold, almost as cold as on the summit of Mount Lowe, and a light misting drizzle began to fall. People—a lot of people—were suddenly there, appearing as strangely as they do at all scenes of an accident, out of nowhere, faceless for the most part. I remember standing apart, holding Mabel Normand in my arms, while she watched everything, feeling her body trembling, now and again, but not from the coldness.

A representative from Pacific Electric was there, asking questions and writing things down in a little notebook, officious as all hell, but damned if I can put a face to him. Just a blur. But I remember answering his questions, and hearing Mabel answer. He kept staring at her, and licking his lips, and smiling—she had her usual effect on him. Two or three touring cars came up the street, honking and speeding, and slamming on their brakes at the last moment. Men piled out. Some lugged big, square, press cameras, and held up T-shaped gadgets loaded with flash powder that flared blue-white, blinding anyone nearby. The flashes went off, again and again, and they crowded around Mabel and grinned at her, and shouted questions. How come we were there? What were we doing? This mean a romance between us? What would Baby Betty Blayne think about it? "Or her mama?" one wise guy asked, and got a roar of laughter.

Mabel posed, obligingly, looking wan, and smiling only wistfully, putting on a shaken act that was so effective one of the reporters finally yelled: "Cheese it, fellas—can't y'see the little lady's worn to a frazzle?"

Davis opened the rear door of the Leach, and we climbed in. I felt my legs give way, and I fell into the seat. My shoulder was numb, and the place on my forehead was throbbing again. Then the car door slammed, and we were getting out of there. Mabel giggled, suddenly, and kissed me, and drove away the cobwebs.

"Damn, sport, you really know how to show a girl a good time!"

"Glad you enjoyed it," I said. "Wait until you see what I've got arranged for the next time."

Everything was strangely quiet after all the hubbub at the scene of the accident. I relaxed. My shoulder remained numb, but the throbbing in my head diminished. Hell, I almost decided that I'd enjoyed the whole damned thing, too! Kissing Mabel, I was sure of it.

The big Leach sedan hurried through the night, the hard tires whispering on the macadam. The windows steamed over, and everything outside was a shadowed blur, just faint light auras, brightening, then dying away. An occasional horn blared, and I heard a raucous siren moaning, far away, police or fire, I couldn't tell. Mabel was softly aroused, not bold or overly aggressive, more a compliant willingness, holding me, pressing against me, seeking and not demanding. These are, to me, the most precious moments of all, because we were closely sharing each other. Sexuality was involved; I wouldn't deny that. But it was more—far more—than just that, and I think, after all, it meant more than that to Mabel, too.

We pulled up in front of Taylor's bungalow court on Alvarado

Street, Davis climbed out and opened the door. I got up, stepped to the sidewalk, then helped Mabel out. She was pressing close against me, and I had an arm around her.

"What about Davis?" I asked.

She looked surprised, arching her mobile eyebrows a bit. "What about him?

"It's very late. I can drive you home—in the morning."

"That's silly—he'll wait."

The subject was closed. The world would always wait for Mabel. For a while, anyway. . . . But that tomorrow seemed very far away, and I wouldn't be sharing it with her. The thought bothered me. No, damn it! I wouldn't accept the finality that what had happened to Taylor before must happen again. Not if I could prevent it!

In the narrow garden-court, Mabel suddenly stopped. There was only one lighted window—a very pale pinkish glow behind one drawn blind. They were common on most windows, then, with most of them made of some kind of dark-green oilcloth, the better ones with an off-white liner, making them opaque. The ones on Taylor's windows were pretty fancy affairs, with scalloped bottoms and dangling crocheted work; even the ring pull was covered with crochet work.

Mabel straightened, looking up at the glowing window, then suddenly, impishly, stuck two fingers in her mouth and let blast with a shrill whistle that would have waked the dead. As I hurried her toward Taylor's front stoop and fumbled out the chain with the ring of keys, lights popped on all over the court, and blinds flew up, and curtains were drawn apart. I could see heads silhouetted against the room lights, as people peered out. I held Mabel close, in the darkness of the little front porch, and heard her giggling.

"What's the matter, Willie? Don't you like an audience?" She raised her mouth to be kissed.

The windows went dark again—in one or two the curtains were held apart for a moment longer. The bungalow court settled back to its usual quiet, and I unlocked the door and let us in. At the door, Mabel turned and whistled, screechingly, again, before I could stop her, then collapsed into my arms, laughing. She went limp, and I had to catch her. She hugged me, and kissed me again, as we went up the dark stairs.

I turned on no lights; it wasn't my idea, but Taylor's. I could sense his embarrassment, which seemed strange. Frankly, I didn't give a damn about Taylor's neighbors or what they thought about my—his—doings, but it was obvious that he did. And it was obvious, too, that Mabel was very much aware of this old-fashioned stiffness he had bottled inside him, and delighted in uncorking it when the opportunity presented itself.

She wiggled out of my arms and backed away from me. I heard rustlings, hurried, and eager, then hands grabbed my shirt— buttons flew as she jerked the front of it apart—and laughed. I grabbed her—felt naked flesh—then she ran from me, threw herself onto the bed. I shed Taylor's clothes, fast, and joined her. Her mood, always mercurial, had changed again, and she was suddenly all wanton.

Mabel's ability to be, instantly, anything she wanted to be—impish, perverse, or loving by turn, or all at once—was now fully demonstrated. She was experienced, and sensuous, and suddenly all female. She was demanding, breathless, and totally uninhibited. Her first seeking passion blazed high and then diminished slowly. Her initial need met, she sought a deeper fulfillment, and took it. But she gave fulfillment, too, understanding my needs and drives and encouraging them.

And when at last we lay still, side by side, she pressed her face against my naked chest and kissed my breast, softly, a gesture of love, warm, yet without passion, which was spent. Her head cradled in my arm, she slept, breathing softly, deeply, content.

I remained awake for a long time. The room was still, save for her soft breathing. I knew beyond doubt that I had found something I had never known before. Just as I knew, also beyond doubt, that too soon I must lose it forever.

13

It was just getting daylight, and the overcast made it seem darker than it should be. I twisted on the round lightswitch knob in the bathroom and blinked in the sudden flood of light. My image in the bathroom cabinet mirror reflected my feelings all too accurately; my—Taylor's—face was drawn and haggard, and there was a dark patch of yellow-brown bruised skin on one cheekbone that was already a match for the ugly spot in the upper center of my forehead, running into the hairline. But it was my shoulder that had awakened me, and the mirror made the reason clear. My left shoulder was red and inflamed, beginning to turn yellowish. It would be a monumental bruise, and I was lucky that it wasn't more serious. Just the same it hurt so much that my lesser bruises felt numb, and I searched the medicine cabinet for a painkiller. I found some aspirin, but passed it up in favor of some patent cough syrup that according to the label had a laudanum extract in it. I swigged some down, the sweet-sour cherry taste a little nauseating, but after a minute felt a little better, even though I knew the drug couldn't be working that fast. The warm glow in my stomach testified almost at once to the strong alcoholic content.

The orange juice and gin had left my mouth filled with dirty cotton, so I brushed my teeth, using the can of Dr. Lyons' Powder liberally. It was while brushing my teeth—Taylor had a perfect set, as far as I could tell, only a couple of inlays of white gold—that I noticed the smeared theatrical makeup on my neck—around my neck. It was quite thick, darker than Taylor's skin, and matched Mabel's darker coloring perfectly. It had probably been blended especially for her. I smiled at myself in the mirror, thinking of the past few hours, of what they meant to me. And then it hit me. *Around* my neck . . .

I don't know why it came as such a jolt; maybe because I had refused to rationalize what I had seen the night before. I had spent a couple of years on the Narco Detail, and I should have known. Mabel's vivacity, slowly running down, then suddenly renewed, like a Japanese toy with a fresh battery. Back in 1922 did they have amphetamines? I didn't think so. But they damned well had cocaine, the worst of them all. . . . And she was mainlining the junk.

I stood there, staring down at her where she lay, still curled up in the bed, her dark hair sprayed across the white pillowcase. My feet and fingers felt numb, and my stomach was solid ice. For an instant it was hard to breathe, then anger flowed and I clenched my fists and wished to hell there was something I could hit, smash into pieces, and then smash the pieces. But there wasn't.

Mabel awoke, lazily, and blinked owlishly at me, then stuck out her tongue and made an impish face. She stretched as lithely as a kitten. I'd turned on the silk-shaded bedside lamp, and in the pinkish glow of it I saw the tracks on her arm. Too many of them. They had been there a long, long time, years. Very carefully hidden beneath her specially blended body makeup.

It was too late. I wanted to shout at her, even strike her with my fists, and damn her for a fool, but it was too late. The numbing coldness gripped my stomach. Now I understood Taylor's reticence about some things.

Mabel grinned and wriggled her fingers to me, and I sat on the edge of the bed. There was no mistake; the tracks were there, plainly visible where the body makeup had been wiped away. I forced a smile and bent to kiss her. Her lips were warm and dry, and the taste of fresh mint was almost gone. Her arms moved up around my neck, and I held her close—very close—aware of how much she meant to me and how little could ever come of it. For a moment she returned the pressure of my arms, then pulled away.

"Hey, papa bear, take it easy!"

"I wish I never had to let you go," I said. There were more—better—things I wanted to say, but the words wouldn't come.

"Nothing lasts forever, kiddo." She made a face. "I hope Doug MacLean doesn't have an early call this morning."

She hopped out of bed, slimly perfect, and turned to let me admire her body, bent to kiss me again, and then ran into the bathroom. I was left to the bitterness of my thoughts.

Charlie Chaplin's Little Tramp came from the bathroom, lifted his battered derby to me, wriggled his tiny square black mustache, and lifted his black eyebrows lewdly. He carried a little bundle, Mabel's clothes wrapped in her bright silk scarf, tied to the end of his skinny cane. The Little Tramp executed a funny skidding turn, made for the door, and blew me a kiss in farewell.

'I'll get dressed and drive you home," I said.

"Don't bother." Mabel giggled. "Davis will be waiting—asleep in the car. See you later, kiddo!"

And then the Little Tramp was gone.

Mabel, beautiful and damned.

I went back into the bathroom and used a towel to scrub away the body makeup from my neck, trying hard not to think about it.

Now you know. God damn it!

Taylor wasn't damning the fact that I knew. He was damning the truth of the knowledge, and I agreed wholeheartedly.

How long have you known?

Not long—a few weeks. I noticed the marks on her arms. I didn't know what they meant at first. And when I learned, I didn't want to believe it.

What tipped you off?

The way she acts—you saw her last night. Then there was a piece in the newspaper, about addicts. Damn, it suddenly seemed—you know?

What have you done about it?

*God damn it, what is there to do? I'd give anything to help her,
but you must know that it's too late. She's been using it too long,
too heavily. . . . There's no cure—no way back. I'm not even sure
that she would want to try. Mabel isn't the kind to face things.
When she's hurt, she hides herself in make-believe, like a child,
making the world go away. . . .*

Do you know how she got herself hooked?

*No, but I can guess. For the sport of it—a new thrill—perhaps
after a fight with Mack—she was hurt badly by the way he is—you
know, with other women. . . . It's why they never married, in the
old days. I don't think Mack realizes how badly he hurt her,
because of the way she always behaves—as if she hadn't a care in
the world, that nothing is really that all damned important, you
know?*

The drug angle in the William Desmond Taylor case was
explained, I thought angrily.

*I'd give anything I possess to fix the sons of bitches doing this! It
isn't just Mabel—I know a half-dozen more caught in the same
web. The dirty swine—just to get their filthy hands on money!
That's why I went to the authorities. . . .*

What about Betty Blayne?

Thank God, no!

Watchdog mama, no doubt.

Perhaps you are right.

Are there any more—dames I mean? Like Mabel and Betty?
Women you're mixed up with?

*That's none of your damned—All right, all right. No. None that
are—important to me. You must understand—*

Believe me, Willie-boy, I do.

*It's—it's not like—what you must think—at least, not with
Mabel. . . .*

I knew then that Taylor loved Mabel Normand, too—at least in
his own way. I could tell by the restraint behind his thought. Did
Mabel love him? I thought she did. But it wasn't an absolute
commitment for either of them. It was for me.

You poor bastard! You must know that it's hopeless—I mean—

I know.

I let it stop there.

You've never talked to Mabel about—being hooked?

No. I told you—it would do no good. Pause, harder: *But I'm going to do my best to see to it that no other poor damned souls get trapped the same way!*

How? I remember you said something about working with the U.S. District Attorney. . . .

That's right. Tom Greene—he's the Assistant U.S. D.A.—I told him everything I knew—offered to work with him. . . .

You told him about Mabel?

Yes—I—I had to! Can't you understand?

What else did you tell him?

The names of everyone I know to be mixed up in or using drugs—the studio people I know to be involved, and those I suspect may be behind it.

It clarified what I already knew about the drug angle in the Taylor case. Had the U.S. D.A.'s office cooperated with the locals after he was murdered? I doubted it, because there was nothing in the official files to indicate it. But why would the Federals be any less secretive in 1922? God knows that in my own time they had played things close to their vests, and ended up being the targets for Congressional investigations because of it. No wonder the Taylor shooting was never solved.

What did the D.A.—Greene—say?

He gave me special authorization to work with him and his men to stop this beastly hop gang. You can't believe how big it has grown, just within the past few years.

You said you named names?

Yes—those I knew. Mabel—and—and Wallace Reid—Alma Rubens—Barbara La Marr . . . some others. He promised me that Mabel and the other victims would not be prosecuted and that there would be no publicity. My God, if the newspapers got wind of this they would tear them apart! There would be headlines around the world. These people are idols.

I thought of the openly acknowledged junkies that dominated the entertainment industry in my own time.

Their problem is, they came along fifty years too soon. Okay, Taylor, how have you been working with the D.A.?

I'm on the inside, and I have access to almost anyone. I've made inquiries at the studio—discreetly, of course. That's the center of the ring—I'm sure of it. There's so damned much money in Hollywood—every featured player is a potential victim—you can't believe how many of them have been snared. The pressures in Hollywood, even for the little people, are tremendous. It's a vicious, depraved racket, growing every day—and it must be stopped!

Not a chance. But it can be slowed down. Have you found any pushers?

Any what? Oh, I know what you mean. A few. Mostly hangers-on. A couple of extra players—a wardrobe mistress—a makeup man—but no one important—not the people behind the whole thing. . . .

One thing puzzles me. You've made no secret about how you feel—I mean, about drugs.

His thoughts were hard, sardonic. Sincerity is not a valuable commodity in the picture business. . . . Everyone puts up a front. I doubt if they believe I really mean it. And I've kept my association with the authorities a secret.

I felt the coldness in my stomach again.

Like hell you have! Those two goons that jumped me—us—last night—did you know them?

No. Neither of them. Pause. Sudden alarm. Do you think—

I sure as hell do! Didn't you realize you'd be sticking your neck out a mile? Junk dealers don't like squealers.

Stubborn thoughts. I'm not afraid.

I am, damn it! Tell me, have you really found out anything important about these bastards? The one that goon called "mad dog"?

I sensed hesitation, and—again—evasiveness. I believe I have. After all, I'm no fool. I thought the point was debatable, but kept it to myself. For that matter, I think I know who is behind the ring—the man who directs the entire operation.

If you are getting close to Mr. Big, no wonder you got bumped off, Taylor. Do the local cops know anything about this, or the part you're playing in the setup?

Not as far as I know. I don't know whom Tom Greene may

have told. He may have asked for their help and cooperation.

No way, man! From what I remember about the case, he never opened his mouth, even when you were murdered. The whole drug thing was just a rumor in the papers. . . .

Taylor's personality subsided into brooding non-thoughts.

It seemed clearer why the Taylor case was never cleared up. The Federals playing it cool, keeping what they knew to themselves; after all, the poor bastard was dead, and murder wasn't a Federal rap. And poor bastard was the right term. He not only had people with personal motives after him, he had the bunch he called a "hop gang" out for his blood. Line them up and take your pick. Edward Sands, after revenge; Betty Blayne's mama, saving the honor of her "child"—not to mention her personal golden goose; a jealous ex-lover of one of Taylor's many women; or 1922-style enforcers out to settle a beef before it got started—complete with tommy guns, yet. But what worried me, knowing Taylor's secretive ways, was the chance there were still more possibilities I had yet to learn about.

The jangle of the telephone cut off my unpleasant thoughts. I crossed to it and lifted the receiver. "Hello?"

"You no good son of a bitch!" Mrs. Denker's strident voice screeched in my ear. "Stay away from her! I won't waste my time telling you again!"

The receiver at the other end banged in my ear. I hadn't had a chance to put in a word. As I stood there I heard a click on the line, and knew that Peavey had gotten an earful. What the hell, he probably knew more about Taylor and his affairs than I did, anyway. I looked at the mussed-up bed, and that made me think of Mabel, and anger burned away the coldness inside me. It wasn't any use going back to bed, for I wouldn't get in any snoozing—not with my disturbed thoughts. And I'd had about all the thinking I cared for this morning. Besides, my shoulder was killing me, making my whole side throb and ache. I went back into the bathroom and took another slug from the cherry-flavored, laudanum-laced cough syrup. A guy could get to liking the stuff; it burned on the way down and set up warm, comfortable, sentry fires inside. As a side-effect it made me feel pretty good, riding a moderate high, almost cheerful about it all, in fact. Screw them all! Me and my cough syrup could lick the world.

I shaved without cutting my throat with Taylor's straight-edged razor. It pulled and scraped like hell, but there was a leather strap with canvas sewn to the back side of it. I tried my hand at stropping the blade, and it seemed a little sharper. Or maybe I was just getting used to the damned thing. I sliced a chunk from the razor strap with an ease that gave me pause and made me slow down. I nicked a few places I had missed the day before, and kept myself from bleeding to death by using a stinging styptic pencil that I took out of its own little glass bottle. A shower made my shoulder ache, and I couldn't raise my left arm much more than waist high, so I prescribed myself another jolt of cough medicine. By the time I had struggled into my clothes—and I had a hell of a time putting on a shirt—I was lightheaded, happy as all hell, and feeling very little pain at all. I made a mental note to tell Peavey to lay in a stock of cough syrup, and even promised myself to try a shot with a little orange juice and gin chaser. Now *there* would be a guarantee of happy time!

The phone rang again and I grabbed it. Let that bastard Peavey listen in—maybe he'd hear something he didn't already know. "It's your dime—I mean nickel," I said. Inflation and moneyitis hadn't yet afflicted Ma Bell as badly as it would in years to come.

"Mr. Taylor?" For an instant I thought that the thin, reedy voice was Mrs. Denker about to tell me off again, then I realized that it was a man's voice, with nothing effeminate about it apart from its high-pitched tone. "This is Bill Hearst. Marion and I are having a few guests on the yacht tomorrow night—a little cruise down into Mexican waters. It should be fun. Can we count on you? There'll be congenial company."

It didn't register for a moment. I started to say something funny-sarcastic, or what I thought was funny-sarcastic, then it hit me. The tinny voice piped up: "Marion is particularly looking forward to seeing you again."

My God, had Taylor been laying Marion Davies, too?

No, you filthy-minded bastard! I could almost taste Taylor's indignation. *Don't ruin everything for me!*

"I'd be delighted, Mr. Hearst," I said to William Randolph

Hearst. "Thank you very much, sir—and please convey my kindest regards to Miss Davies."

Taylor traveled in the best Hollywood circles, that was for damned sure. But wasn't there a rumor about Hearst taking a shot at somebody, way back when, for monkeying around with his gal, Marion? No, that was somebody else. My—Ernie Carter's—memory stirred. It was Thomas H. Ince, after he died under somewhat mysterious circumstances. Was it aboard Hearst's yacht? My memory was hazy, just old Hollywood legends, still talked about—something about a party aboard Hearst's yacht. Only rumors—half-assed myths with no facts to back them up, as I remembered. Hell, it turned out that Ince wasn't even shot, but died at home of natural causes.

Thomas H. Ince—shot? The incredulous query came from Taylor. *How could a story like that get started? Who would want to shoot Ince, for God's sake?*

I'm a hell of a lot more concerned about who shot *you!*

And that called for one more shot of joy juice. I stuck the bottle in my coat pocket. You never know when you'll develop a cough.

Funny, but thinking about Taylor's murder didn't really get to me this morning. So, to hell with it, too! I went down to breakfast humming "The Age of Aquarius" loudly, enjoying the paradox that the man who would write it wasn't yet born.

I was hungry, and scooped up some of Peavey's watery scrambled eggs, and some bacon, onto my plate, and he brought out some warm toast, oozing melted butter. There were some strawberry preserves, and I washed it all down with the chickory-tasting coffee. Peavey had taken the hint, and had brought me the *Examiner* along with the *Times*. Hearst's paper was an eye-opener. I saw a half-dozen stories that would have got my time's paper sued for millions. No punches were pulled; the writing went all out, anything for the sake of sensationalism, openly casting slurs and naming names. Hell, it reminded me of my own TV newscasters' way of slanting every story, either by emphasizing their own political convictions or by playing up only the downbeat, catastrophic, or unpleasantly sensational elements.

By comparison the *Times* was its own drab self. But at least the gist of the stories was there, plain to see, and not hidden behind a façade of eye-catching bad taste. In the *Examiner* Fatty Arbuckle was characterized as a pervert and a grossly obscene murderer, already convicted by the yellow press. In the *Times* there was a brief story on a back page about the second hung jury, filling in the details not given the day before. It was thought he was on his way back to L.A. As I remembered it, Fatty, the poor damned soul, would be tried a third time before he was found not guilty. A verdict that must have given the *Examiner*'s biased, hate-mongering staff the hickies for days.

A third trial? My God! It doesn't seem possible. Not Fatty. I know the man!

Did you know Virginia Rappe, too?

I detected a slight smirking tone in his thoughts. *Yes—I mean, after all, the girl—well, she was hardly any better than she had to be. . . . I mean, damn it, Fatty wouldn't have had to—*

You mean she was balling half of Hollywood.

If you must put it that crudely.

You should talk!

Sulky withdrawal.

I found *Gasoline Alley* in the *Examiner,* and it brought back a wave of nostalgic enjoyment. Uncle Walt was more like the grown-up Skeezix that I remembered as a kid, only fatter. Walt hadn't married yet, apparently, and Skeezix was a baby, about to have his first birthday. . . . But the strip was the first completely familiar thing I'd seen here in 1922. That wasn't quite true. I remembered *The Gumps*, and *Bringing Up Father*, with Maggie and Jiggs doing their same old thing, neither one of them aged a minute in fifty years or more. In *The Gumps*, it was a continuing story, and in this morning's episode, Uncle Bim, Andy's rich relative, was involved with the Widow Zander, and there was a contest for the readers to decide whether or not he should marry her. The first prize was—good God!—a bale of hay. I'd seen horses and some horse-drawn vehicles on the streets yesterday—even one horse-drawn fire engine, come to think of it—but a bale of hay? It had to be a put-on, a bit of vintage humor, or did enough people still own horses to make it a practical prize? I still am not sure.

Peavey brought in the mail. There was a big, thick manila envelope. "From the Director's Association, suh," Peavey announced. "Papuhs fo' yo' to sign." He did his Mantan Moreland bit, almost shuffling. "As president, yo'ah a mighty important man, Mistuh Taylor!"

"President? Of what?" I stared at him, taken off-guard.

"The Screen Directors' Association, suh—yo' thuhd term, suh!" Peavey stared at me. "Yo' told me what an honor it was."

"Of course it is, Peavey." I forced a laugh. "Just joking—and not doing very well at it, I'm afraid."

"Yessuh." Peavey almost-shuffled out, leaving a puzzled look behind him.

Peavey will think I've lost my senses.

He'd be right.

That isn't amusing.

I looked at the rest of the mail. There was a cheap manila envelope, addressed to:

> Mr. William Desmond Taylor, Esq.
> 404-B Alvarado Street
> Los Angeles, California

No zone number and no zip code—they wouldn't be slowing down the mails for years to come. There was a silver curved-blade scimitar letter-opener on the table, and I used it to open the envelope. A batch of pawn tickets—more than a dozen in all—fell out, representing something over five hundred dollars in pledges.

I sensed Taylor reacting, then carefully hiding it. He had caught something I hadn't. Undoubtedly because it meant more to him than to Ernie Carter. Damn him and his secrets! I looked closer at the pawn tickets and suddenly caught on. Every one of them was made out to William Cunningham Deane-Tanner.

Somebody else knows our little secret, Willie. Sands?

I detected quickly hidden amusement. *Of course, you stupid fool!*

If Sands found out about your dark past, you sure as hell

weren't very careful about keeping it secret. And that's not your style, Willie-boy.

That's idiotic—how could I keep him from knowing, once he had found me?

Found you? What in hell are you talking about?

Silence. Withdrawal. I had the feeling that Taylor had almost let something slip—but damned if I knew just what. But he had gone back into his hole and pulled it in on top of himself. But I caught one final, blurry thought: *He had as much to lose as I did, and I never thought he'd prove to be a despicable thief. . . .*

Do you know any other kind? Come on, Taylor, what gives with you and Sands, anyway? Silence. Okay, okay, never mind. Come on back. I need your help.

Nothing, damn him!

I put the pawn tickets back into their envelope, and noticed that in 1922 they were still using real postmarks, with time and date and place clearly stamped. The envelope had been mailed in Long Beach at 10:30 A.M. yesterday, just a short while after Sands had called Taylor and talked to Peavey on the phone. Knowing that didn't help me a bit. There was no way I could be certain that it had been Sands who sent me the pawn tickets. I put them back in their envelope and stuck it in a pocket; no use letting Peavey know any more than he did already.

There was no junk mail at all, not even a *Reader's Digest* Sweepstake giveaway. For that matter did the *Digest* go back to 1922? I doubted it, although it had been around for all of my—Ernie Carter's—life. The twenties were the heyday of the adventure pulps. Too bad I couldn't cart a few thousand back to my own time—they were collector's items, now.

A tiny perfumed envelope caught my eye, and I opened it.

> Dearest, Darling Billy-Love:
> I love, love, love you! You touch me and I burn like a candle. I need your love—all of it! Forever and forever! Nothing must keep us apart. I have to feel you, a part of me, always.
> Your love-child,
> B. B.

My God, if her gimlet-eyed mama had read the note! If she owned a .38, she would be loading it, right now! I stuck this one into my pocket, too.

Betty Blayne's note didn't get a rise out of Taylor. He was still making himself scarce, for reasons of his own.

There was a large envelope with ARTCRAFT PICTURES, JESSE L. LASKY–FAMOUS PLAYERS STUDIOS, HOLLYWOOD, CALIFORNIA, printed on it, and it held two slim movie scenarios. They meant nothing to me. The top had *Limberlost* in the title, with a note clipped to it:

> How do you feel about directing a sequel, again with Betty Blayne?
>
> JESSE

More important, how would Mama Denker feel about her little moneymaking darling being involved with Taylor on a picture? I found the thought amusing. Serve the old bag right. Still no response from Taylor. To hell with him, too.

The bell on the front door rang, and Peavey went to answer it. He was back in a minute. He looked a little uptight.

"A gentleman to see yo', suh," he said. "A policeman, suh—Sergeant Cahill of Homicide."

Police routine check—or trouble? Knowing Taylor, I figured it had to be trouble.

14

Dan Cahill was wearing a derby hat, which he removed as he came into the dining room from the front hall, proving that the old movies on TV had it right. He smiled pleasantly, as usual, his upper lip permanently lifted, slightly. His bright-blue Irish eyes took in the room, and me, quickly—and I would have bet he didn't miss a thing.

"Sorry to disturb you, Mr. Taylor," he said.

"No bother at all, Sergeant Cahill," I replied, smiling back. "As a matter of fact, I was hoping that I would hear from you today."

"Why?" The smile remained just as pleasant, but his eyes seemed a bit harder. "I mean, police officers aren't usually all that popular with the taxpayers."

Even back then? "They are when they can satisfy the taxpayer's burning curiosity," I said, smiling just as insincerely. "What about those two fellows—the one that shot the other?"

"That's what brings me out here, Mr. Taylor."

"Good. Would you care for some coffee?"

"Yes, thanks."

Peavey vanished and came back with a silver pot of coffee and an eggshell china cup and saucer, which he placed on the table. He then pulled back a high-backed chair for Cahill, who handed

Peavey his derby and sat down. Peavey left the room, but I had the feeling he wouldn't miss a word of what we said. Cahill stirred in sugar and cream. The cream was so thick it had clotted in the pitcher, and required a spoon to lift out, making greasy, butterlike streaks shine on the surface of the hot coffee. His eyes traveled around the room, but I sipped my own coffee and outwaited him.

"Out-of-towner," Cahill said slowly. "The dead man. Name of Patterson. Police record in New York, Chicago and, lately, in San Francisco. Strongarm type. A hired messer for the mob."

"Fascinating," I said, in a puzzled tone, as if I found it difficult to catch his drift. "You mean he was a gangster?"

"That's right, a real bullyboy, Mr. Taylor."

"A bootleggers' war right here in Los Angeles! Exciting notion, isn't it?"

"I could get along without it." Cahill drank his coffee and smacked his lips. "You're sure you've never seen or heard of this man before, Mr. Taylor?"

"Patterson? Quite sure. I'm afraid I don't travel in his circles, Sergeant."

"No, of course not." Cahill studied me. "I'll level with you, Mr. Taylor. We aren't sure that it was a bootlegging ruckus at all. In fact, we're pretty sure it wasn't. Patterson hasn't been running with alky mobs. He's always been associated with junk graft."

The slang was a little strange to me, but I got the message, even though I pretended otherwise. "I'm not certain that I follow you."

"A dope ring—traffickers in narcotics, Mr. Taylor."

"I see." I thought fast. "I won't say I'm shocked, Sergeant, because I'm not. Hollywood is filled with addicts, I'm afraid. It's common on every lot in town—too damned common to suit me, as I've made known."

"Mind telling me why, Mr. Taylor?"

"In confidence, no," I countered. "I'm sorry to say that certain . . . friends of mine have become involved. But I'm sure I'm not telling you something you don't already know."

"Would you name some of these friends—in confidence, Mr. Taylor?"

"I would rather not—at least at the moment. I'm sure you can understand why."

Cahill hesitated, then nodded slowly. "As a matter of fact, I'm not even sure that I want to know," he said. "My business is homicide, not the drug racket."

"Thank you," I said, then frowned. "But tell me, why did you ask me—again—if I knew this Patterson? Surely you don't think I'm involved in this—this junk graft as you call it?'

"No, Mr. Taylor, as far as we know, you're clean," Cahill replied quietly. "As a matter of fact, I got word from upstairs to take it easy with you."

"Then, why—"

"You swore out a warrant for the arrest of Edward F. Sands, who once worked for you. Is that right?"

"You're damned right! Sands stole me blind. While I was in Europe last year—"

"I read your complaint, Mr. Taylor," Cahill interupted. "How much do you know about Sands' background before he came to work for you?"

"Why, I'm not sure," I said. I needed time to think—and help from Taylor. I didn't get it. He was gone. "Not much, really. He gave references, I believe, good ones. . . ."

"Probably forged. Did you check them out?"

"As a matter of fact . . . no," I replied. "I know that sounds odd, but the man was forthright, rather nice-looking, certainly he seemed honest, and after all—"

"It pays to be sure, Mr. Taylor."

"I found that out to my cost. But I still don't—"

"Sands has a record, too. Served a year in Joliet five years back." Cahill paused, his bright eyes fixed on me, watching for any reactions. "His cell bunkmate was Patterson. They were released on the same day and left Joliet together."

"You're sure it's the same man—Sands, I mean?"

"We're satisfied that it is."

"I see." My thoughts were churning, trying to add up things that didn't match ends. "But even if true, it doesn't mean that Sands has been involved with him since then."

"No, it doesn't. But it does add up. Sands worked for you for two years, and you're very well known and respected in the motion picture industry. Being close to you, Sands would have had a golden opportunity to make time with other people in the business. Frankly, a man in Sands' former position would make an ideal setup for a hop gang."

"I suppose so." I left a doubt in my—Taylor's—voice, but there was very little in my mind. "Still, it seems that I would certainly have known about it."

"Not necessarily. Like you said, your antihop attitude is pretty well known, Mr. Taylor. You made a perfect cover for Sands—if what we suspect is right."

"Yes, well, at least he isn't using me—not any longer." I frowned. "But if you are right, would Sands jeopardize his position by stealing from me?"

Cahill's frown matched mine, although his quirked-up lip made his smile constant. "Not unless he was stupid—or thought he could get away with it."

"He isn't stupid—and why would he think I'd allow him to get away with thievery?"

"If you don't have an answer to that, Mr. Taylor, I'm sure I don't." Cahill's blue eyes were frost-cold. "There was something else. The medical examiner says that Patterson was pretty badly battered—he had been in a fight—and somebody worked him over pretty good just before he was shot."

"His killer of course? There's your motive, Sergeant Cahill. 'When thieves fall out'—isn't that the old saying?"

"I guess it is, Mr. Taylor." But it was clear that Cahill wasn't buying it. He finished his coffee and placed the cup on the saucer, his eyes steady on my face. "You had a narrow escape last night, I understand. A runaway trolley?"

"That's right." I shook my head. "It was a damned close call. But how did you—"

Cahill's smile remained coldly fixed. He pulled a folded newspaper from the side pocket of his coat. He unfolded it and laid it on the table in front of me. The *Examiner*—the Morning Final.

FAMED FILM STAR ESCAPES DEATH
MT. LOWE RAILWAY DISASTER
MABEL NORMAND IN
CLOSE CALL
Noted Director
With Her

In a box below were two photographs, a large one of the wrecked trolley car and a round insert of Mabel Normand, looking pertly at the camera and wearing a pillbox hat with a long feather thrusting up from the back of it. I picked up the paper and scanned the story below the headlines. It had the facts straight.

"You were both lucky," Cahill said. "Neither you nor Miss Normand was hurt at all?"

I shook my head, still reading the vividly written account. The conductor was seriously injured and in a hospital. There was a brief interview with the motorman, who said Mabel and I had acted "heroically" in trying to help stop the speeding trolley car. I had the feeling the reporter had put words in his mouth.

"Just a badly bruised shoulder. Miss Normand got off scot-free, thank God!" I looked at him. "Have they found out what caused the accident?"

"Air hose, badly frayed—it gave way and you had no brakes. It must have been a pretty wild ride."

"Better than a roller-coaster—and more scary, too." I shook my head. "Frayed hose, eh? I suppose those things do wear out—or chafe against something."

"Yeah. A wood file, for instance," Cahill put in quietly. "We found the chewed pieces of rubber on the ground at the top of the hill, near the cable car tracks."

I stared at him, and the cold, cold feeling in the pit of my stomach made it easy to register shock. "You mean that it was done deliberately?"

Cahill's expression didn't change. "That's right."

"Are you certain?"

"Yes. Those air hoses are checked before a car is put into service—especially on the Mount Lowe run. And the rubber scrapings between the tracks leave no room for doubt. Somebody wanted that accident to happen."

"But—but why?" I stared at him. "Miss Normand and I were the only passengers on that car."

"There are several possibilities. There usually are when things like this happen. A disgruntled Pacific Electric employee, someone who had it in for the motorman or conductor, a lunatic—or someone trying to kill you or Miss Normand." He paused, frowning. "Can you think of anyone who might be carrying a grudge against you?"

"No." The slight tremor in my voice was natural.

"You're sure, Mr. Taylor? An old enemy? Have you received any threats on your life?"

"No—I did get a telephone call from Sands, but it wasn't a threat—not exactly—I mean, it doesn't make any sense—not Sands . . ."

"Your life was endangered twice in one day, Mr. Taylor," Cahill said. "Doesn't that strike you as strange?"

"Of course it does, old man," I found myself saying, and forcing a smile. "Damned strange. But things do happen like that, you know. I mean, they say accidents come in sets of three. . . ." And I was suddenly wondering if number three was a .38 in somebody's fist.

"Let's hope not—for your sake, Mr. Taylor," Cahill said. "As for Sands, when we find him, we'll soon learn if he was involved." He smiled at me. "You don't happen to know where he called you from—Sands, I mean?"

"No. Actually, I didn't speak with him. My man, Peavey, talked with him, but I gather the conversation was brief."

Cahill stood up. "Thanks for the coffee. I'll be in touch with you again, Mr. Taylor."

"Please do, anytime."

I walked to the front door with Cahill and saw him out. I closed the door behind him and leaned against it, aware of the tremble in my—Taylor's—legs. I felt tired, drained, and badly frightened. My high had worn thin. Time for a little cough medicine. I pulled out the bottle and took a swig. The warmth from it failed to obliterate the cold, hard knot in my stomach or the trembling of my legs.

I had the feeling that it hadn't been good luck that had saved William Desmond Taylor's life last night, but the fact that he would be shot to death, right here in this bungalow court apartment, between 7:30 and 8:00 P.M., on Wednesday, February 1, 1922, with a single bullet from a .38 caliber handgun, type and make unknown. The certainty of that struck me hard. I had just six days left to live.

Peavey came in clear up the breakfast mess. "Yo' wanted Mistuh Howard to drive yo' to the studio this mohning, Mistuh Taylor."

"The studio?" I drew a blank.

"Youah meeting with Mistuh Lasky, suh."

"Oh, yes, of course. What time was that meeting?"

"Eleven o'clock, suh. Yo' talked about it the day befo' yestahday, suh."

The day before yesterday was another age, another life; I was on the night watch out of Hollywood Division, cruising Hollywood Boulevard in an unmarked police car with my partner, Jacobs, and William Desmond Taylor was just a name in a tattered old file in the Unsolved Murders drawer, downtown in the Central Division Archives, along with those other forgotten sensations of their day, the Wanderwell murder on the yacht down at San Pedro Harbor, the oddball Thelma Todd case, and the Black Dahlia killing. . . .

I dug out the platinum pocket watch; my fingers began automatically winding it. No self-winders or electronic timepieces here and now, in 1922. My God, the whole world— Ernie Carter's world—was not yet born. . . . And everything about me, all of it, in every last, finite detail, would change in the next fifty years. The differences were strangely easy to accept— probably because of the latent presence of William Desmond Taylor—until I thought about them, and then they overwhelmed me, numbed my mind, and the sickening strobe-jumps started up again. In self-defense I pushed the conflicting memories away. It *was* 1922 as far as I was concerned, and remembering a tomorrow yet to be only made matters unbearable. My fingers trembled slightly as I stared at the face of Taylor's expensive watch. It wasn't yet ten o'clock.

The pain in my shoulder was a dull, throbbing ache, and the laudanum in the cough syrup wasn't killing it, just making me lightheaded. I began to think that taking it hadn't been such a hot idea after all. I decided a few minutes with my eyes closed might help, and went back upstairs. Peavey had made the bed, but I could still detect the delicate fragrance that Mabel had worn, mingled with a haunting smell of mint. I took off my coat, remembered the letter from Betty Blayne and the pawn tickets, took them out, and eyed the room for a place to put them out of Peavey's sight.

Boots. Closet.

Taylor was back again.

Why the hell did you duck out? I suppose you sat in on what's happened, what Sergeant Cahill had to say? You know he's no dummy; he's got a hunch about what's going on, and trying to fool him could be dangerous, Taylor?

Nothing, damn him!

I went over to the closet, opened the door, and pulled on the drawstring. Light flared. A pair of tall, black, highly polished riding boots stood in a far corner, and I bent over to reach for them—and instantly regretted it. The pain from my shoulder was blinding in intensity, but passed after a moment, leaving me feeling weak and sick. There was a packet of perfumed letters, all from Betty Blayne, in the toe of one boot, tied with a pink satin ribbon. Probably from her hair, I thought, and grimaced. I added the newest letter to the bundle, dropped the envelope with the pawn tickets on top of them, and shoved the boot back. A thought struck me, and I pulled out—moving carefully—the other boot. I was right—there was another packet of letters in the toe of this one, too.

Leave them alone, damn you!

Screw you, Willie-boy!

It wasn't hard to guess who had written them. Mabel. I carried them back to the bed, ignoring Taylor's vehement mute protests, and lay down. I went through them one by one. I suppose they could be called love letters, but next to Betty Blayne's little erotic masterpieces they seemed more friendly than sexy. Like Mabel herself they did not commit her beyond a certain point, warm, but not gushy, and again I found myself wondering if this was as far as she would go, or if it was all she had to give. It was a disturbing thought.

I drifted off into blurry half-sleep. It lasted a half-hour, then Peavey woke me up. My shoulder was agonizing, especially whenever I moved or jarred it. I regretfully passed up the cough syrup and took four aspirins; they were one thing that hadn't changed a bit. These Bayers looked, tasted, and acted exactly the way they did a half-century later. No, on second thought, TV advertising had had one effect; the aspirins to come crumbled in your mouth before you got them well-swallowed, and these didn't. They went down whole.

"Yo' feeling okay, Mistuh Taylor?" Peavey had a solicitous expression on his face.

"I'll be all right, Peavey." I stifled a groan.

"Yo' shouah, suh? Ah could call Mistuh Lasky, an' say yo' ah feelin' a mite undah the weathah. . . ."

"No need to, Peavey," I said. "Banged my shoulder pretty hard, and it hurts like hell. That's all." But I couldn't keep back a groan when he helped me on with my coat.

"That could be serious, suh." Peavey looked worried.

"I'm sure it isn't—there's nothing broken. Just a bad wrench, I imagine."

"Yo' bettuh see Doctah Jameson, anyway, Mistuh Taylor, suh."

Who the hell was Dr. Jameson?

The studio physician—I play handball with him every week.

Thanks. Now stick around, damn it!

No reply, but I felt his presence. Somehow it didn't reassure me much.

The aspirins seemed to help, or maybe it was just getting up and moving around. I took a fuzzy tan-colored hat and a thin walking stick from Peavey and stepped out the front door. The garden in the center of the bungalow court was pleasant, although the patches of grass were yellow, and I could smell fertilizer—natural cow product and not chemicals. A strikingly beautiful young woman passed me, coming in from the street. She gave me a quick, shy smile. I glanced back and saw that she turned into the far half of Taylor's bungalow. That made her Edna Purviance, Charlie Chaplin's long-time leading lady, and by all accounts his ladylove.

You could have spoken to her, you clod.

Forget it, Taylor—you've got enough problems.

Seeing her—the perfect features, and slim, shapely body—I found myself wondering why Charlie had been so interested in so many other women. But embarrassment of riches never bothered Hollywoodites—and that included William Desmond Taylor.

Me, Ernie Carter, if I'd had Mabel Normand for my own, the rest of the women in the world could sleep in Chaplin's bed for all I cared—all those, that is, that didn't already do just that. If I had Mabel—but I knew, with sudden absolute certainty, that nobody would ever really have Mabel. Not all of her, not in the way that counts . . . . And maybe that was one reason for Taylor's continuing fun and games with little Betty Blayne.

How about it, Taylor?

No response. But no feeling of snide mockery either. Misery might love company, but it didn't seem to do me any good.

Howard Fellows opened the door of the big Packard sedan. He was wearing a dark-blue uniform and matching chauffeur's cap. Something made me look at him, study him for a moment.

"Glad to see you are all right, sir," he said.

"Thank you, Fellows." I climbed into the back of the sedan, careful not to bump my throbbing shoulder, and relaxed on the soft rear seat. I shut my eyes. Fellows got in and pulled away easily from the curb. He drove with a little of the dash of Mabel Normand's chauffeur, Davis, for which I was grateful. Every bump made my shoulder ache that much harder.

It was a perfect Southern California day. The sky was blue as hell, the sun warm, and there was a mild breeze smelling of good earth and sea winds. A place like this could attract a hell of a lot of people, and would. I tried to think of a way of buying up a half-mile or so of Wilshire Boulevard, on the chance I would ever get back to my own time and cash in on it. The idea fascinated me. *If* I got back—and I had serious doubts that I would—even I wouldn't believe what had happened to me. So my cop's mind began working on the problem of proof that would satisfy me when I got back. I didn't give a damn whether it satisfied anybody else or not. It was a game, at first, something to amuse myself, get my mind off the almost intolerable aching of my shoulder.

How would a man in 1922 leave something behind him to be delivered to someone fifty years later? Bury it? Not a chance, not with all the building that would be going on during the next five decades. Find a hole way out in the desert? Possibly, but there would be no safeguards. Leave a legal bequest? Who were William Desmond Taylor's heirs? Probably the wife and daughter he had abandoned in New York before World War I. I didn't remember reading anything in the old police files about that angle of the case. Taylor didn't leave that much of an estate, actually; a few thousand in cash, his cars and furniture. That was one puzzling factor in the case; Taylor had made damned good money for several years prior to his murder, and despite his lavish spending—relatively speaking, since everything was a hell of a lot cheaper back in 1922—he had very little savings. There was one item, suddenly I remembered. He had made a cash withdrawal of $2,500 the day before he was murdered, and the money was never found. What did he do with it? Did he pay off somebody— Sands? Or what? Now, wait a minute! It wasn't Taylor who drew out that $2,500—it was *me* . . . or would be me. Now there was something to think about.

But the question of Taylor's estate and heirs made something stir in my memory. There was someone else. That was right! A brother. Damn it, what was his name? Douglas—no, *Dennis!* Dennis Deane-Tanner. Something peculiar about him. . . .

I felt Taylor stirring, trying to block my thoughts, almost frantically, but I mentally pushed him away.

Dennis Deane-Tanner. I remembered. He disappeared, too, about four years after Taylor had pulled his vanishing act, which made it in 1912, before Taylor showed up in Hollywood. Dennis Deane-Tanner had left behind a wife and two children, and it had been Taylor's sister-in-law who had spotted him in some old movie. Taylor was supposed to have denied the relationship, or that he was William Cunningham Deane-Tanner, but there had been records indicating that he had paid out money to Dennis' wife. . . .

Taylor! You're not much help.

I got the feeling that he didn't intend to be, either. The son of a bitch would end up getting us both killed if he kept on keeping things back from me.

Fellows turned the Packard north on Vine Street, although I didn't recognize it. No way. It was lined with small homes, and huge poplar trees on both sides for shade, as we neared

Hollywood Boulevard. It had a rural, rustic look. A group of small frame buildings stood on the east side of the street, and a painted sign over a wire auto-entrance gate read: FAMOUS PLAYERS— LASKY CORPORATION—WEST COAST STUDIOS—PARAMOUNT PICTURES. What the hell was Paramount doing here on Vine Street, just south of Hollywood Boulevard, when it belonged a mile south, on tiny Marathon Street? No matter, here is where it was.

There were lowered striped-canvas awnings over the front windows that faced west, but despite them, and the shade of the poplars, the frame buildings must have been sweatboxes in the summer months. The guard at the gate was wearing a heavy dark-blue serge policeman's uniform, and swung the high wire gates open, then saluted as we drove in. Being a big shot—even back in 1922—made me smile despite the pain in my shoulder.

Fellows pulled around to the front—inner—street. The buildings were a little more elaborately trimmed on this side, but not much. The day of the grandiose stucco-builders hadn't yet dawned. There was a tiny patch of yellowed grass, and trees everywhere for shade, except near the huge, rickety-looking stages themselves. Almost all of them had been built with glass-windowed roofs for light; film speeds were a lot slower in 1922, and emulsion not as sensitive to incandescent lights. The lot was busy, but it was an orderly turmoil; a bunch of costumed Arabs came from what must be the wardrobe building, farther down the studio street, and filed across into one of the stages. In the tiny parklike area, a couple of cameramen were enjoying the sunshine while they worked on their cigar-box shaped cameras. Both of them wore caps, with the bills reversed—just the way you see Billy Bitzer in old Hollywood stills, cranking away alongside D. W. Griffith in his wide-brimmed panama hat. . . .

On the street in front of a small window topped by another awning, there had been a couple of benches, with a motley assortment of people lounging on them, blocking the sidewalk, some seated on the curb, and they had all given the Packard and me the eye as we drove in. Extras, waiting for the chance to make a couple of dollars in a mob scene, or whatever. . . .

Fellows jumped out and opened the door of the Packard for

me, and I managed to climb out, although the pain in my shoulder almost knocked me out. We were parked at the curb in front of a two-story frame building with an awning over double glass-topped entrance doors, and potted fern-palms to either side. A girl with high-piled hair that must have dangled below her hips when unbound dabbed at a carbon smudge on her nose with a tiny hankie and held the glass door open for me. She smiled at me, exposing yellowed teeth. A little fancy brightener toothpaste from my own day and age would have made her pretty—so maybe the Madison Avenue TV peddlers weren't as wrong as I'd always thought.

At a desk in the reception area, another girl wrestled with a clattering typewriter that looked and sounded like something from the Age of Dinosaurs, and I wondered what she would have made of the IBM Selectric IIs that dotted my Hollywood. She didn't look up.

"Mr. Lasky is expecting you, Mr. Taylor," the girl who had been waiting for me said.

I followed her into the building. There was no carpeting over the wooden floors, and her high heels clunked. But her hips swayed nicely as she went up the stairs ahead of me. My shoulder didn't ache *that* much, to keep me from noticing a well-rounded fanny. I figured it was Taylor's influence.

Bastard!

I smiled, and followed the secretary down the cool, dark upper hall. I wasn't kept waiting in an outer office. Jesse L. Lasky bustled out to greet me. He was beaming, a genial smile. His little round glasses perched on his nose, and he had a mild-mannered look that would have been just great if he was playing Clark Kent.

"Bill! I've been looking forward to seeing you!" He took my hand. His grip was firm and hard, to my surprise. But Lasky's outer appearance didn't reflect the man at all, as many people learned to their cost. But, considering the company he kept, as one of the first Hollywood moguls, he sticks out as one of the few nice guys—if not the only one!—around. He had grown up playing a silver cornet, and worked the vaudeville stages in a family act for years. But he had also, when seeking quick money, and dead broke, played cornet in an Alaskan whorehouse during the Gold Rush in 1898.

He studied me from behind his gleaming round eyeglasses. "You all right, Bill? I mean, not hurt?" He shook his head. "I'm beginning to think you'll be dead in a week, the way you're going!"

15

For a second his words shook me, then I figured out that he was referring to the trolley-car accident last night. He wouldn't have known about the shooting downtown—or would he?

"The thought's occurred to me, too," I said.

"Damn it, be careful, Bill!" He frowned. "Is Mabel okay?"

"Fine. As a matter of fact, I rather think she enjoyed the whole thing."

"That's Mabel Normand for you—anything for a laugh or a thrill." He frowned. "Arbuckle's a problem that way, too. I suppose you've heard his second trial ended with a hung jury? It might almost have been better if they had convicted him."

"I doubt if Fatty would agree with you, Jesse."

Lasky smiled his meek little-man smile, but his eyes remained blued steel behind his lenses. "I was thinking of the industry, not Arbuckle," he said. "Selfish, I suppose, but the damned fool brought it on himself."

"Don't we all?" Especially Taylor, I thought to myself.

"You're right of course." Lasky frowned, looking off. "He's not the worst chippie-chaser in this town, but he's the one who is going to be made an example of, believe me, Bill!"

"Does there have to be a whipping boy? These things always die down if you give them time."

"Not this one. Every newspaper from coast to coast is giving it a big play. And the image they're projecting isn't doing Arbuckle's case any good. The public's ready to believe anything of Hollywood people, and the idea of a three-hundred-pounder raping a ninety-pound girl, forcing himself on top of her, hurting her—you get the picture."

"But Virginia Rappe was no innocent little dove. The girl was sick—there was something wrong with her internally. Fatty wouldn't intentionally harm her or anyone else."

"Even if you're right, Bill—and I'm not saying that you're not—this isn't the first time Arbuckle's been in a jam. The studio bailed him out in that East Coast mess a year ago. We can't go on doing it forever." He sighed—either a good act or he was really a little disturbed by the situation, I couldn't be sure which. "At any rate, it isn't up to me alone. And it's clear that motion pictures can't tolerate many more scandals like this. We're all being tarred with the same brush."

I thought, he was going to have a lot more jolts coming to him, with the drug scandals and the William Desmond Taylor case coming up fast.

Lasky shook his head. "I talked to Zukor in New York last night, and he's coming out here next month. We're having a general meeting to work out the way to keep the lid on. One thing in our favor, Will Hays will put a stop to such affairs if we let him have the power to do it."

Will Hays—the Hays Office. My God, how far away that seemed. I wondered what Mr. Hays and Lasky would have made of the porno flicks saturating the theaters in my own time. They might have shaken Hays, but I had a strong suspicion they wouldn't have bothered a man who once played a silver cornet in a Gold Rush whorehouse.

Lasky smiled at me. "At least we have no publicity problems with you, Bill, thank God!"

I had to fight back a laugh, but found myself nodding, with poise and dignity. Taylor, on top of everything else, was a sanctimonious bastard who couldn't see his own faults, even when they threatened to get him shot.

"I try to stay out of the headlines," I found myself saying modestly.

To keep from laughing out loud I eyed Lasky's office. It was paneled in dark wood, with heavy velvet drapes over the windows. An Eskimo electric fan stood on a table to one side—the latest in air conditioning, 1922 style. With the drapes closed, the room was dark. A couple of silk-shaded lamps burned on tables beside heavy club-type chairs that looked too hard to be comfortable.

Lasky paced for a moment, then shook his head as if pushing away dark thoughts for something more pleasant. He went behind the huge desk, shuffled some papers, brought out a blue-backed folder, opened it, read a few lines as if to make certain it was what he wanted, then nodded and smiled at me again.

"Your new contract, Bill. Nice one. More money—and more important, you get your name above the title from here in." He announced it the way you might have knighthood. He chuckled pleasantly. "You and the De Milles."

I smiled back dutifully, De Milles—plural? That was right, C.B. had a brother. William?

"I think you'll find it satisfactory," he added, again nodding a benediction. "Your choice of properties, even approval of stars and locations—once the budget's set, of course."

"I'll take it along with me and read it tonight," I said—or let Taylor say. "Thanks, Jesse."

Lasky beamed more broadly, his eyes guileless. "Hearst has been talking to you about his Cosmopolitan Pictures? He'd like you to direct Marion Davies, I know, because of the great job you did for Pickford. How many of Mary's productions did you make, Bill?"

I had no idea, but Taylor said, smoothly: "Three." I realized that Taylor was smiling and playing them close to his vest, as usual. "It's all in the family, anyway, isn't it? Mr. Hearst releases his productions through Famous Players."

"At the moment," Lasky replied. "But one can never be sure where you stand with William Randolph Hearst. He's serious about making pictures—at least those starring Marion Davies.

But there is always the chance he'll decide to distribute his productions himself. There's been talk that he's been shopping around for a studio staff. Have you heard anything along this line, Bill?"

"No, I can't say that I have."

"He hasn't made you an offer, then?"

"I haven't talked business with him, but I've been invited for a weekend cruise on his yacht."

"He'll make his pitch then," Lasky said. "Well, you listen to what he has to say, my boy, but don't commit yourself until you get back to me. I'm sure we can match his offer."

"Thanks, Jesse," I said.

"Fine, fine." He beamed again. "Just to whet your appetite a bit, I've spoken to Zukor about doing a special—something new—an all-star motion picture. You'd be the man to handle it, I think. How does the notion of teaming Wally Reid and Betty Blayne strike you?"

I felt Taylor's immediate reaction, and it was negative. "I've never worked with Reid."

Lasky studied me. "I know. I understand there was a little difficulty between you, but after all, a personality conflict can't stand in the way of a successful picture."

"There's more to it than that," I found Taylor saying. "I doubt if Reid would want me on his picture—any more than I would want him."

"Because of Betty Blayne?"

"It's a personal matter, Jesse," Taylor replied stuffily. "I'd rather not discuss it."

"Any romance between Reid and Betty is ancient history. He's all wrapped up in his wife and baby—a real family man nowadays, Bill."

"So the magazines say."

"Your attitude surprises me," Lasky said. But I could tell that it didn't surprise him at all. "Still, you'll be the best judge of what you'd like to do for us, eh?" The same soft chuckle. "We're dickering for the film rights to Harold Bell Wright's new novel, which you should read. Sounds promising for the new year, eh?" He paused, then added offhandedly—just a bit too offhandedly—

"C. B. asked if you'd drop by his set while you're on the lot today—he wants to speak to you about something. Important, he said." Lasky smiled. "Everything that interests De Mille is important."

Lasky sat down and picked up a sheaf of papers. The meeting was over. I folded the blue-wrapped contract, stuck it in an inner pocket, and went out. Lasky's secretary opened the anteroom door for me and closed it behind me, showing her badly tarnished smile. I felt fuzzy-headed, and my shoulder was a numb hotness, throbbing constantly now.

"Is Dr. Jameson on the lot today?" I asked.

"I'll find out, Mr. Taylor." She flicked switches on a wooden intercom box while holding a round earphone to the side of her head. She hung it back on the box and nodded. "Yes, he is. He's playing handball right now."

"And where's De Mille—C.B.—shooting?"

"Stage Two."

"Thank you." I started out, but the buzzer on the intercom sounded. She picked up the earphone. "Yes, Mr. Lasky." She hung up and smiled at me. "Mr. Lasky has an open table at the Blue Front for lunch today, Mr. Taylor. He'd like you to join him."

"The Blue Front?" I'd never heard of it.

"Armstrong-Carleton's," she said. "It's a little passé now, but Mr. Lasky likes it—and it is better than Brandstatter's."

"Of course," I said. I had never heard of either one of them. But there was still, in my heyday, one old-time Hollywood café on the Boulevard. "What about Musso-Franks'?"

"Musso? I didn't know that Frank had a new partner. The food is good there, but Mr. Lasky says it's very old hat." She smiled. "The real hotspot is the Montmartre, across from the new Christie Hotel. I've been trying to get my boyfriend to break loose and take me there."

"You'll love it," Taylor said. I caught his vague notion that if her boyfriend couldn't be broken loose, an eminent director might be available some night. He was remembering the lithe waggle of her hips on the stairs, but I remembered only the ugly, discolored teeth, and disagreed with him. So I kept silent and left the office. I felt Taylor's annoyance. The bastard was woman crazy.

I let Taylor's ego take over long enough to find the handball court. One end was the thick-slab wall of a stage; but with silent pictures, noise didn't matter, and you could hardly hear the slap-bang of the hard-rubber ball over the multitude of sounds of the busy studio. Two men were playing hard. Each had a white linen band around his forehead to keep sweat out of his eyes. They were both prime specimens. The tallest of the two was probably the handsomest man I had ever seen. He was big, lithe, as fast as any professional athlete. His body and face were his trademark, and for my money he would give Paul Newman a run for his money in the looks department. *The All-American Boy.* The thought was sharp, jeering, loaded with mockery. Taylor didn't like him one damned little bit, and I was to find out that the feeling was mutual. *Wallace Reid—hophead.* Bitter anger underlay the thought.

But I caught something else, too. Betty Blayne—and another woman—a young girl—hazy impression—hell, Taylor didn't even remember her face clearly! But his resentment was plain.

Reid had beaten his time, more than once, and Taylor had broken up Reid's little play for Betty Blayne—that pleased his ego, no doubt.

The other man was somewhat older, probably past forty, but also in perfect physical condition. His hair was almost gone in front, but he was sun-bronzed, even in January, and if anything, faster on his feet than Wallace Reid. Dr. Jameson was a lot of man. I remember thinking I'd hate like hell to take him on in an all-out scrap, even in Taylor's rugged body.

I watched them go at it, and Jameson really bore down. It was close, but he beat Reid. They were dripping sweat and breathing hard as they shook hands. They saw me approaching at the same moment, and their reactions were totally different. Reid's handsome face darkened in a scowl; Jameson grinned and waved a mittened hand.

"Bill! How's the boy? Get banged up in the accident? Saw it in the paper this morning." Jameson moved to clap a hand on my shoulder, but I dodged away, making a face. One touch and I felt I'd go down to my knees. Jameson stared at me. "Hey, boy—what's the matter?"

"Bad shoulder," I said. "I thought maybe—"

"Of course! Let me take a look at it." He glanced from me to the silent Reid. "You two fellows not speaking?"

"How are you, Reid?" Taylor asked coldly.

"I'm fine." Wallace Reid glared back at me. "Which is more than you'll be able to say if you don't keep your yap shut."

Another unfriendly native. Taylor had a talent for making enemies. One of them was going to kill him, and damned soon. "I beg your pardon, old man?" Taylor's stuffy Britishness took over.

"Hey, Wally, come on, now!" Jameson's attempt at cooling it got nowhere.

"I'm warning you, Taylor—keep your nose out of my affairs or I'll bust it for you." He meant it, too. "And if you have anything to say about me, make damned sure it's said in front of me and not behind my back."

With that he stormed away. Jameson looked after him, then frowned at me. He shook his head.

"Hey, now, what was that all about?"

I could have made an educated guess. Taylor was only reticent about himself, and by his own account he had named Reid to the U.S. D.A. And, knowing Taylor, he had probably talked to others about the drug racket, too. It wasn't unlikely that word had gotten back to Reid. Bad news travels a little faster than light. But Taylor would have shrugged if my shoulder hadn't hurt too much to move it.

"Damned if I know," Taylor lied smoothly. "Something's twisted his tail for sure."

Jameson eyed me, started to say something, then shook his head again. "Come on over to the dispensary. I didn't intend working today, but we can get a look at that shoulder."

The studio dispensary-hospital was in a corner of a carpenter shop, two small rooms, one with two narrow metal bunkbeds, carefully made up and covered with gray blankets. The other served as Jameson's office. There was a desk, a filing cabinet, and a locked glass-fronted medicine case, atop which sat another Eskimo electric fan. Jameson had to give me a hand getting my coat and shirt off. He whistled when he saw the bruise, and also looked closely at the bruises on my forehead and cheekbone. He shook his head. "From the newspaper account, I didn't realize you got banged up so hard, Bill."

"I didn't think I had," I answered. "I felt okay last night—just a bit sore and stiff. Now I can't move my shoulder at all."

He nodded and slowly raised my arm. It felt like it was being ripped off. I almost yelled, and had to clamp my teeth shut. He eyed me, then took a good grip on my wrist; his fingers held incredible strength. He stood still for an instant and then jerked with all his strength. I damned near fainted on the spot. I felt something give, wrench, then grate sickeningly into place. My whole left side felt numb. Jameson let go of my arm, moved to his desk, brought out a large pharmaceutical bottle, and unstoppered it. He used tiny glass beakers, and poured out two stiff drinks. It was scotch—good scotch with the taste of smoke in it. I downed it, and suddenly felt better. I could even move my arm a little, and the numbness was wearing off.

"Simple dislocation," Jameson said. "It'll be sore, but you can move it. If it pops out again, call me." He went to the glass-fronted case, unlocked it, and brought out a large brown dispensary bottle. He used a small white paper envelope, and casually dumped out white tablets from the bottle, a dozen or more. He folded the flap of the envelope inside it and handed it to me.

"Codeine. If your shoulder hurts much, take a couple. If you need more, let me know."

"Thanks, Jameson," I said. "Much obliged."

"Any time, old sport," Jameson replied. He frowned, hesitated. "I'm sorry there's bad blood between you and Wally. Can anything be done about it?"

"It's between the two of us, Jameson," Taylor said stiffly.

"Sure. But you're both friends of mine, Bill. May I exercise the prerogative of a friend, and butt into your affairs a bit?"

"Must you?"

"I think so." He frowned, then shook his head. "Damn, it isn't as easy to talk about as I wish it was! When these things happen to people you don't know, it doesn't matter much, but—" He stopped, met my eyes evenly. "If it was just woman trouble . . . but the talk is—damn it, Bill, after all, you're not your brother's keeper—and certainly not Wally's!"

"And you're not mine, Jameson," Taylor said coldly.

Jameson frowned, then slowly nodded. "Of course. Sorry. It's just that I'm fond of you both. I hope it straightens out between you." He turned away. "Don't do anything strenuous for the next few days."

"I shan't." Taylor's charm was back in place. "As a matter of fact, I'll be going on a little cruise over the weekend."

"Really? With Hearst?" Jameson smiled. "Funny thing—I'll be along, too. I'm not his official medico, but I'm invited quite often." His smile widened. "Even Croesus wants free medical advice—it goes with the license!" He laughed. "At any rate, I'll be handy if your shoulder acts up."

"Most reassuring," I said. Also in case one of Taylor's buddies decided to bash in his head a few days early. . . .

"Are you joining Lasky for lunch? He's got an open table at the Blue Front."

"If I can. I'm not sure yet. I have to see De Mille."

Jameson frowned, slowly, and his eyes narrowed a trifle. "C.B.? He's supposed to be directing Wally's next film, isn't he?"

I smiled. "I thought I was."

"You're kidding!"

"Lasky's idea, not mine. Thanks again."

I left him still frowning thoughtfully, and went out.

It's funny, but despite all the differences, the movie lot felt the same. I'd spent a couple of weeks a year or so back in my time, on special loan-out to Universal Television in the Valley, as a technical adviser, and official representative of the Department, on a new Jack Webb cop series. And when I was in Hollywood High, I'd made a few bucks as an extra, and I had worked on several major lots, most of them now closed or changed beyond recognition. But, as I stepped aside to permit a little jitney-truck towing some flats on a big dolly to go past, it all seemed much the same. Bustle and hurry. But in 1922 there was no sound to worry about, and no red warning lights in the street, or over stage doors, when the camera was turning for a take. The huge doors of one stage were rolled open, and I saw two sets, put up side by side, inside, the warm sunlight shining down on them from the big glass overhead panels. Even the side walls on one stage were of clear glass.

Down the street, past the stages, was a tenement city street, and a company working. Huge reflectors brought sunlight where they wanted it, and cheesecloth flies filtered, softened the glare. There were two cameras, with men standing behind them, reversed caps on their heads, grinding steadily away, while another man shouted out directions through a small megaphone to the actors on the street. No crab dollies, no smoking, monster lights.

I found myself turning away, down a narrow street between two huge stages, and ahead of me, standing by itself, a larger single stage, with a big number 2 emblazoned on the sliding doors that fronted it. I walked toward it. Carpenters were banging away on a set to one side, and I could hear music. Muslin sheets were across the overhead skylight, while fierce glare came from a solid rank of huge, clear-glass bulbs. These monstrous lights were set, row upon row, in a steel framework that stood twelve feet high. The heat in front of them must have been brutal. *Cooper-Hewitts*, Taylor volunteered. *Makes night shooting possible. But they are hard on the eyes.* A second bank of the huge bulbs stood against one wall of the big stage, not lighted. Cables writhed across the splintery wooden floor, to the big lights. A pair of cameras were set up atop a wheeled wooden platform that rolled on wooden planks across the set, and in a canvas chair to one side, a man lifted a small white megaphone to his lips.

"No, Mr. Nagel—to your *left!* Your *left!* That's better—now hold it in, please—let me see what you feel in your eyes—all right, that's good for me."

I recognized Cecil B. De Mille's voice, oddly enough, yet he had been dead for years in my own time. But I'd grown up listening to him on *Lux Radio Theater* before a squabble over a union assessment for a political contribution took him off the air for good.

The Cooper-Hewitt wall of lights went dark, not all at once, but slowly, as the huge filaments inside the grotesque clear-glass bulbs remained glowing redly for seconds, before cooling into blackness. One bulb shattered with a sound like a thousand mirrors cracking, and a workman methodically moved over with a long-handled dustpan and broom to sweep up the debris. It was done matter-of-factly, and no one even jumped when the bulb exploded.

I recognized Conrad Nagel, on the set with a dark-haired girl I didn't know. *It's Leatrice Joy, damn it!* Trust Taylor to know any good-looking doll. The set was a frilly feminine boudoir, and elaborately done. The wallpaper was silk, and the fluffy curtains were cloud puffs. The wicker chaise longue was covered in white silk edged in fluffy feathers. Miss Joy's negligee might have been hot stuff in 1922, but it looked like something out of a prehistoric Sears Roebuck catalog to me.

Cecil B. De Mille was a slim, bald man, the dome of his head edged with dark-brown hair, wearing britches, puttees, and an open-necked white silk shirt, the sleeves rolled up muscular arms. He was about average height, but seemed taller. A monocle-filter dangled from a cord about his neck, and he had a wooden-sided viewfinder in one hand. It wasn't difficult to recognize him. Who could mistake him, for that matter? He had personified Hollywood and the movies for generations. He had the poise, assurance—and sheer arrogance—of royalty. No one crowded him, but at least a dozen men were within reach of his softest call. He saw me and motioned me to him. He didn't proffer his hand, and somehow I didn't expect him to. Kings don't shake hands with commoners.

"Nice to have you on the set, Bill," he said. "You'll stay for a moment. I've got to wrap these retakes." He wasn't asking, he was telling. He turned back and raised the megaphone. "Places, please! Now, Miss Joy—you love Mr. Nagel, but you have married someone else—a man beneath you . . . your chauffeur. You have found to your cost that your marriage in haste hasn't worked. . . . And you, Conrad—you're own marriage is broken. You have come to see the woman you really love, for the last time. . . . Both of you—make me feel it, please!"

He sat down in the canvas chair. I stood behind him, not too close. He raised a hand. An assistant called out: "Music!" As the Cooper-Hewitts sputtered into life again, glaring onto the set, I heard a piano and a violin playing, to one side. The actors took their places, smiled at each other. They remained still. The music and the sputtering lights were the only sound.

"Action, please," said Mr. De Mille. The two beautiful people went through their silent scene. Although they seemed to be speaking lines, neither of them voiced them aloud. While the sound wouldn't have been recorded, anyway, it struck me as totally unreal, something totally bizarre. I'm not sure why. Logic says that if your words serve no purpose, why speak them out loud? The camera will record only the lip movements, anyway. I saw De Mille nodding, then he raised his hand. "Cut. Thank you. That's a wrap. Thank you, Miss Joy and Mr. Nagel." He stood up and turned to me. "All right for you, Bill?"

I smiled. "Perfect. You make it look easy, C.B."

"Come along." He strode away, followed by his small entourage. He glanced at his leather-strapped wristwatch—one of the few I saw in 1922. The Cooper-Hewitts slowly darkened. Men were moving in, starting to strike the set.

I saw Conrad Nagel—funny, but during the last of his long film career, he had had a TV series—some sort of a game show, with aspiring actors and actresses making simulated screen tests—wasn't *Screen Test* the name of the damned thing?—and while I was at L.A. City College, studying Dramatic Arts—don't laugh, because a future chief of police of Los Angeles was in the same class with me—I'd worked a couple of days on his show. For scale—which was about ten times what the extras in 1922 were making. The strange thing was, Conrad Nagel didn't look that much different—or younger—than he had in the 1950s, and his fine speaking voice—wasted in silents—was just as I remembered it. He died in 1970, still handsome in his seventies. For an instant I had the impulse to go over to him, where he was talking, audibly now he wasn't in front of the cameras, with Leatrice Joy, and see if he remembered me. The notion made me smile. Hell, I wasn't *me*, and this was fifty years before I met him, anyway. . . .

Nagel looked up, spotted me and, to my momentary shock, waved a hand and started toward me. He came up and gripped my hand.

"Good to see you," his resonant voice said.

For an instant I was confused, completely disoriented. Time was twisting, contorting, meshing me in senseless, anachronistic coils.

"How have you been, Bill?" he went on, and everything turned back right-side up.

"Just fine, Con," Taylor said smoothly.

"Good. Let's have lunch soon, eh?" Some things hadn't changed, especially cliché dialogue.

"Count on it," Taylor replied. "Got to toddle—just wanted to say hello."

Nagel smiled and returned to Leatrice Joy, who smiled at me and waved a hand. *No!* Taylor put in, before I could frame the thought for him.

You mean there are broads in this town you've missed?

There's still time, old boy. Taylor had a sense of humor, after all.

I hope to hell you're right!

I hurried after De Mille, who hadn't waited, but was some distance up the narrow studio street, striding along. *De Mille wouldn't wait for God*, Taylor put in. But at a doorway De Mille paused, looked back, and motioned impatiently for me to join him before entering. A little wooden sign over the door read PROJECTION ROOM TWO, and beside it a typed notice on a white filing card declared: *Reserved for Mr. De Mille.*

No question about which Mr. De Mille, I suppose?

His brother spells it with a small "d." Jesus! Taylor was being serious, too!

I followed the crowd into the projection room. Two big leather chairs dominated the narrow, windowless hall, De Mille's entourage dispersed to the smaller wooden theater seats in front. De Mille took one of the leather chairs and waved me into the other, with all the commanding presence of a pharaoh granting a favor to a captured Nubian soldier. Damned if I didn't actually feel honored!

Cecil B. De Mille was forty-one years old in 1922, totally self-assured—self-centered?—and master of his own private world. He had yet to discover the glory of filming *The Bible*, but it was already in his mind. He was the first great film director after D. W. Griffith—and I'm not sure but what it should really be the other way around. At least, while in his dominant presence, I felt that way. He patted my hand and nodded at the small, dirt-streaked screen at the end of the long room. The lights went out, I heard a projector whirring behind the thin partition in back of us, and light flickered on the dark screen. But, before the picture appeared, the side door opened, spilling sunlight into the darkened projection hall, silhouetting the figure of a small, slender woman.

"*Damn* it!" De Mille shouted. The whirring of the projector stopped, and the overhead lights went back on. In the light, the woman smiled brightly and waved a hand at the men in the room.

"Hello, everyone!" Jeanie Macpherson called out. "Am I late, Mr. De Mille?" She always spoke to him formally whenever there was anyone else present. In private, she had been his mistress since they had made *Rose of the Rancho* back in 1914.

"Damn it, Jeanie!" C.B. said angrily. "*Can't* you ever be on time for anything?"

"Of course I can, Mr. De Mille," Jeanie Macpherson returned, tipping up her slightly pug nose. "If you would stop sending me on ridiculous errands any moron could do just as well!"

Nothing C.B. enjoys more than a good, hot argument—but Jeanie's the only person on the lot with the guts to quarrel with him. I think that's why he fell in love with her. Taylor's old-fashioned instincts had made me stand up, but now De Mille tugged at my arm.

"Sit down!" he ordered, and Taylor meekly did as he was told. Around De Mille most people did. "Now let's get on with it." He glowered at the woman. "That is, if you're ready, *Miss* Macpherson?" His voice dripped sarcasm.

"Any time you are, C.B." she returned, sweetly venomous. and as the room darkened, I heard somebody chuckle. It was De Mille.

Again the projector whirred into life, and images flickered on the screen. "My new picture, *Saturday Night*," De Mille said. "This morning's retakes were for it. Zukor premiered it in New York last Sunday night—went over great, I'm pleased to say." If it hadn't, God—or De Mille—would have smitten the recalcitrant audience with thunderbolts. "Zukor thought that the boudoir scenes were too explicit—that Nagel kept staring at Leatrice Joy's bosom too much. . . ." Again he chuckled. "I was tempted to reshoot it bare-bosomed, just for the old bluenose's benefit."

It's funny how many of the faces in De Mille's old-timer, *Saturday Night*, were familiar to me—not Taylor, *me*—even though I couldn't put names to them. However, it wasn't necessary, anyway, as C.B. identified each one with a comment, invariably complimentary. He never lacked for enthusiasm, deserved or otherwise—not for a De Mille picture.

Edith Roberts, playing a laundress, was "very good"; Theodore Roberts, who would precede Charlton Heston as Moses in De Mille's first production of *The Ten Commandments*, played Leatrice Joy's father "Superbly, as always!" I never found out if they were related. She was young enough to be the old man's real-life daughter. The fourth side of the story's quadrangle was Jack Mower as the chauffeur Leatrice Joy unhappily married, "Great future for this lad!" The rest of the cast received De Mille accolades ranging from "Well done!" to "Coming along smartly—be a star someday!"

The story was a corker. Iris Van Suydam and Richard Wynbrook Prentiss, played by Leatrice Joy and Conrad Nagel, are in the Top 400, real class and engaged to be married. But Leatrice gets the hots for the handsome young chauffeur and jilts Conrad at the altar. Nagel promptly falls for the beautiful young laundress and marries her. The plot thickens. Upper and lower classes—ne'er the twain, etc. . . . All this is told at the expense of the "lower" class representatives, of course. The chauffeur and the laundress can't handle the society life, so unhappiness sets in. The two fancy-dress pigeons moan to each other about the cruelty of Fate. There is a fight between Nagel and Mower, but a four-alarm fire signals the dramatic climax. The laundress marries the chauffeur, and the two society specimens are free to enjoy upper-crust bliss forever. My reaction was they all deserved each other. But the funny thing was, the damned picture—ridiculous as it was—was slickly made, and once into it, you found yourself enjoying it, even buying the fantasy of the story line. But, in all honesty, dramatic values have changed over the years, so being able to even watch the picture was an indication of how good it must have appeared to a 1922 audience. Surprisingly enough, none of the actors overdid it much, playing low-key, for the most part, although Theodore Roberts did an effective bit of eye-rolling, which was apparently standard with him. Tricks of a trade that no longer existed in my time.

The screen went dark and the lights came up. De Mille stood up. "What do you think?" He was looking at me.

"Just great!" Taylor said, beaming. It was the right answer.

De Mille bobbed his bald head, said, "Stout fella!" and headed outside. He dismissed his personal crowd—except Jeanie Macpherson—with a wave of his hand, gestured imperiously to me, and strode on ahead. Jeanie smiled at me and fell in step beside me. The main titles of *Saturday Night* had given her credit for having written it.

"I tried to make it true to life," she said. "Did you think it came across?"

True to life! I looked at her. Taylor came to the rescue. "It was most effective," he said smoothly. "I don't suppose C.B. would let you work for another director?"

Hold it, Taylor! You don't need another broad—or another enemy.

Jeanie Macpherson blushed and smiled a bit shyly. "Why, you'd have to ask Mr. De Mille," she said.

"I'll do that," Taylor promised.

Over my dead body. Forgive the expression.

De Mille slowed his stride a bit, frowning. He gave Jeanie a look.

"Did you want me for anything, Mr. De Mille?" she asked. "Otherwise, I've some work to do."

"Fine, fine," he said, and Jeanie left us. He kept frowning slightly as we entered a bungalow building. "We'll talk, now," he decreed.

Cecil B. De Mille's office was bigger and more elaborate than his movie set. It had a high, vaulted ceiling, and reminded me of a cathedral—everything but the stained-glass windows. A desk dominated the big room, wider than any I'd ever seen before, and polished until it gleamed. He backed up against it and studied me from the coldest eyes I've ever seen.

He didn't waste time coming to the point. "I'm thinking of using Wallace Reid for the lead in my next picture—it's called *Manslaughter*, from Alice Duer Miller's best seller of last year." He frowned, raised his wooden viewfinder, aimed it at one wall, and peered into it. "I discovered Wally," he said pontifically.

"Oh, Griffith used him in a bit in *Intolerance*—but I saw his potential first. I made his first starring picture—*Maria Rosa*, six years ago—gave the boy his chance." He paused and focused the viewfinder on me, then slowly lowered it. "After the Arbuckle thing, I can afford to take no chances with an actor. There's talk that you're behind an investigation into narcotics use in the industry."

I was right; Taylor had been talking too damned much for his own good.

De Mille paused, then looked directly at me. "Is Wallace Reid a hophead?"

Taylor had got himself into this, so I drew back and let him handle it. He said, "Yes, he is."

C.B. sighed, unhooked the cord of the viewfinder, and laid it on his desk. "You're certain, Bill?"

"I am."

"Damn, damn, damn!" De Mille said slowly. "I knew that some of our people would be tainted, but Wally Reid. . . ." He shook his head sadly. "All right, thank you, Bill. I'll have to see what can be done."

He straightened up from the desk, walked to a draped window, and stood there. The pharaoh had dismissed the Nubian. I went out.

16

My shoulder was hurting again, and remained a little numb, but it no longer gave me the excruciating pain I had felt before. I looked around for a water cooler, and realized the day of the electric fountain was yet to come. But I spotted a bottle of water in a stand at the end of the hall, and headed for it. There was ice in the stand, and the water was cold. The big blue-glass bottle was familiar, too, as was the black-and-white printed label that said ARROWHEAD SPRINGS. I drank two paper cupfuls, then dug out the tablets that Dr. Jameson had given me. I took two with another slug of water. There were still plenty of codeine tablets left in the little white envelope he had given me so casually; it was obvious that either codeine wasn't counted as a narcotic drug or doctors weren't required to keep as close tabs on the stuff as they were in my time. Come to think of it, did doctors just hand out pills anymore? They did when I was a kid, but in recent years, in my time, all you got was a prescription. An expensive one, usually. The medicine wasn't a part of the doctor's fee.

Back on the studio street, I felt a bit fuzzy, used up, and I let Taylor take over. He didn't waste time, but struck out at a long-legged pace, and knew exactly where he was going. But I suddenly felt that someone was watching me; maybe it was a cop's instinct, highly developed, I don't know—but I trusted it, and it had saved my bacon more than once. Because, whoever it was, wasn't casual; they hated my guts. Call it a hunch. Most cops have it. Funny that it would work here and now, but it did.

I stopped, as if thinking, and looked around. Taylor's platinum watch said it was a little past twelve thirty. Lunch for the executives lasted into the afternoon, but not for the wage-slaves; they were already back at work. Carpenters pounding away, property men wheeling an ungodly array of artifacts around, and an incredible motley of extras, dressed in a greater variety of costumes than you'd see at a masquerade. But no one paying any particular attention to me.

A little jumpy, aren't you?

To hell with you, skirt-chaser!

But I drew back and let Taylor go his way. It led to a tiny frame bungalow set past the last stage, backed by a row of towering palm trees. There was a patch of grass and a shady poplar tree, even a wrought-iron, white-painted garden table, lawn umbrella, and ice-cream-parlor chairs. The door opened as I came up, and Betty Blayne saw me, and squealed, then flew into my arms. She was wearing a badly tattered—in all the right places—white silk little-girl's party dress, her ringlets a bit straggly and forlorn, and her perfect face smudged with Dirt #3 makeup. She was bare-legged, without shoes, and one rent in the dress revealed a nice length of milky-white thigh.

"Just in time to save me from the cannibals, Cap'n Jack!" she cried in a childish falsetto. She giggled. "I like you in the part better than I like Johnny Bowers! Will you save me from a fate worse than sex?"

"Absolutely not," Taylor replied, and rolled his eyes leeringly. Her kiss almost brought me back into control again, but holding her made my shoulder hurt again. My face must have shown it, for she let me put her down then made a face at me.

"I'd say I'm sorry you got hurt, but I'm not. Fine thing, gallivanting around with Mabel Normand!"

"I was in the mood for sex—and your charming mater wasn't available," Taylor said.

Betty Blayne stared up into my face, then peeled out her little girl's lascivious laughter. "You're terrible—you know that, don't you?"

"I must say I've had a suspicion about it now and then," I said, before Taylor could come up with something charming. "And speaking of the devil, where is your mother today?"

"Who cares where the old whore is? Come on—you'll have lunch with me!"

"My shoulder hurts too much to work up an appetite," I said, and again she laughed.

"Even if I do all the work?"

"Afraid so." I smiled. "Besides, I'm supposed to join Lasky at the Blue Front."

"All right, I'll forgive you—this time. But I do want to talk to you about the picture."

She led the way inside the tiny bungalow. It was all pink and white, with frilly lace curtains and white-painted wicker furniture, more like a little girl's dollhouse than anything else. She closed the door behind us and kissed me again. Then she backed away and raised her tattered dress to her waist. She was wearing nothing under it.

"Are you sure your shoulder hurts too much?"

"You little devil!" Taylor reached for her, but the pain in my shoulder cooled his ardor fast. I made a face. "Sorry as hell, darling, but—"

Betty Blayne was instantly contrite, dropping her dress and ushering me into a wicker chair, fussing over me. She used a tiny wisp of a hanky to mop my sweaty face, and kissed me, gently.

"I'm so sorry, Billy-love," she whispered.

"It's all right," Taylor said nobly. "You wanted to talk about your new picture?" He frowned. "I can't remember the title."

"*Castaway*—but that isn't the one."

"It seems like a change of pace for you."

"Being fed to cannibals? I suppose so—but I'm still twelve years old, and the jungle isn't all that different from the Ozarks." She made a grimace. "But I was thinking about the one we're going to do together—the one Jesse told me about."

"It isn't settled yet."

"But you are going to do it with me? Please? It would give us time together, and Mama couldn't do a damned thing about it!" I wasn't sure whether the idea of being with me, or spiting her mother, appealed to her the most.

"I may not be the one to make the decision—it will star Wallace Reid, too, and—you know how he feels about me—about us. . . ."

"Oh, pooh!" She made another face. "Just because I didn't give him a tumble."

"Not many girls say no to Wally."

She stuck her tongue out. "So maybe I'd better let him lay me, huh?"

"Over my dead body," Taylor said.

You keep saying that, and somebody's going to take you up on it, Taylor.

Betty Blayne moved in to kiss me again. "I'll take care of Mr. Spoilsport Wally Reid! Besides, I like Johnny Bowers better, even if he doesn't have all those muscles! And I'll just tell Jesse Lasky so, too!"

The name rang a memory bell with me, this time. John Bowers. Sure! He was the actor who inspired the character of Norman Maine in the classic film *A Star Is Born*. The guy who swam into the sunset, oh, so romantically ending it all. Only the police report, which I'd once looked up, said that Bowers used a sailboat, which was found a few days later floating upside down. He probably wasn't as athletic as Fredric March in the movie.

"They'd better use him while they can," I said cynically.

Betty Blayne eyed me and shook her head. "You're not funny when you act like you know something I don't."

"Sorry," Taylor put in smoothly. "I was just thinking he was a bit old for you."

"He's years younger than Wally Reid! What's the matter with you today, Billy-love?"

"My shoulder," I said. "Took some pain pills, and they've made me a bit woozy, I'm afraid."

Instantly she was all sympathy again, leaping up to come over to me and fuss over me. And, of course, with Taylor's luck, she was kissing me at the very moment Mama Denker chose to pop into her baby daughter's dressing bungalow.

The door banged wide open, and Betty Blayne leaped away from me as if I'd suddenly grown red hot. Her fear of Mama was all too real. The woman who surged into the little room damned near filled it. She was tall as most men, and nearly as broad in the shoulder. She was heavy, but not soft-fat. Her body was gross, and as hard as a rock—which matched the craglike features under her cinnamon-colored mop of hair. The riot of colors in her print dress added to the effect, and the hat she wore must have been a yard wide. She was sweating, and in an ugly mood—which didn't improve a bit when she recognized me.

I found myself wondering how any man had ever summoned up enough courage to impregnate Mama Denker. A hired gigolo would have charged triple-time just to *dance* with her.

"*You!*" Her strident voice resounded angrily.

"Mama!" Betty Blayne squealed, running to her. "The most wonderful news! About my career!"

Mrs. Denker's monstrous bosom heaved three or four times as she glared at me.

"Mr. Taylor was just telling me—he's going to direct my next picture—it's going to be a special—the biggest picture Realart has ever made!"

I stood up. I had been wrong. Mrs. Denker was taller than most men. She sure as hell was taller than Taylor, and outweighed him by seventy pounds.

"Is that right?" she demanded, barely controlling her rage.

"The—eh—deal is being worked out now." It was the first time I noticed Taylor stumbling over a word, but I didn't blame him. Mrs. Denker had the same overpowering effect on me!

"There had damned well better be more money for my baby!" Mrs. Denker shouted. "A hell of a lot more money! Look at the rags she's wearing—"

"They're just for my picture, Mama," Betty said.

"So what?" Mrs. Denker bellowed. "The pittance they're paying her, she's lucky she's not bare-assed naked! I want a wardrobe for her—one she can keep when the picture's finished. You understand me?"

"That really isn't up to me, Mrs. Denker," Taylor said. "But of course I'll see what I can do . . ."

"I'll just bet you will!" She took a deep, angry breath. "What the hell are you doing in here, anyway? I warned you—"

"I told you, Mama!" Betty put in hastily. "It's Mr. Taylor's picture, and the casting is up to him—they're talking about using Wallace Reid in it, too."

Mrs. Denker's greed won a close decision over her hatred of Taylor. She softened her look to an angry glare, and then plunked down in a wicker chair that squeaked in protest. She used one foot to force a shoe off, then the other. The leather had cut into her puffy feet, and she rubbed them together, making ugly gurgling sounds in her throat.

"Well, I'd best be going," I said. "I'll talk to you later, in more detail, Betty, when the matter's finally settled. Nice seeing you, Mrs. Denker."

"You just be goddamned sure I'm around when you do all that palaverin'!" Mrs. Denker shouted. "None of this sneaking behind my back shit!"

"Certainly not," I said, and hastened to close the door behind me. I hadn't released the knob before it was torn from my grasp, and Mrs. Denker lumbered out after me.

"You listen to me, you slimy English son of a bitch!" Her voice had risen in volume, a strident screech. "Don't let me catch you fucking around with my baby—do you hear me?"

"I'm sure the entire studio can," I answered. "But I assure you, I'm an honorable man—and my intentions are the same. After Betty and I are married, of course, things will be different." I don't know why I said it, nor am I sure who was more shocked, Mrs. Denker—or Taylor. I felt his stunned reaction. *Are you mad?* But I kept my attention on Mrs. Denker. She looked like she had been poleaxed, her face gone white, her eyes bulging.

"Goddamn you," she said, almost quietly, then jerked back inside the bungalow and slammed the door in my face.

Only then did it occur to me that I'd given her a real incentive to put a bullet into Taylor. Defending her "baby girl's" honor was one thing, but threatening to wipe out her hold over Betty Blayne's career—and money—was something else. I would have regretted saying it, except I found the expression on her beefy face so rewarding after all the shouting she had done at me.

17

Occupied with my thoughts, I'd walked blindly, and Taylor had retired into his sullen shell. As a cop, the crime always came first, and in this instance I was forced to work ass-end to. Preventing a murder should be easier than fingering somebody for the job after it was done. Knowing what had happened should have made figuring out the *who* a simple job. But it wasn't. The most obvious thing, of course, was the fact that Taylor had mixed himself up dangerously in a drug ring investigation, but I had a strong hunch—I just *knew*—that wasn't all there was to it. Too many crosscurrents were involved.

Motive and opportunity—how damned many people had them? Too many, that was for sure. And, to make matters worse, this time I was personally involved—too damned personally to suit me. And time was running out.

I did my best to put the pieces in some kind of order, without trying for final answers—not yet. They would come. They usually did. *But not always?* I couldn't be sure if the doubt was Taylor's—or my own.

The sudden roar of a lion brought me to a shaky halt. I was aware of the strong smell of wild animals, and now other sounds penetrated. A goddamn zoo—lions, three or four of them, and a magnificent tiger, pausing in its endless pacing to look at me through the flimsy-looking bars of a cage, its feral yellow eyes burning resentfully. I stood there, looking at the row of cages that covered a big area. There was even a ponderous Indian elephant, one leg chained to a heavy stake driven in the ground, bales of hay in front of it, swinging its massive head from side to side. Where the hell had I walked to?

Animals are required for pictures. Taylor rejoined me. *Every studio has its own zoo. Famous Players has one of the best.* Taylor was proud of the fact.

A keeper came up, lugging buckets filled with raw meat, with which he fed the carnivores. The yowling and roaring grew louder. He grinned at me.

"Doin' a jungle romance next, Mr. Taylor?" he asked.

"Not if I can help it," I said, and started walking.

In other cages I passed wolves, coyotes, and bears—Northwoods epics were big in the 1920s. The back lot was big, and sets sprawled everywhere, tacky, some of them falling into disrepair. They were flimsier than those of my own day, many of wood framing and stretched and painted canvas. But a Western street I came to would have been right at home at Universal in the 1970s. Two companies were shooting at the same time, not far apart, with cameras grinding and directors shouting through megaphones. It looked like total confusion to me, but they knew what they were doing, and the two outfits worked away, not really interfering with each other, even when shots were fired on one set. Without sound, it didn't matter. In that respect, movie life was simpler in 1922.

The feeling of being watched struck me again, and I jerked around, quickly, but saw nothing. People working, walking past—I recognized none of them.

I headed back for the stages, and the main gate. I'd be late for Lasky's open-table lunch. As I passed Stage Two, I saw that one huge rank of Cooper-Hewitts had been wheeled out through the high doors and secured against the siding of the big wall. I was abreast of the giant light-framework when I heard a noise—a rumbling, and shrilling of metal—someone shouted loudly: "Run! Look out!"

Like a dummy I was caught off guard, and paused to look

around. Someone hit me from behind, in a flying tackle that sent both of us tumbling down the street, while at our heels the whole world, it seemed, crashed into glass splinters. The entire bank of Cooper-Hewitts had toppled, and I'd been standing directly under them. They had crashed to the street, and exploding bulbs hurled glass fragments everywhere, many of them studding the wooden walls on both sides of the street. The Cooper-Hewitts were a tangled wreck of smashed glass, twisted metal, and broken wires.

I was sprawled out—but I'd landed on my right shoulder, luckily, and my injured side throbbed painfully, but the joint had not been dislocated again. The man who had tackled me, and driven us both out of harm's way by his charge, now sat up, looked at the smashed Cooper-Hewitts, then at me.

"You goddamned stupid Limey!" he said.

I recognized his voice first, throaty, husky, and while not loud, it carried clearly. But this wasn't the John Barrymore who had died when I was a twelve-year-old kid, puffy face and shaking hands, the wreck of an Adonis; this was Adonis himself, as a youth. He could give Wallace Reid cards and spades in the handsome department and beat him without trying. His aquiline features matched perfectly. He raised one eyebrow quizzically at me and started to chuckle, his Barrymore chuckle that I still remembered from the pictures I'd seen as a boy.

"You silly fuckin' Englishman—you trying to get yourself obliterated?" he asked. He got up, lithe of movement. There was a feline quality to his body. No one took worse care of himself than John Barrymore—or showed it less.

"If at first you don't succeed . . ." I said, favoring my left shoulder as I got up. It didn't seem to be hurting much worse than it had before, and the codeine still kept it below the threshhold of severe pain.

"Eh?" Barrymore stared at me, then suddenly laughed. He did everything in an odd player's way. Not "on" like the comics of my own time, but fully aware of any audience, even a watching child. " 'Wherein I spake of most disastrous chances, Of moving accidents by flood and field, of hair-breadth 'scapes i' the imminent deadly breach . . .' Eh?" He shook his magnificent head. "I didn't think you were the type, you English bastard!"

"Neither did I," I said ruefully.

People ran up, staring at us and at the wreckage of the Cooper-Hewitts. Dr. Jameson came up quickly, eyed me.

"Are you hurt?"

"No—Barrymore shoved me out of the way in time."

"Thank God!" He looked around. A workman was standing in the open doorway of Stage Two. "God damn it, why weren't those lights secured?"

The man gave him an angry look. "They were. I tied them down myself."

"Then you did a hell of a poor job!" Jameson barked. "You two look like you can stand a drink."

"Do we need an excuse?" Barrymore asked. "Where've you been, my good leech and sawbones? Been looking for you to ask if you'd seen our chubby friend this day."

"Arbuckle? No. He hasn't been on the lot. This business has hit him hard, I'm afraid. He isn't up to facing things yet."

"Fuck the bloody bastards—they've all done as bad—or worse—than our good Fatty. Sanctimony is the curse of mankind! Now where in hell's that drink?"

Jameson's scotch was as good as I remembered it. I finished my liberal glass beaker and looked at my watch. "If I'm going to join Lasky, I'd better run."

"No problem," Jameson said. "There's still time."

We had another drink. It felt warm, but didn't have much effect otherwise. To Barrymore it might have been branch water, the way he took it aboard. They both walked to the gate with me, Barrymore keeping up a running commentary on Life, Hollywood, Sex, and other Misfortunes.

"What are you working on? I haven't seen you since *The Lotus Eater*, Jack." Jameson got a word in as we drove toward Hollywood Boulevard.

"Did you have to mention that piece of shit?" Barrymore raised an eyebrow. "Dirigibles, yet! I still cringe at the thought of playing that benighted, innocent son of a bitch who was twenty-five years old and had never had a piece of ass in his miserable life!" He sighed. "Ah, Hollywood—may reality never soil your bedsheets." He blinked owlishly at us. "As for what I am now essaying—'tis a bit better, methinks! 'The game's afoot, Watson—and don't forget the needle, eh?' I'm doing Sherlock Holmes for the ex-Mr. Samuel Goldfish—alias now being Goldwyn. . . ."

Armstrong-Carleton's was a single-story Spanish-style—stucco facing and red tile roof—building, with blue Mexican ceramic tiles around the front door. We were conducted past the front dining room, down a passage, to a "garden room" styled like a Spanish enclosed patio, complete to tiled fountain, paper roses climbing green wires to fake balconies. At a big table near the fountain, Jesse L. Lasky held court. Waiters were busy pouring orange juice and gin "tea" from chinese porcelain pots into white china cups. Lasky saw us and waved us toward him. There weren't three seats together, but Jameson said, "I'll see you fellows later," and moved around to the far side of the table. Barrymore magically provided two chairs, took one, and immediately collared a waiter.

"Libations, my good man!" he shouted.

We were quickly provided with cups filled with the perennial Prohibition cocktail. Barrymore commandeered a tray loaded with sandwiches and fruit salad. I found I was hungry and, eating, began to feel better. The orange juice and gin was watery, and Barrymore made a face.

"Who's been pissin' in my orange juice?" he asked, making an owlish, blinking face.

A laugh went up—then suddenly thinned out, went off-key. Everyone looked toward the door, where a huge man had appeared. He was alone, smiling, almost shyly, looking at the people at the table, slowly, one by one. No one smiled back.

"Hello, everybody!" he called out.

His round face and round body marked him. He was Roscoe "Fatty" Arbuckle—but a sad clown at the moment. He had lost weight, for his suit bagged a bit on his huge frame, and his face seemed to sag, like a softened clay image.

No one spoke. He stood there for a moment longer. His broad grin crumbled slowly. Then, silently, he turned and walked away. The room remained silent. Then Barrymore's chair went over with a crash as he leaped to his feet.

"You lousy bunch of cocksuckers," he said scathingly, then ran after Arbuckle.

I started to get up. *Don't be a fool. You'll do Fatty no good, and Lasky won't like it.* The thought was urgent.

Fuck you!

I got up and walked out.

But Barrymore and Arbuckle had left the café, and were gone.

18

I slept most of the way back to Alvarado Street. Fellows woke me up by opening the door of the Packard. My shoulder still throbbed, numbly, and my tail was dragging. Peavey opened the door of the bungalow apartment and flashed his gold teeth at me.

"Everything go all right, suh?" He was careful helping me off with my topcoat. "Yo' see Doctuh Jameson?"

"Yes, Peavey. It's all right—just sore."

"Glad to heah that, suh. Yo' had me worried!" He shook his head. "Oh, yessuh, Miss Mabel called—she's expectin' yo' to pick her up at her place—seven o'clock."

I thought about it, feeling the sudden, warm desire to have Mabel with me again. It was clear that I couldn't trust my feelings about her, and seeing her again, being close to her, perhaps making love to her, would only make it worse. Breaking it off now would be the smart thing to do, for me, and certainly for her, because if I couldn't keep Taylor from being murdered, she'd be in it up to her beautiful neck. Her film career would suffer badly, and never recover. But since when does a man in love play it smart or count the cost? And I knew I loved her, knew with absolute conviction that it was for real, and for keeps.

"I'll be there," I said. I wouldn't have changed it for the world—and at the same time, I found myself wondering if I *could* change anything, or if what had happened before *must* happen again.

I went upstairs to rest awhile, took a couple more codeine tablets, and flopped across the bed.

I woke up suddenly, sweating, and yet cold. I had a brief memory of somebody pointing a gun at me in my dream. The room was dark. My head felt clearer, and my shoulder had stopped throbbing. I pulled on the silk-shaded bedside lamp. My watch lay on the table. It was a little before six. I sat up, and still felt pretty good; at least the sodden weariness had left my bones.

I felt still better after a shower. Peavey heard the water running and came in to ask if I needed help. I didn't, not even to pull on my pants and shirt, which Peavey had carefully laid out. The shoes were patent leather dancing pumps, with a little black taffeta bow on the front of them. As Ernie Carter, I'd never worn—or even seen—anything like them, but they were light and comfortable on my feet. Peavey came in to attach the funny little standup-wing collar, and to tie the butterfly-shaped black bowtie.

"Will yo' want Mistuh Howard to drive yo, suh?" Peavey asked.

My shoulder felt pretty good; Jameson knew his business. I shook my head. "No. I'll take the Pierce-Arrow."

Thinking about the lively roadster was pleasant. Mabel and the Pierce-Arrow—two things I'd give anything to take back with me when I returned to my own time. *If*. But if I *did* prevent Taylor's murder, would I live out the rest of his life, in his body? The thought was disturbing as hell; maybe I didn't like a lot of things about Ernie Carter and the world he was stuck with, but the idea of never getting back shook me. Still, I'd have—as William Desmond Taylor—the kind of life most men would gladly swap their own for. Plus Mabel Normand. . . .

The flickering strobe-jump returned suddenly. I forced the thoughts away.

Peavey was holding up a lightweight topcoat, which he helped me into. He handed me a black fedora, and in the full-length dressing-table mirror, Taylor was a strikingly handsome man. Maybe not in the same league with Barrymore and Reid, but not out of the ball park, either. . . .

Peavey walked with me down the stairs. "Mistuh Sands called again, suh."

"I hope you told him to drop dead?"

"No, suh . . ." Chuckling. "But ah'll be glad to do it next time."

He went with me around the bungalow to the garage, and I got the impression he was there to protect me, in case I needed it, and I was grateful. At least there was one person back in 1922 not out for Taylor's blood—I hoped!

Fellows had left for the night, but the garage was unlocked, the door behind the roadster standing open. I climbed into the Pierce-Arrow, feeling again the warm glow of possession; I would never look enviously at a Rolls-Royce driver again! I set the spark and gas levers, pulled out the choke a notch, and hit the starter. The big engine turned over smoothly, whispering powerfully to itself. I pulled on the lights and twisted in the seat to look behind me. There were no backup lights, and the notion of "inventing" them for 1922 struck me, and made me smile. If I kept Taylor—us—alive long enough, I just might put one of these ideas into practice.

"Shall I leave the door open fo' yo', suh?" Peavey asked. I shook my head, and when I backed into the street, he slid the garage door shut.

A streetcar clanged down Maryland, and I waited for it to whisk past before backing on out into the street. Only then did it strike me that I didn't know where Mabel Normand lived. *Seventh and Vermont!* Taylor was more obliging than usual with the information, probably because of the way he felt about Mabel, too, the bastard! I turned the nose of the roadster toward Alvarado, and headed for Vermont. The night was cold and clear, with more stars glinting overhead than I'd ever seen above L.A. before. A few wisps of cloud edged the sky to the west. It was a dark, moonless night. The moon would be in its last thin quarter, and wouldn't rise until almost sunup. Vermont was busy, but the traffic cops kept the flow of cars constant, doing a better job than electric signals ever would.

At five minutes before seven I pulled up in front of Mabel's apartment house. She was standing at the curb, wearing something black, silky, and sleek, the skirt raised with one hand, revealing her trim, perfect leg, encased in sheer, glistening black silk hose, the other raised, thumb extended in the classic hitchhiking gesture. I squealed the brakes and leaned over to open the door.

"Going my way, Kewpie-doll?" I leered.

"Absotively, big boy!" she returned, with an impish grin, and hopped in, and gave me a big kiss. I kissed her back, looking into her eyes and letting my feelings show.

"I could learn to like this," I said, and reached past her to tug the door closed. My shoulder protested and I winced.

"Now you've hurt your shoulder," she said. "Doc Jameson called me this afternoon. He was worried about you. Are you sure you're feeling up to tonight?"

"Never better."

She looked doubtful for a moment. "Doc said you shouldn't do anything strenuous."

"Sex isn't strenuous," Taylor replied before I could think of anything. "Not as far as my shoulder is concerned."

"You are a terrible man, Willie—and oversexed, too, I'm happy to say." She laughed merrily. "But you're out of luck tonight. I promised Doc I'd get you home early and tuck you into bed—alone."

I pulled the Pierce-Arrow back out into the traffic and drove in silence for a moment. I grew aware of Mabel's odd look. "Something wrong?" I asked.

"I hate to tell you," she said, studying me. "But you're going the wrong way—the Montmartre is way out—next door to the Hollywood Hotel. Willie, I do believe you've got something on your mind."

"And it'll be the death of me yet," I said, more harshly than I intended it to be.

She was looking into my eyes as I spoke, and suddenly shivered. "You're certainly acting strangely, lately. What's wrong, Willie?"

"Everything—nothing," I said lamely.

"Doc told me about the close call you had this morning, but you can't let accidents bother you. They do happen, you know."

"Especially to me." I smiled at her. "Truth is, I'd forgotten about that. I was just thinking about us, you and me, Mabel."

"What is there to think about—besides having a hell of a good time while we can, Willie?"

"A lot of things."

"If you're going serious on me, Willie-boy, you can damned well take me back home."

"Not a chance," I said, firmly. "Fun it is!"

The Montmartre was upstairs in a building directly across the boulevard from the New Christie Hotel. There was a cleared space at the curb in front of the entrance, and drivers waiting to whisk unchauffeured cars off to some parking place. One of them opened my door and hopped in as I climbed out of the roadster. I helped Mabel out and we pushed our way through a crowd of onlookers. They recognized Mabel and started yelling and waving. She loved every second of it, and hurried over to touch their waving hands and grin at them.

At the curb, a big Rolls limousine pulled up and a uniformed driver hopped out to open the rear door. A small, dark, and very shapely woman climbed out, to wave and blow kisses to the crowd, poised and regal, very definitely "on" for their benefit. Behind her came a gray-haired, burly man, with heavy shoulders and chest. Mabel turned to look at them, then giggled and called out, "Oh, Miss Busch! Can I have your autograph, huh?"

Mae Busch was strikingly beautiful, with a row of perfect spit curls plastered across her forehead. She smiled graciously, looked toward Mabel—then tensed, her expression furious. She grabbed the burly man's arm and tugged him toward the entrance. Mabel grinned at the spectators, who were wise to the little comedy-drama. They gave her laughter and applause, obviously on her side, and she did a little Chaplin walk and bow, then ran lightly toward the doors.

"That two-timing bastard Mack!" she said, actually half-angry. The burly man was Mack Sennett, I gathered. Mabel, like most Hollywood people—then and now—lived by a double standard; one set of rules for herself and another for the rest of the world. As if she had caught my thought, she gave me a quick look.

"You want to know something? I was true to that two-timer for ten years—until I caught him with his pants down with *her!*" Her expression was indignantly righteous for a moment, then a thought made her smile, and abruptly laugh again. "At least I was true to him mostly. . . ."

The maître d' was bowing and separating the wheat from the tourist chaff, parting his velvet ropes like Moses doing his Red Sea bit, to admit the important clientele. The Red Sea parted wide for Mabel. A captain led us to a tiny table near the dance floor. The place was crowded, a bit smoky, and expensive perfume failed to cover the smell of stale human sweat. Beyond the postage-stamp dance floor was a small orchestra stand, with a big bass drum in front, with an interior light lettered BERT FISK AND HIS SYNCOPATORS.

Mack Sennett and Mae Busch were directly across the floor from us. Mack smiled at Mabel and nodded to me. Mae Busch's beautiful features were frozen, and she didn't intend to see us at all if she could help it.

"Von Stroheim's new picture will make her the hottest thing in films," Mabel said. "You don't have to guess how she got the part! Poor, blind Mack—the stupid bastard!"

Maybe she was right, but the only thing I remembered Mae Busch for was her roles in a couple of Laurel and Hardy comedies—and Jackie Gleason's old put-on, in the early days of TV, of ". . . and the ever-popular Mae Busch . . . !" It would be a long, long way down for Mae Busch.

The walls of the Montmartre were gilded, and the ceiling was draped with canopies of bright blue satin that moved with the air currents. Everything was new, shiny—matching the sleek, too-perfect beauty of the people gathered around the little dance floor. Familiar faces, many of them, a few whose names I knew; but these people, world famous in 1922, were forgotten in my day, just names in nostalgic reminiscences about Old Hollywood, sneered at by the equally forgettable superstars of the 1970s. . . .

"Golly, everybody's here!" Mabel said, looking around, seeing—and being seen. A curly-haired, round-faced man stopped by, a lovely woman on his arm. "Mickey Neilan—I thought you were in New York!"

"Hello, Mabel—Bill! Jack tells me he saved your life this afternoon."

News traveled fast in Hollywood.

"Knowing Barrymore," Taylor said, smiling, "he'll never let me live it down."

"Oh, hey—don't you two know Anna? Miss Anna Q. Nilsson—Mabel Normand and Bill Taylor. . . ."

"You're beautiful!" Mabel said, smiling and holding out her hand. "As always. We've known each other for years, Mickey."

Marshal Neilan and Anna Q. Nilsson moved away. There was a sudden round of applause, a stir of excitement, and the maître d' ushered a little man and a beautiful woman to the table next to ours. The little man, his hair already graying, a bushy mass of curls, smiled, bowed, and kissed Mabel's hand. I knew Charlie Chaplin and Edna Purviance, my next-door neighbor. Then, behind them, to a second-row table, came Wallace Reid, by himself. He smiled at Mabel, saw me, and frowned. He came over, bent to kiss Mabel. He stumbled slightly. Too much hop or hooch. His eyes showed it.

"We're going to do a picture together, Wally, someday. I swear it," Mabel said.

He nodded, glared at me, and returned to his table, a little unsteady on his feet. Mabel gave me a knowing look.

"He acts like you've been poaching on his females, Willie."

"Hardly," Taylor said stiffly. "His interests lie in another direction."

"I can't say the same thing about you, Willie." Mabel laughed again. "I seem to be fated to fall for womanizers."

"You could put an end to it as far as I'm concerned," I said slowly.

She stared at me, then quickly shook her head. "Don't tempt me, Willie—I'd just wreck both our lives."

A waiter came up, carrying the symbol of Prohibition, a white china teapot that tinkled with ice. He poured drinks into our cups—for once not gin and orange juice, but whiskey and ginger ale. He took our orders and hurried away. The orchestra filed onto their platform. A drum roll, and then into "Wang, Wang Blues." I let Taylor take over—Ernie Carter's two left feet weren't up to close-coupled dancing—and he moved very well.

The orchestra dug into the 1922 Top Forty: "June Moon," "Leave Me With a Smile," "The Sheik of Araby," and "How Many Times," then, "My Sweet Gal," "I'm Laughing All the Time," "Just a Little Love Song," "Ty-Tee," "The Happy Hottentot," "Second-Hand Rose," and then really turned on with "When Buddha Smiles."

And Taylor and Mabel didn't miss a one. Mabel was a professional dancer, quicksilver on her tiny feet, and Taylor must have been taking lessons, because he somehow held his own. Twice the rest of the crowded floor cleared away to let them dance alone with a blue spotlight on them, as everyone applauded. I could tell that Taylor really dug it. But, good as they were together, they took second place to the most beautiful couple in the joint. The man was slim, athletic of build, graceful as a bullfighter, and his tiny partner matched him, easily, in a tango.

"Rudy and Natacha," Mabel whispered in my ear. "He shouldn't be here, in public—not with his divorce from Jean Acker still in the courts. She's going to take poor Rudy for every dime he's got."

Rudolpho Valentino, the soon-to-be greatest romantic idol in films, took his bows with a wide, toothy smile. He blew a kiss to Mabel. She giggled.

"If he was as good in bed as he is on the dance floor, I'd give Natacha Rambova a run for her dollars."

"Hey, now, how would you know?"

She waggled her eyebrows archly and did her Little Tramp smirk. Chaplin came up to our table.

"Shall we show El Vaselino how it's done?" he asked, grinning and bowing.

Mabel hopped up and they moved onto the dance floor. The orchestra started another tango and Mabel and Charlie danced. He bowed, gracefully, promptly tangled up his feet, did his famous little walk-step, sliding on the sides of his shoes. He backed a step, made a nose-lifting grimace, and pretended to kick something offensive from the floor. Mabel swayed toward him, slipped, and skidded into him. They grabbed each other frantically, to keep from falling, their feet slipping and sliding every which way, as the audience clapped and howled laughter. Then, just for the hell of it, these two consummate artists stopped the pratfalling and *danced.* They matched Valentino and his lovely Natacha step for step—and ended with a riot of applause.

Hollywood of 1922 knew how to enjoy itself. But the main event was yet to come.

It was warm, and the drinks were cold. Mabel was dancing with me again, to a waltz. But I kept thinking about the unhappy fat man who had faced silence when he needed applause more than ever before in his life.

"I saw Fatty Arbuckle this afternoon," I said. Mabel didn't raise her head to look at me. "Jack Barrymore was the only one who even tried to greet him. The rest of them just sat there, acting like they were embarrassed that he existed. They deserved the name Barrymore called them. . . ." Mabel was silent, and I felt her stiffen slightly in my arms. "You've known and worked with Arbuckle, and—"

"Damn it! Don't spoil my fun!" Mabel looked at me. Genuine anger was in her eyes for an instant, then it faded and she made an impish face. "Don't let's talk, Willie. Just dance, huh?"

Arbuckle brought reality too close to her dream world, and she couldn't bear it. A whole world, built on dreams, and fun and games, shared by all these other beautiful shadows of the silver screen who surrounded us. Sweet music, and a satin sky, and carefully subdued lighting designed never to make you feel old, or ugly, or tired. For an instant I hated them, all of them, even Mabel, because I understood them, and why they couldn't let down their guard, even to help one of their own who had fallen headlong into sordid reality, as Arbuckle had. . . .

I was going to suggest that we stop by Arbuckle's house, later—but I knew it was no good. She wouldn't go. If she had known that scandal would soon destroy her, too, would she have felt any differently? I don't think so. The world might love her—for the moment—but Mabel was a loner, and she played by her own rules, win or lose.

I had been favoring my shoulder, avoiding contact with the other dancers as best I could. But now someone collided with us, hard. My shoulder sent agony through me, and I staggered, trying to grip it, to ease the pain. Then I was spun around and a fist smashed into my face, sending me crashing into Mack Sennett's table. The burly Mack was a powerful man—he'd been a steelworker in his younger days—and he caught me, held me up until my head cleared. On the dance floor, Wallace Reid was glaring at me, his fists knotted.

"I warned you, you son of a bitch!" he yelled, and came for me.

"Don't mess up his face!" Mack yelled at me.

My shoulder had gone out of the socket again, and I had no intention of letting muscleman Reid pound on me. I went low, reared back, and kicked, hard. It spun him around, his feet sliding on the waxed floor. I went in fast and hit him in the stomach with my left hand. I had plenty of room to move around in, and I meant it. My first punch doubled him over and the second dropped him on his butt. Then men jammed between us, and Reid was hustled away. He jerked free, his face contorted.

"I'll kill you, you son of a bitch!" he shouted.

Then he was gone.

I added Wallace Reid's name to the list of people out to do Taylor in. I was beginning to think that the police investigation into his murder had barely scratched the surface.

Dr. Jameson was suddenly beside me. He led me through the crowd, to one side. Everyone was still gawking, but the orchestra was taking up the beat, and dancing was beginning again.

"Jesse Lasky's going to have a job keeping this out of the newspapers," Jameson said cheerfully. "Man, you certainly fight dirty, you know that?"

"With one arm what did you expect?" I snarled. "What the hell lit his fuse?"

"Your little meeting with De Mille. C.B. told Wally he was out of the picture—and he blames you for it, naturally." Jameson grinned—and suddenly jerked my arm. I felt it slide sickeningly back into the shoulder socket. The whiskey and ginger ale turned to water.

"That better?" Jameson asked. "I suggest that you keep that wing in a sling for a few days. It won't help the injury, but it may keep someone from punching you."

"I doubt it," I said. "Thanks again, Doc."

"Need a shot to help the pain?"

"I've got those pills you gave me.

"Take a couple—but don't mix them with too much booze. They can have a devastating effect."

He helped me back to my table, where Mabel grinned up at me. She was flushed with excitement, and had obviously forgiven me for mentioning Arbuckle. She raised her cup of hooch in salute. "One-round Taylor wins again!"

"I feel more like the loser."

She was contrite, instantly, and kissed me, gently touching my shoulder. "We can go now, if you'd rather?"

"Not a chance." I forced a smile. "Isn't this our dance?"

The pills and booze kept me going. Or maybe it was being with Mabel, and holding her close in my arms. For some reason, she was warm and attentive, holding my eyes with hers, and snuggling up against me. It was a night I'd never forget. I just wish— But beggars only ride in dreams.

It was eleven thirty when, at her insistence, I dropped Mabel Normand off at her apartment house. She wouldn't let me come up. She kissed me gently. In the last hour she had quieted down, almost like a film being projected too slowly. All the way back to Alvarado Street I thought of the tracks on her beautiful arm.

I put the Pierce-Arrow away and was thankful that the garage door slid so easily. I locked it and went between the bungalows. My place was dark; Peavey had gone to bed. I let myself in and went upstairs.

Betty Blayne was sprawled on my bed, in a sheer silk, pink nightgown, with *B.B.* embroidered in blue letters across one small, round breast. She was asleep, more little-girlish than ever. She woke up, stared sleepily at me, smiled—then stuck her tongue out at me.

"The hours you keep!" she said.

"Only because I didn't know what was waiting for me at home," Taylor replied, smiling.

She hopped up from the bed and helped me out of my coat, unbuttoned my vest and shirt. She tossed my clothes any which way, copped a feel as she undid my trousers, and laughed her perfect little-girl's laugh. She oohed over the bruises on my chest and shoulder—they looked as colorful as a print by Technicolor—then half-pushed me into bed.

"Hold it," I said. "What about Mama?"

"I saw her on the night train to Santa Barbara—her sister's in the hospital. She would've made me go, too, but I've an early call in the morning." She giggled. "So we've got all night. Mama won't be back until tomorrow afternoon."

Then she stepped out of the flimsy nightgown and hung it in my wardrobe closet. She pirouetted her naked child's body in front of me, then hopped onto the bed.

"Look," I said, hesitantly. "I'm pretty well banged up. . . ."

"Then relax and enjoy it!"

I thought about the initialed nightgown. It would be found hanging in William Desmond Taylor's closet—after he was murdered—one more part of the puzzle surrounding his death.

Then Betty Blayne's soft hands and gentle persuasion drove all other thoughts from my mind. She climbed astride me, awkwardly, at first, then slowly picking up a rhythm. After a few moments she paused, breathing a little hard, and grinned at me.

"I've never done it this way before—I didn't know what hard work it was!"

"In that case let me take my turn," I said.

My shoulder didn't hurt a bit.

19

Betty Blayne left while it was still dark, insisting she would drive herself home. She had left her car a block or so down on Maryland, out of sight of anyone in the bungalow courts who might have recognized it. Her concern for the proprieties reflected the hypocrisy of the 1920s; they had no qualms about indulging themselves in any way they liked—so long as their public image wasn't tarnished. In Betty Blayne's case, she had maintained the pure little-girl image on the screen for so long, even a whisper of scandal could—and would—wreck her career. The moviegoing public expected their heroes and heroines of the silver screen to be in real life the paragons of virtue they were on celluloid, preposterous as that seems. When the truth came out—which it occasionally did, as in the case of Fatty Arbuckle, and during the police investigation of the William Desmond Taylor murder—then the crap really hit the fan, dirtying every-one it touched. But the fact that Hollywood then—as now—indulged itself in any kind of pleasurable vice known, shows that people—unlike times and places—never really change a hell of a lot.

After Betty Blayne had gone, I relaxed in bed. I felt pretty good, a little beat up, but my shoulder hadn't gone out again, and despite my sexual activities there was only a minor dull ache. This was Friday morning. William Desmond Taylor had five days to live, if I didn't come up with something—and I was noplace. Sure, I was beginning to sort out the pieces, maybe even get a glimmer of what would really happen, and why. But there were still too many items missing. Important ones. I was pretty sure of one thing—Taylor's murder wasn't just a professional rubout; whoever shot him hated his guts, too. I had no facts or logic to back this up, just a feeling in my gut. But that feeling seldom proved wrong. The list of names of people in the film industry involved in the use and/or sale of narcotics that Taylor had given the U.S. Deputy D.A. was enough in itself to get him killed. Maybe it had, despite my hunch to the contrary. One way to make sure, I thought, was to eliminate that angle before next Wednesday night, if I could. . . .

I slept another hour, then got up. I still felt pretty damned spry. Taylor's sex life was doing wonders for my morale, if not my physical stamina. But the weekend on William Randolph Hearst's yacht wouldn't provide much opportunity for sexual acrobatics—and even Taylor's gonads could use the rest. *Like hell!* I ignored him.

Peavey had another enormous breakfast ready, a half-dozen dishes under silver lids, and in chafing dishes, keeping hot. I found I had an appetite—Betty Blayne was right, sex does make you hungry—and even tried some kippers. They were too salty, and too damned fishy for me, although I gathered that Taylor relished them. I didn't feel in the mood to indulge him, so I settled for a piece of ham and a couple of coddled eggs.

I glanced at the *Examiner*'s ratty headlines, even read something about a love-nest raid in Pasadena—in *Pasadena!* The *Times* was beginning a campaign to raise funds for some starving Russians in the Crimea. The political world was stable, and the Congress was playing things close to its vest for the moment. *The Gumps* still continued the contest for its readers to advise on the marital-romantic affairs of Uncle Bim—and the damned bale of hay was still the first prize. I thought it still had to be a put-on.

There was mention of a drug bust. The story named Under-sheriff Biscailuz—William I. Traeger was sheriff in 1922—as one of the principals making the arrest. When I was growing up, Biscailuz was *the* sheriff of Los Angeles County, with an international reputation in law enforcement. The D.A. for the county was Thomas Lee Woolwine, and I'd never heard of him. A dozen stories, scattered through the news section of the *Times*, told of Prohibition problems; a man went blind from drinking tainted—probably wood—alcohol in San Bernardino; a blind pig in Barstow was raided—a *blind pig?* Two murder trials in the state were covered, one dealing with a man defending the honor of his home, whatever that meant; the other was a stage actress who had pumped a couple of shots into an unfaithful lover; her husband was standing beside her, which proves times haven't changed so much, and people are just as stupid now as they were then. . . .

I read the entertainment page with some interest. At Loew's State, Mae Murray was starring in *Peacock Alley*, and the review was pretty good; Richard Dix—hey, I remembered him in Westerns when I was a kid—he played The Whistler, too, in his later years—was the star of something called *The Glorious Fool*, playing at the California Theater. At Grauman's Million Dollar Theater, Lionel Barrymore—of course I remembered him, especially as Dr. Gillespie with Lew Ayres as *Young Doctor Kildare*—in *Boomerang Bill*. The Kinema had Hope Hampton in *Star Dust*—five years before Hoagy Carmichael first wrote it as a piano rag, and longer than that before it became a standard ballad—while the Superba featured Marie Prevost in *Don't Get Personal*. Miller's Theater was showing Strongheart, a dog star, in *The Silent Call*. The Alhambra had Douglas Fairbanks' *The Three Musketeers*—I'd seen it at John Hampton's Silent Movie Theater on Fairfax, just this past—Ernie Carter's past—year. At Clunes', Bebe Daniels starred in *Nancy From Nowhere*, and the Symphony Theater featured Harold Lloyd in *Sailor Made Man*.

Pavlova was making her farewell L.A. appearance at the Philharmonic Auditorium, while at the Mason Opera House, a hit New York play, *The Bat*, was doing big business. The Pantages had a featured vaudeville bill—and I didn't know a single name on the "All-Star" program. At the Morosco Theater was a play called

Scrambled Wives. I did better with the vaudeville bill at the Orpheum, which featured:

KELLAM & O'DARE

FRANK FARRON

and

EDDIE FOY & THE YOUNGER FOYS

in

"THE FOY FUN REVUE"

At least I remembered Eddie Foy, Jr., who must have been one of the Younger Foys in the big-time act, and I'd heard of his father. Bob Hope had played him in *The Seven Little Foys*, which still played the Late Show on TV.

On the next page was a listing of the top-selling new phonograph records, which featured the All Star Trio doing "My Sweet Gal" and "I'm Laughing All the Time," three big Paul Whiteman hits, including "When Buddha Smiles," a woman named Elsie Baker, and another popular gal singer named just Miss Patricola—which shows rock 'n' roll didn't invent oddball performer names. Then another familiar name, and song title, too: Fanny Brice singing "Second Hand Rose" and "My Man"— from the *Ziegfeld Follies*, read the plug. It proved that Bert Fisk's Syncopators kept up with the hits, for we had danced to all of them the night before.

On the sports page, Jack Dempsey was in New York, looking for a match; there was still talk he would meet Harry Wills. I knew he wouldn't, and found myself smirking a bit and feeling superior. The fact that most of the then-famous names were strange to me brought everything back into perspective. I was still a stranger in a very strange land.

The phone rang, and I thought it was probably Mama Denker about to give me hell for laying her baby daughter again, then remembered she was out of town. It was Mr. Hearst's secretary—male—to say that a car would pick me up at six— dinner would be at eight—informal, on the yacht, the *Oneida*. Thinking of Hearst reminded me of the blue-covered contract I'd brought home yesterday. I carried a cup of coffee over to my desk and opened the contract. It was pretty good money, even for my time, guaranteeing Taylor thirty-nine weeks out of fifty-two, at

$1,500 per, or almost sixty grand. His name would be above the title, like a star's. On the desk was also a half-filled-out income tax form, due on March 15. Clipped to it was a folded slip of paper, indicating Taylor had made a little over $37,000 in 1921—which wasn't bad, either. Especially when I saw that the tax rate was just 4 percent. He might make more in my time, but he'd keep a hell of a lot less.

On the slip of paper was a note in Taylor's handwriting: *Call Margie Berger.* My God, another broad?

My income tax expert, damn it! Taylor was almost indignant. Almost. If the Berger dame was a looker, ten would get you fifty he was laying her. *You son of a bitch! I've had enough of you!*

Margie Berger. The name rang a bell in my memory. I'd run into it before. A Hollywood case. . . . Hey, got it! In the police report covering Jean Harlow's husband's—what the hell was his name? Bern—Paul Bern, that was it!—suicide, there was mention that he had talked to her the afternoon of the day he blew his brains out.

Paul Bern? I know him. He's Barbara La Marr's sweetie—Jack Gilbert's longtime buddy. But who is Jean Harlow?

After your time, Taylor. Harlow—her real name was Harlean Carpenter—would be an eleven-year-old student at the Barstow School in Kansas City, Missouri, right now. But one of these days she's going to set this town on its ear. She's still the hottest thing in pictures, excepting only Marilyn Monroe. . . .

I'll take your word for it. The future wasn't one of Taylor's big interests—he had too much going for him *now.*

The phone rang again. It was Mabel Normand. Suddenly I felt guilty because I had spent the night with Betty Blayne, even though I felt certain that Mabel wouldn't give a damn.

"I love you," I said. "Will you marry me?"

Are you mad? You've already told Mrs. Denker you're marrying Betty Blayne!

What are you worried about, Billy-boy? You've been handling the two of them up until now.

"Oh, Willie, I just got a call from Goldwyn—he thinks he's found the right property for my next picture. . . ." A sudden pause. *"What did you say?"*

"I asked, will you marry me?"

"No!" Mabel's delighted laughter made the day brighter. "Now be serious! Have you read the new Ethel M. Dell book, *Rosamundy*?"

"I'm afraid I haven't."

"Would you get it, read it, and tell me what you think, please? Whether you feel it's right for me? I'll do something nice for you in return—just as soon as your shoulder's up to it."

"I'm a fast reader—what about tonight?"

"You terrible, terrible lecher! No—I've got a date with Mack. He wants to talk about my doing another picture with him— *Molly O* is doing big business, now he's taken it from the shelf and dusted it off." She laughed again. "Besides, you need the rest—in more ways than one!"

"Not as far as you're concerned," Taylor returned. "But if you insist, I'll keep my nose in the book. What did you say was the name of it?"

"*Rosamundy*, by Ethel M. Dell—you can have Parker's Book Store send it out to you this afternoon."

"I'll do that. And, think about marrying me, please?"

"It would serve you right if I did!"

After she hung up I asked Peavey about Parker's, and he said he'd order the book sent out by messenger. It would cost an extra quarter, he informed me later—and the book was priced at $1.90—no sales tax either.

I told Peavey to pack a bag for the weekend; he'd know what I should have along, and I sure as hell didn't! He brought in the mail, and it proved to be uninteresting. The doorbell rang and I heard Peavey talking. He came back, frowning.

"A reporter from the *Examiner*, suh," he said. "He won't go away 'thout seein' yo'."

"Then bring him in."

The reporter looked very much like he had been created by Hecht and MacArthur for *The Front Page*—rumpled suit, a hand-rolled cigarette dangling from one stained corner of his mouth, dirty shirt with loose collar, and ink-stained fingers. There was a sour smell of sweat and whiskey that came in with him. Deodorants for men were unheard of in 1922. He grinned at me.

"Had a little ruckus last night, heh, Taylor?"

"Not that I remember," I replied coldly.

"Don't bullshit me, mister. I got the straight dope from an eyewitness."

"Good for you," I said. "Then you don't need me to tell you about it. Good-bye."

He blinked, then scowled. "Oh, yeah? Well, what's your side of it? You decked Wally Reid last night at the Montmartre—and that's news, mister!"

"I doubt it." I picked up the phone. "Can I have the number of Mr. William Randolph Hearst's home in Beverly Hills? Thank you." The reporter stared at me, still grinning. The same male secretary's voice answered. "This is Bill Taylor," I said. "I'm not sure that I can make Mr. Hearst's party on his yacht, after all. You see, there's a reporter here from the *Examiner* who has made up a cock and bull story he intends to print, and—oh, all right." I held out the receiver to the reporter. "For you."

He took it. I heard the murmur of the secretary's voice. The reporter said, "Yeah. Gotcha. Okay, okay, already!" He hung up, squinted at me, wobbled his frayed cigarette to the other side of his mouth, then nodded. "Next time, bozo," he said, and turned and walked out. I had the feeling that Taylor's murder would get a bad press in the *Examiner*.

Sergeant Dan Cahill showed up at ten o'clock. His odd, crooked lip made his smile seem sinister. He was carrying his derby hat in his hand when Peavey showed him in. We shook hands. Cahill looked around.

"Nice place you've got here," he said.

"I like it. Will you have a cup of coffee with me?"

"I haven't got the time, but thanks anyway. I just wanted to ask a couple of questions, if you don't mind. You were driven up to Mount Lowe, night before last, by Miss Mabel Normand's chauffeur—named Davis. Is that correct?"

"It is."

"Davis is a dark, Latin type—it strike you as odd his name's Davis?"

I smiled. "Not really. I'm in the movie industry, remember? Nobody uses his right name, it seems. And, with the hit Valentino's made with *The Four Horsemen of the Apocalypse* and

The Sheik, Latin surnames are all the rage—but a few years ago they were poison with the studios. I'd guess that Davis—if he is a Latin—has movie ambitions, and changed his name."

"There could be another reason. A legal reason. He seems to have been the only person hanging around that trolley line that night."

"You're working on the assumption that the trolley wreck wasn't an accident, then?"

"We have to until things are cleared up. That air hose was weakened by somebody using a file or rasp."

"You said it might be a grudge against the Pacific Electric Company."

"We've checked it out—it isn't likely."

"I see." I frowned, thinking fast. "But it's still possible?"

"If somebody tried to kill me, I'd want to find out who and why—unless I already knew the answers," Cahill said slowly, watching me.

"I couldn't agree with you more, Sergeant."

"Who wants to kill you, Mr. Taylor?"

"I suppose I have some enemies," I said. "I imagine there are people who would do you in, too, Sergeant, if they could get away with it. But would you want to accuse them—with no more to go than what you have now?"

"Maybe not," Cahill said grudgingly. "I don't know. But Davis—has he anything against you?"

"I hardly know the man!"

"That's not really an answer, Mr. Taylor."

"I meant there's never been anything personal between us. He's driven Miss Normand and me a few places—that's all. To the best of my knowledge I've never even held what you might call a conversation with the fellow."

Cahill's expression didn't change. "What about the fight you had with Wallace Reid at the Montmartre last night?"

I smiled. "A push and a punch doesn't make a fight—except in Hollywood, Sergeant. It didn't mean a thing. Mr. Reid had been drinking—and so had I."

"So I gathered. You took him out pretty easy—and he's a rugged guy."

"I've learned to take care of myself, Sergeant. I've knocked about the world quite a bit, and seen a few tight places. And others grabbed us before it got serious." I forced a smile. "Wally would have knocked my block off if he'd been sober."

"Would he, now?" Cahill studied me for a moment, then nodded his head. "Thanks for talking to me, Mr. Taylor. I'll be in touch." He paused. "You're going away tonight, I understand."

"You do believe in doing your homework, don't you, Sergeant? You're right, but I'll be back Monday, or before. I'd be interested in learning how you knew, though, if it isn't a trade secret?"

"I'm afraid it is," he said quietly. "If you have nothing to add to what you've told me, I'll be on my way."

"I'm afraid that's all."

He nodded and went out. Cahill was a cop doing his job as best he could, and my holding out on him wasn't making it any easier. Maybe if I leveled with him—

No! Mr. Greene, the U. S. Deputy District Attorney, made me swear to keep my mouth shut!

Nobody's going to use Mr. Greene for a target next Wednesday night, either! Believe me, Taylor, if I need his help to stay alive, I'm going to yell cop to Cahill—real loud!

But I had suddenly had enough of William Desmond Taylor and his troubles. I got my hat and stick and went for the Pierce-Arrow. I backed it out of the garage. Howard Fellows was polishing up the Packard. He had already worked on the yellow roadster, and it looked great. I kept my mind off my problems, just driving and enjoying the clean smell of the air. There were high-piled white clouds over the mountains to the north and to the west, but nothing that looked like rain. The sun was bright. There had been a heavy overcast the night before, and the moisture had darkened the sidewalks a bit.

I headed west on 6th, turned north on Cahuenga. The Hollywood Bowl didn't have its cement-shell backing, but the mountains on both sides were green from the winter rains. There were houses, but more bean fields than anything else. I drove past Universal Studios—in Universal City, right where Uncle Carl Laemmle had planned it, and where it still remained in the 1970s—scattered single-story frame buildings, sprawling up a sloping hill, and several glass-topped stages, their roofs visible high above the surrounding fence, reflecting the bright sun. Along Lankershim Boulevard, in front of the studio, a row of signboards advertised their new movies, *Outside the Law*, with Lon Chaney—the original Man of a Thouasand Faces, not his son, Creighton, who changed his name to Lon, Jr.—*Mad Marriage*, *The Dangerous Moment*, and a batch of Westerns starring Ed Gibson, who was also called "Hoot" on the billboards—including *Action*, *The Fire Eater*, and *Red Courage*. A double-length signboard announced the Universal Jewel Special, *Foolish Wives*, starring Erich von Stroheim and Mae Busch.

The San Fernando Valley was empty, just miles and miles of bean fields and truck gardens. Ventura Boulevard became a dirt road not far from Cahuenga Pass. The street where Ernie Carter had bought his condominium didn't exist, and I wasn't even sure where it would be in fifty years. I left a cloud of thick dust in the wake of the Pierce-Arrow. The temperature guage was climbing into the red, so I looked for a filling station. There were none, but I found a clapboard general store, nestling among some native California pepper trees, their long, green tendrils providing shade that must be a godsend in the summer months. There was a gasoline pump in front, so I pulled in and honked. A man wearing alpaca sleeve-protectors and a dingy white apron came out and worked a long handle at the side of the pump to fill the big glass tank on top of it with colorless gasoline.

"Got any ethyl?" I asked.

"Who?" The man looked puzzled. "Nobody of that name here."

For a moment I felt like a man treading water, then I realized that tetra-ethyl lead was probably unheard of in 1922. With the new no-lead fuels, we'd come full circle in my day.

The man in the apron unscrewed the gas cap and inserted the nozzle. The pump dinged away the quarter gallons. I raised the hood. Everything looked fine. I let the man unscrew the radiator cap; steam hissed into the air. He used a garden hose to put in water.

I went into the store. It smelled great, a mixture of pleasant, old-fashioned smells, compounded of tanned leather, dry goods, smoked hams dangling on cords from the ceiling behind the little meat counter, even pungent coal oil, and open barrels of pickles and pickled fish. It's a funny thing, but I remember the smells of 1922 better than most other things about it. The labels on boxes and canned goods looked strange, even those with familiar names on them. And the half-dozen open cartons of cigarettes included Camels—looking the same as now, as far as I could tell—and Lucky Strikes, which were in green packages. Sweet Caporals had a Turkish fez centered in a red and gold sunburst design on the package, while Sunshine Cigarettes were in a dull red package with an idyllic yellow river and a golden sun featured. Home Runs had an old-fashioned baseball batter and catcher at home plate printed on a gray-green background. There were Fatimas, in a tan-yellow package with a veiled harem beauty, a Maltese cross, and star and scimitar printed in red; and Murads, with the fanciest label of all—a sunburst, Egyptian temple, and a lounging Cleopatra on a golden divan. . . . In the same case was an assortment of chewing tobacco, some in paper-and-foil-wrapped bars and others in little round tins; Bull Durham and Golden Grain tobacco in little cloth bags, hanging from paper cards; a few dried-looking cigars in a wooden box that looked like it was made from cedar; and some tins of pipe tobacco. The other half of the same glass case held boxes of penny candies, jellies, jawbreakers, Juju Beans, and shriveled-up marshmallow bananas, as well as cartons of candy bars. I bought a nickel Hershey as big as those sold for a quarter in my day and munched on it as I went back outside. The chocolate tasted a little different, and seemed to be waxier, somehow.

A big black sedan was parked in the shade of a pepper tree down the road a short distance. Picnickers, I thought, and returned to the yellow roadster. The gasoline cost me fourteen cents a gallon—a little over a dollar's worth had filled the tank. I paid the man in the apron, started the motor, and drove back to the road. I headed west, planning on cutting over the mountains through Topanga Canyon.

I drove steadily, enjoying the warmth of the sun on my face. I passed only a few cars, but several horse-drawn wagons. There were houses scattered along the boulevard—or the dirt road that would someday be Ventura Boulevard—at the foot of the hills. A

sign on one side of the road announced TARZANA RANCH, and
there was an isolated little cluster of buildings, all of them frame
or adobe. As I drove on, I noticed a car in the rearview mirror. A
black sedan. The same one I'd seen back at the general store?
Following me? I couldn't be sure. It kept pretty far back—too far
to identify anyone in it. When I turned south on Topanga—
another dirt road—it was still there. I still couldn't be sure that it
was following me, as there was a little settlement in Topanga
Canyon. I drove past the dusty pepper trees and scattered
houses—most of them just shacks—and the dirt road began to
climb the Santa Monica Mountains.

It was nothing like the Topanga Canyon Road that was still
dangerous in my day, far from it! It was badly graded, graveled
only in spots, rutted when muddy during heavy rains, and
rougher than the old Baja California Highway. Chuckholes
abounded, and minor landslides had completely obliterated the
road in places, but the high wheels and narrow tires of the
Pierce-Arrow had been made for this kind of cross-country travel,
which would have shaken my Chevelle to pieces, and the big
engine purred like a cat with a saucer of cream as I fed gas to it. I
got the feel of the heavy roadster, the peculiar mushiness of
brakes only on the rear wheels, and even learned how to use the
handbrake to supplement the foot pedal. The trick was not to
brake in a curve, but just before bending into it, then to give her
hell as you came out of it. The Pierce-Arrow loved it, and I loved
the big roadster.

Dust ballooned up behind me. At first the big black sedan fell
back, but the driver was only biding his time. He had to eat dust
to do it, but he stayed with me. Some of the curves were sharper
than hell, and the roadster skidded; the heavier body of the sedan
gave it an advantage in some of the turns. We were climbing
steadily, and I saw that the temperature gauge fluid had risen into
the red, high into the red. There must be a minor radiator or hose
leak. I slowed a bit and thought about pulling over to let the
engine cool. But the ugly black nose of the sedan behind me
changed my mind.

With the engine overheating, and loving the car too damned
much to burn it up, I slowed still more. The sedan stayed on my

tail for a moment, then suddenly gunned it, swung wide to come alongside. I saw it coming, and I saw something else, too. The black ugly snout of a tommy gun as the man holding it leaned out his window to take aim. I jerked the wheel, nearly creamed a fender on the rocky cut-out hillside, as I heard the stuttering thunder of the shots. None came close, but they chewed hell out of the hill.

Overheating or not, I didn't care for the idea of dying five days early, and fed the big motor more gas. The Pierce-Arrow *went*. I took a sharp curve on two wheels, with a five-hundred-foot drop inches away. There was a shallower straight stretch, and I opened up the roadster. The speedometer wheel began to turn, past 60, 70, 80, and still climbing. I left the sedan lumbering behind me, hit the first curve ahead fast, just made it, the rear wheels spinning dirt over a steep canyon drop, and I had all I could do to twist the wheel the opposite way for the next one! I cut it sharp, hit a shoulder of the road, bounced, swayed dangerously, but made it. The road was narrower then hell here, and I felt the big engine shuddering. I jammed on the brakes and jerked the handbrake as hard as I could. The roadster skidded, spun sideways, then half-straightened. The engine stopped. The radiator cap blew with a thunderous *bang!* Steam geysered straight up.

Then the sedan, the driver obviously thinking that I'd gotten away from them, came barreling around the bend as fast as he could make it, tires screaming, motor thundering. He saw me—the big yellow Pierce-Arrow roadster was filling all of the narrow road. His driving instincts betrayed him. He jammed on the brakes and jerked the steering wheel—but he jerked it the wrong way. I stood up to look back. It was like something you see in an old gangster movie on the Late, Late Show. The sedan kept going, but there was no road under its madly spinning wheels, just vacant space. It soared straight out, a hundred feet or more, over a canyon that didn't bottom out for nearly a thousand feet. That sedan arced out as gracefully as the flight of a tennis ball over a net. Then, almost like slow motion, it began its long, long drop. I watched it go. A door jerked open and a dark figure started to climb out, the useless tommy gun still clutched in its arms. I could see the man's face, recognize it. He was the smaller, thinner man of the pair who had jumped me outside Paulais'—Patterson's buddy who had gunned him down, probably with that same ugly-snouted gun. Patterson had called him Corbo, and cursed him as he died.

Then the car, the man, and the tommy gun were gone. I followed them with my eyes, down, down. Still soaring gracefully. I could hear a man screaming incoherently. Then they hit. The sedan went to pieces, as if dynamite had exploded inside it, bounced, burst into flames, and then tumbled, end over end, pieces flying, and spilled gasoline, burning brightly, down the steep canyon wall. Thick black smoke churned upward, then thinned quickly in the mountain breeze.

I could scratch the man with the tommy gun from my list. He wouldn't be the one who murdered William Desmond Taylor. That was for damned sure.

20

After the echoing thunder of the crash died away, there was only stillness. Dust blossomed into the sky, then blew away. The dark smoke puffed, thinner each time, faded into dark gray, lightened still more. The whole thing seemed suddenly unreal, as if it had happened in a dream, without meaning. I leaned back against the leather seat of the Pierce-Arrow and felt my body—Taylor's body—trembling violently. The steam hissed steadily from the radiator of the big roadster, only slowly dying down.

The faint chugalug of an engine came to me, echoed faintly against the rocky hillside. Then, over the rise ahead of me, an ancient—even by Taylor's standards—Model T poked its black nose. The windshield was long gone, just the naked black metal arms that had once held it remained, and the body behind the front seat had been sawed away and replaced by a homemade wooden flatbed. A rawboned, weathered face beneath an incredibly twisted, torn, and battered old fedora moved rhythmically, a cud of tobacco swelling one lean cheek. Some wooden crates—empty—were tied on behind the tattered seat, which had been covered with a cheap cotton Navajo-design blanket, now faded by the sun from its original garish coloring to a muddy gray, except in the folds, where the colorful design remained. Seeing the Pierce-Arrow blocking the road, the farmer driving the old Ford half-stood up, jamming both feet onto the floor pedals. The Model T jerked, then slowed, reluctantly, the rivets in the worn-out brake linings screaming against the steel drums. Eventually the Ford slowed to a stop. Without missing a chew, the farmer eyed me and the roadster.

"Just gawkin' or you got yourself some trouble?" His voice was a rusty squawk, totally compatible with his ancient car.

"Overheated," I said. "Blew off the radiator cap."

"Probably got yourself a cracked block, then," he said, and just sat there, as if waiting for me to do something about it.

"Can you give me a lift? I'm afraid I can't drive my car. I can send a tow truck up after it if I can get to a phone."

"Your car's blocking the road."

"If you'll give me a hand, we can push it to one side."

"That's an idea," the farmer admitted, after giving it some thought. He chewed for a moment, without moving.

"Well?"

He eyed the situation again, held his own silent debate, reached a decision, then slowly nodded. He got out, and thin as a fishing rod, he towered up inches over me. But he was strong and willing once he got moving, and we shoved and pushed and got the Pierce-Arrow off, onto the gravel of the shoulder of the narrow road. It would be all right there unless somebody ran into it coming around a curve too fast. But this farmer's was the first car I'd seen in more than half an hour, so that possibility didn't worry me too much. Riding down the steep road in the Ford with the liningless brakes did, but he kept the Model T's low-gear pedal engaged and worked his handbrake efficiently, and at a steady 7 or 8 mph we returned down into the San Fernando Valley.

I looked off, over the edge of the long drop, and thought of that delicately arching flight to disaster made by the black sedan, but remembered, too, the ugly muzzle of the machine gun, and felt no great qualms of either guilt or regret.

The farmer dropped me off at the little general store–service station. They had a telephone on the wall inside. It was wood encased but had a coin slot. The call to Hollywood cost me a nickel. The operator's voice asked, "Number, please?" And for an instant, panic hit, as I didn't have the faintest notion what Taylor's number was.

"Hollywood 7643, please," Taylor said. There was a racket on the line, then clicks, and finally I heard Peavey's voice. "Mistuh Taylor's residence."

I told him my car had broken down, had to ask the aproned clerk where I was, and told Peavey. I also told him to have Fellows pick me up in the Packard. I had time to kill, so I looked over the shelves at the vaguely familiar labels, then bought myself a cold drink. There were, of course, no dietetic drinks, and although there was a Coca-Cola calendar on the wall, there were no Cokes in the icebox. I chose a bottle of something called Moxie. Apart from being a little medicinelike, it tasted okay, but not great. Maybe I've been conditioned by Tab and Fresca and Diet Pepsi. The soft-drink cooler was filled with ice and water, and the tank was badly rusted. The lid advertised Hires Root Beer, another familiar name.

I wished I'd remembered the flask of booze in the sidepocket of the roadster, but I hadn't. I walked over to the counter, and the aproned clerk watched me closely. I smiled at him.

"Beautiful day."

"Suits me."

"Me, too."

"You want a drink? Look like you can use it."

"You just saved my life," I said, fervently. "My car overheated going up Topanga Canyon—shook me up a little."

He hesitated. "I guess you're okay," he said. "Can't be too careful these days. Sold an old lady a coupla bottles o' home brew, an' she turned out to be a Prohi agent. Cost me a hundred bucks. Lucky I didn't get sixty days."

"That right?" I shook my head in sympathy. "Sorry to hear it."

"Mr. Volstead's Law's made a lot o' people damned unhappy. I don't mind. Money in bootlegging. Cost you six bits." He took the lid off a pickle barrel, pulled on a string attached to a nail driven into the side of it, and out came a brown bottle. He wiped the brine off on his apron, brought it over to the counter. He reached behind it, brought up a shot glass, and filled it to the brim. I put a five-dollar bill—the old large-sized money still didn't seem real to me—on the counter. He put the bottle under the counter, out of sight. "You got a chaser—you want some water, too?"

I shook my head—and drank my first genuine bootleg hooch. It was an eye-opener. The taste was raw and violent, coated with fusel oil. For a second I thought I'd choke, then it burned its way down. I struggled for breath, swallowed convulsively to keep it down, and then swigged Moxie. For an instant my stomach churned and I thought I was going to lose everything right down to my toenails. Then it settled, and I felt the heat of the alcohol beginning to burn. The storekeeper grinned proudly at me.

"Pretty smooth, huh? Best moon I've had in months. Made up in Barstow."

Barstow would never grow famous for its whiskey. But the raw alcohol did its job. The trembling in my legs stopped. I'll admit I gave a passing thought to being struck blind, but what the hell? I nodded, and he poured me a second jolt. It went down easier; either my stomach knew what to expect or it was still in a state of trauma, because it churned lethargically a moment, then gave up. More Moxie put out the glowing embers.

"You can take a bottle along with you for five bucks," my benefactor said obligingly. "You won't find nothin' like that in L.A." I hoped not.

When Howard Fellows showed up with the Packard, I told him where the Pierce-Arrow was, and he stayed to wait for the tow truck, and would ride up with them to get it. He didn't look too happy about it, so I told him there were a few drinks coming out of the five I'd paid the bootlegger. He smiled and nodded. He took the refilled shotglass, held it up, nodded his appreciation of the color and the beading of fusel oil, then downed it neat. He smiled. "Smooth as silk!" he said.

I kept looking into the rearview mirror on the long drive back to Hollywood. Nerves. Nobody followed me. Those that had would never tail anybody again. The thin guy had tried for Taylor twice. His luck wasn't worth a damn. But it brought up the question of why. It wasn't hard to guess. Tayor had run to the Federal D.A. about the drug racket in the film industry; he had named names and offered to work undercover. Somebody had found out about it. Either Taylor had told someone or there was a leak in the D.A.'s office—or Taylor had given himself away by being too damned nosy. In any case it had earmarked him for an early demise. With the money at stake in the hop racket, they'd try again—and again. Of that I was sure.

Which meant, if I wanted to keep Taylor—and me—alive, they would have to be stopped. Just one they? That was the question I couldn't answer. The attempt outside Paulais' Restaurant and this one today were obviously motivated—and carried out—by the same bunch. But if Sergeant Cahill was right, and the air hose on the trolley car had been tampered with, I couldn't be sure it was the same gang—it might mean that more than one party was out to kill Taylor. And, knowing Taylor, I was beginning to find that easy to believe.

The uneasy feeling of being watched I'd experienced at the studio this morning, and the accident with the Cooper-Hewitt light standard. Were they tied in? I couldn't be sure. And yet, the drug operation could be big-time, even cover more than one studio—hell, they could be milking all Hollywood for all I knew. And Taylor seemed to think that the drug business was centered on the movie lot. If he was right. . . .

And, where the hell did Edward F. Sands and his vicious and oddly phrased threats fit in?

Hey, Taylor—you getting all this loud and clear?

Nothing. Taylor's ka had done its disappearing act again.

My cop's mind brought me back to one thing: It was possible that Mabel and I had been followed from the Winter Garden out to the trolley line up Mount Lowe. Possible. Just. But we had left the Winter Garden suddenly, in mid-show. Which brought up the possibility that someone had been told we were atop Mount Lowe. We had stayed up there at the Alpine Inn for three hours—enough time—more than enough!—for someone to fix the air hose on the trolley car. Davis, Mabel's chauffeur? Cahill suspected him. Davis could have called someone and told them we were up there, or he could have fixed the air hose himself. But thinking about the way he had looked at Mabel, I had doubts that he would have tried to kill her, no matter how badly he wanted to knock off Taylor. There was one more possibility. Mabel herself. She had excused herself and left me alone twice. She had been gone each time long enough to give herself a fix—and also make a phone call. Why would she do it? A junkie can't be figured out. And Mabel was hooked, bad. Still, she had ridden that crazy trolley car down the steep side of Mount Lowe with me. And, in that case, she would realize—must realize—that someone had tried to kill not only me, but her, too. . . .

I shook my head. I just couldn't buy the idea that Mabel had set me up for a killer. Unless she didn't know that murder was intended.

Mabel. Laughter and the taste of fresh mint. No way, man! But the cop side of me locked the thought away for future reference, just the same.

I got back to Alvarado Street before dark and put the Packard away. I thought of Fellows—he'd be stuck with the Pierce-Arrow for hours probably. *He's paid for his trouble!* Taylor was back, now that I didn't need him. The thought was strong and arrogantly righteous. I had the feeling it was just as well he didn't survive into the time of civil rights protests.

Peavey had a cold lunch waiting. He took my hat, and the phone rang. I answered it.

"Have a nice ride, Mr. Tanner?" Edward F. Sands asked in his unpleasant British accent.

"Splendid," I said. Sands' remark made it clear that he, for one, was mixed up with the drug angle, which made Sergeant Cahill's guess correct. "Saw a terrible accident, though, Sands. I even thought you might have been involved."

"You son of a bitch!" Sands shouted. "Do you think your luck will last forever?"

"Why don't you ask your little playmates, Sands? They're at the bottom of Topanga Canyon—what's left of them."

He was silent. I could hear him breathing, hard. "Damn it, Billy, why don't you get wise to yourself and lay off? I can still fix it for you, I think. Play it smart. It'd be made worth your while, and I could stop worrying about you. . . ."

"I doubt if you or anyone else could fix it now," I said. "And pushing hop's really not my thing, old boy."

"Ain't you comin' it a bit thick, William?"

"But I won't be facing a drug or murder charge, Sands," I replied, making my tone harder. "Now speak your piece."

"Look, Billy-boy." Sands' strident nasal voice became a second-gear whine. "You owe me a break—for old times' sake. . . . I'm sorry about takin' your things—but I sent you the pawn tickets, didn't I? You got money—you can afford it. And I—I had to have some cash—and with you gone to hell off to Europe, what else could I do? Look, you help me this time, Billy, and I swear I won't bother you no more! I'll just disappear—like before—and that's best for both our sakes, ain't it?"

I let Taylor handle it. "I told you—no more money from me!"

"I'm desperate, Bill! You don't know the trouble I'm in—and after the way you been carrying on—what you done today—"

Taylor slammed up the receiver, cutting him off. After a moment the phone rang again. Peavey started for it.

"Let it ring," Taylor ordered.

"Yessuh, Mistuh Taylor."

After a minute or two the phone stopped ringing. My shoulder was hurting again, but mainly just stiffness. I took another pair of Jameson's little white tablets and then ate some cold lunch.

"Parkuh's sent out that book you wanted, suh," Peavey said.

"Fine. I'll take it along with me. Did you pack some things?"

"All done, suh. Hope yo'll have a right good time."

"I hope so, too."

The chances were I would. If there was someone else out for Taylor's head, they would find him hard to get at aboard William Randolph Hearst's yacht.

I hoped.

21

Hearst's Rolls-Royce—a 1921 American-made model, man-ufactured in Springfield, Massachusetts, closed coachwork by Locke & Co., which sold new, in that year, for a little less than $14,000—picked me up at precisely six o'clock, and I wasn't prepared for the surprise that had been arranged for me. I hadn't had much time to rest, but the codeine tablets had eased the soreness in my shoulder, and I'd had time to wash up. All in all, I felt pretty good; my lunch had settled the queasiness in my stomach from the *s-m-o-o-t-h* bootleg bathtub bourbon, and my mind was clear. I'd phoned Mabel a couple of times, but she was out, according to her maid. Probably with Mack Sennett, the bastard, I thought jealously.

There were three women in the back of the big Rolls limousine, and the atmosphere was colder than an Eskimo's backside as I climbed in. Mabel Normand was in the right-hand window seat; Mrs. Denker's bulk was stiffly erect in the center, taking up most of the seat; and Baby Betty Blayne was squeezed in on the left. I paused, halfway in, just staring.

"Surprise!" Mabel said sweetly. Betty Blayne started to giggle, then cut it off as her mother glared at her, then Mabel, and finally me, in that order. If her eyes had been lasers, Taylor would have been in very small pieces.

"You're right, it is," I agreed, still stunned. I slid into the jump seat that had been unfolded from the wide floor of the rear compartment. The chauffeur closed the door, then carried my heavy black leather gladstone bag to the luggage rack on the rear. In the silence I could hear the thumping noises as he strapped it down with the rest of the luggage. Still more bags and cases were piled in the open driver's compartment up front, behind me.

"You should have seen your face, Willie," Mabel said, and went into peals of laughter. Mrs. Denker glowered at her and tugged her coat closer around her, as if to avoid contamination.

"Well, one of you should've told me you were coming along," I said lamely. I sensed that Taylor didn't share my embarrassment; the son of a bitch was amused by the situation, enjoyed it, and in fact even delivered a brief fantasy of having two beautiful young women in his bed at the same time.

Mama Denker would not only make it complete, she'd take up most of the bed!

Damn, must you share my every thought?

We have no secrets from each other, Billy-boy—and that one wasn't bad. . . . You're a hell of a swinger, in my book!

He thought up something most unpleasant back at me.

"We didn't know it ourselves until the last minute, Mr. Taylor," Betty Blayne said in her little girl's voice. "But Mama said nobody ever turns Mr. Hearst down, so she hurried back from Santa Barbara . . . and I think it will be fun!"

"More than I expected," Mabel agreed, grinning and winking at me. "But you know Willie well enough to call him by his first name, don't you, Baby?"

Betty Blayne studied Mabel for a moment, but her voice remained a happy little girl's. "Please call me Betty," she said sweetly. "And I do call him William, sometimes. . . ."

Mabel looked owl-eyed at me. "I'll just damnbetcha you do. . . ."

Mrs. Denker made a rumbling noise, glowering at me. "If I'd known that you—" She broke off, obviously thinking better of voicing her sentiments. Not insulting Taylor cost her a lot of effort.

"We're Marion's idea of an interesting weekend group," Mabel said, and laughed. "It'll spoil her fun if we don't play up to it."

"I don't know what you mean!" Mrs. Denker snapped.

"Gee, that's too bad," Mabel said. "But don't worry about it—maybe you'll catch on later." Again she laughed, and Betty Blayne had a difficult time suppressing her giggle.

Mrs. Denker turned her laser-look on Mabel. Mabel ignored it and winked at me again. It was no put-on, she was really enjoying the moment! I saw that Betty Blayne was watching me, and I forced a smile.

"It will be an interesting cruise," I said.

If only the old harridan wasn't along—

Forget it, Taylor!

The chauffeur finished securing the luggage, and climbed behind the big wooden steering wheel, and the huge limousine purred away. I still preferred my yellow Pierce-Arrow roadster. *Yours!* I let it ride. We turned west on Maryland, then south on Vermont, to Santa Monica Boulevard, where he speeded up in the light traffic, heading west. The traffic thinned to nothing as we drove steadily toward the ocean. Mrs. Denker fell into a sullen, brooding silence, but Mabel and Betty were obviously well acquainted and could handle the situation—and themselves— without effort. They kept up a steady stream of chatter, dropping famous names effortlessly, alluding to scandals, rumors, and Hollywood shoptalk that meant nothing to me.

". . . that they're going to try Fatty again," Mabel said angrily. "As if they hadn't done enough to him already. . . . If two juries couldn't convict him of anything, why bother with a third trial?"

"Mama says it's a juicy headline-maker for an ambitious district attorney, and he isn't about to let it drop." Betty made a face.

"Poor Fatty," Mabel said, and sighed.

"Poor Fatty, my ass!" Mama Denker bit out. "The bastard's been askin' for it for years! He was in trouble last year about the same thing—a wild booze party, and forcing a girl into—having relations with him!" The way she said it, it sounded worse than any four-letter word.

"Since when did anyone have to force a Hollywood tramp like Virginia Rappe?" Mabel lashed back. "She's been living openly with Pathé Lehrman for over a year—there was even a lot of talk about her having an abortion—that *that*'s what was wrong with her!"

Mama Denker forced a shocked expression over her thick features. "If you don't mind, Miss Normand, I must ask you to watch what you say. Betty's very young, and—"

"Your ass!" Mabel said, and covered the words with a quick, artificial sneeze. "I'm sorry—I forgot that we had such tender ears present, Mrs. Denker." Again she closed one big eye in a deliberate wink, not caring whether Mrs. Denker noticed or not. Betty Blayne quickly stuffed her tiny wisp of handkerchief into her mouth to stifle a giggle.

"What picture are you doing?" she asked, when she had recovered.

"We just finished shooting *Head Over Heels*—for Goldwyn. Nalbro Bartley's story's a scream. I play an acrobat—me!"

"Who's your director?"

"Victor Schertzinger—he's good, but all business. I like Paul Bern better—he did some of it." She looked at me. "I'm trying to find my next story." She laughed again. "I suggested to Sam Goldwyn he ought to put me in Jack Barrymore's picture, *Sherlock Holmes*—I'd make a great Watson, I think."

"I like that idea," Taylor said. "What did Barrymore say?"

"He was all for it, but Sam Goldwyn nixed it. He says he has enough of a problem with just Jack."

"Drunk as usual, no doubt," Mrs. Denker put in. "Men!" She sniffed audibly.

"Don't you like them?" Mabel inquired innocently.

"Not drunk—and not in my bed!" Mrs. Denker declared.

"Gee, I *do*—although not in that order. . . ."

This time Betty Blayne couldn't stop from laughing, but it was quickly strangled under Mama's glaring look.

We drove through Santa Monica, smaller than in my day, quieter, no high-rise buildings. Hearst's yacht, the *Oneida*, was tied up at a lighted dock. Deckhands were wheeling aboard supplies. The chauffeur drove through an open, guarded gate, onto the pier, and pulled up at the gangplank. The *Oneida* was a miniature oceanliner, some 220 feet in length, with the old-fashioned rakish look to her hull and bowsprit, smoke rising lazily from her funnel. All white paint, polished hardwood, and shining brass, the yacht had colored electric lights strung from her stubby masts, stern to bow, giving her a festive air. Jazz music sounded clearly—the *Oneida*, I learned, carried her own orchestra. The only way to travel—if it's 1922, and you're William Randolph Hearst.

Dr. Jameson, decked out in nautical blazer, cap, and white flannels, smoking a handsome bruyère pipe, met us at the head of the gangplank. He greeted the three women warmly.

"I've been appointed the welcoming committee," he said. "Marion's pleased you could all come."

"I'll bet she is!" Mabel said, and laughed. Mrs. Denker gave her and Jameson a glower to divide between them, and then led Betty Blayne on ahead, down the glistening mahogany deck. Mabel grinned at us, winked, and followed them, imitating Mrs. Denker's free-swinging, hip-rolling stevedore's stride.

Jameson looked after her, amused, then shook his head. "I suppose you know this is Marion's little joke, eh, Bill?"

"I hope she enjoys it more than I do."

"No doubt about it—she will," he replied, taking my arm. "You haven't seen the half of it. . . . But, come on—I guess you can stand a drop of bonded stock, can't you? Good for the nerves."

"You give me the feeling I'm going to need it."

Jameson led the way aft to the main deckhouse, then down carpeted stairs and along a hallway forward again, to his stateroom, which was as big as most motel bedrooms, with two built-in double bunks against one wall, and heavy overstuffed furniture giving it a comfortable look. He closed the door behind us and winked.

"Our host doesn't approve much of boozing—one cocktail before dinner is it, usually, and he frowns upon your bringing your own emergency supply aboard. However, the stewards have been trained by Marion, so you won't go thirsty. The best, too. If a bootlegger had Hearst's sources of supply, he'd be a millionaire in a week."

"Nothing like having a few million dollars," I said.

"That's right," Jameson agreed, and smiled. "It's a style of living I can appreciate. I'm told that before the Volstead Act went into the books last year, Hearst bought up a wholesaler's entire stock—a dozen warehouses jampacked with the best liquor in the world—thousands of cases—just to make sure he'd have it when he wanted it. . . ."

Jameson pulled a squarish bottle of scotch from a drawer, held it up for me to admire the label. Johnnie Walker Black Label hasn't changed much over the years.

"Prewar," Jameson said, smacking his lips—and I realized he was referring to World War I.

He poured two stiff jolts into cut crystal tumblers that stood beside a sparkling carafe on a table. He nodded at the carafe, but I shook my head. He poured a little water into his glass.

"The water's brought in bottles from Baden-Baden," he said. "You get used to the taste." He eyed me, lifted his glass in a silent toast, and we drank. The Johnnie Walker really was Johnnie Walker, and the tumbler was hand-cut Bacarat, with blue-red glints in it. I appreciated them both.

"I'd better get my bag and get settled in."

"Don't worry, the steward will take care of everything. Our host and hostess won't make an appearance until a few minutes before eight. First night's always informal and early to bed." He frowned. "Besides I wanted to talk to you."

"The other half of it?"

He nodded. "First off—Wally's on board."

"Reid?" Somehow it didn't surprise me.

Jameson nodded, sipped his scotch, freshened it with another dollop, and eyed me. I shook my head again. Not before dinner. "Marion loves making mischief—I suspect she's hoping you two will stage another bout for her benefit."

"Thoughtful of her."

"Wally learned his lesson—you're a tougher customer than he's ever run up against before. He'll behave himself, especially since Dorothy Davenport's with him.

I started to ask, "His girlfriend?" but Taylor cut in with: *She's his wife—and has been for years.*

I thought he had the hots for Betty Blayne?

That was a long time ago, when they were on location for a film together. . . . There was talk he might marry her, but it cooled off.

With your help. . . .

Ah, Hollywood—it hadn't changed in that respect a damned bit in fifty years. Who was screwing whom was still anybody's guess.

"I'll do my best to do likewise," I said to Jameson.

"I was sure you would, Bill," he said slowly. Whatever else he had in mind he was having difficulty putting into the right words. "Look, Bill—when De Mille spoke to you—about Wally, I mean—did he ask you—you, know—about his—problem?"

"Yes, he did. I told him that I thought Reid was badly hooked on the stuff."

"An addict, you mean?" Jameson shook his head, drank more scotch, sweetened his glass again, and drank again. "Jesse Lasky asked me to keep an eye on Wally—tell him what he faces if he doesn't break the habit."

"Do you really think he can kick it?"

"I don't know." Jameson finished his glass of scotch and held the cut crystal tumbler up to the light, staring at its sparkling facets. "Adolph Zukor's coming out from New York next month. There's going to be a reorganization of the studio, as I suppose you know. Realart will become just a part of Paramount Pictures, with no separate identity. That means a shakeup on the lot, of course. Wally's contract terminates next year. Jesse thought I could get it across to him easier than to have Zukor lay down an ultimatum." Jameson set the glass down. "They owe Wally every consideration—he's made a lot of money for them. But they can't take a chance of dope-fiend publicity about one of their major stars, on top of the Arbuckle mess. . . . Did you know they're shelving Fatty's unreleased pictures—just swallowing the loss?"

"I hadn't heard that," I said. It even surprised Taylor. *That packs it in for Fatty. He'll never work in pictures again.*

"The poor bastard will find it impossible to get a day's work—even if the third trial proves him innocent. He's all washed up—and Famous Players–Lasky can't afford another scandal. They'll pitch Wally to the wolves, too, if they have to."

"The idea doesn't make me happy."

"Ummm." Jameson studied me, hard-eyed. "You've taken a stand against the use of drugs in the industry. There's talk you're behind an official investigation."

"There's always talk."

"True." Jameson nodded. "But can I ask you—as a friend, Bill—what you've found out?"

"Not a hell of a lot," I answered. "There is a hop gang behind the wholesale distribution of the stuff in Hollywood. Drugs have wrecked other lives and careers besides Wallace Reid's—and I'm determined to put an end to it."

"That could be dangerous for you."

"So I've discovered. There have been attempts on my life—but I think the men behind it know they can't stop me."

He was thoughtful for a moment. "You're certain—I mean about the attacks on you?"

"You saw the bruises."

He looked surprised. "That trolley accident? But Mabel Normand was with you!"

"The people I'm after don't give a damn who gets hurt. There's too much money at stake for pussyfooting."

"A hop gang . . ." Jameson spoke slowly, thoughtfully. "Is there—I mean to say—" He had trouble getting it out. "Is there anyone—someone—in the industry—someone we know?"

"Behind it? I think so."

"You're not sure?"

"As a matter of fact, I am. Proving it is something else."

"I see. . . ." His expression was troubled, and he again shook his head. "It would mean another scandal, of course—and the studio is trying to avoid that. . . . I mean, perhaps if you were to—er—"

"Cool it? No way. It never ends, Doc. But I intend to slow it down."

He blinked. My words were strange to him, but it was obvious that he caught their import. His eyes met mine direct and hard. "What is your stake in this game, Bill? What do you expect to get out of it?"

"Not a damned thing." I finished my drink and put the glass down, watching him. "Are you offering me a bribe, Doc?"

He smiled suddenly. "Hardly. I'm only interested in the effect the whole affair will have on our business. . . ." He sobered. "But tell me, Bill—why?"

"Mabel," I said slowly. "Alma Rubens, Barbara La Marr, Olive Thomas, Wally Reid—how many more do you want me to name?"

I started for the door, then paused to look back at him. "What's your stake in it, Doc?"

His smile held steady. He chuckled. "I like that! You even suspect me, don't you, Bill?"

"Thanks for the drink, Doc. I'll see you at dinner."

He nodded, then shook his head and poured himself another drink. He didn't add water from Baden-Baden this time.

I walked out, closing his stateroom door behind me. I found a steward, who led me to my stateroom. My bag had been unpacked and my things laid out. My room was a bit larger than Jameson's, with comfortable—and expensive—furnishings. Even the two paintings on the wall were signed originals—and I found myself impressed. Who wouldn't be by Corot and Picasso? And in a guest stateroom on a boat, yet! Hearst's reputation was for real, it seemed.

I investigated the desk. In the file drawer was a built-in bottle rack. It held gin, bourbon, and scotch—a quart of each, and all bottled in bond. I took out the bottle of scotch—Dewar's, and thirty years old—and admired it. I didn't admire the hairline cut all the way around the lead-foil cap over the cork. It had been made by a very, very sharp blade, carefully used. My first thought was that the bottle had been refilled with bootleg hooch—but on William Randolph Hearst's yacht? I carried the bottle over to the desk and held it over the top of the lamp. The pale amber of the whiskey was faintly murky. A few tiny particles of something were suspended in it, swirling around slowly. No, it wasn't bathtub booze in a legitimate bottle. Something had been added to Dewar's Finest. Something that wouldn't improve my health a damned bit if I drank it.

I considered dumping the bottle down the toilet, then had second thoughts and carefully restored it to the drawer. As long as it was there, untouched, waiting for me, whoever had doctored it might not try something else.

Might not.

Who? You're the detective—so you claim.

Don't remind me.

One thing I was sure of: It was going to be one hell of a weekend.

22

A steward went down the corridor outside my stateroom, tapping musically on a chime board, a sound I remembered but had forgotten. I'd spent a half-hour on a soft bunk, not thinking, just letting things run through my mind. They were a jumble, but facts in a case usually are, and sorting them out is what a cop is selected for and trained to do. I'd found out, early on, that pressing didn't work for me; I had to relax and let things stew. Developments always pointed the way, and I had a strong feeling that I was getting on top of this case, that the answers were close at hand. My hunches were almost always good, so I'd just relaxed, letting my brain idle, barely ticking over.

The stateroom was dark, so I snapped on the wall light over the head of the bunk, and blinked in the soft glare. I got up, feeling the stiffness still in my shoulder. In the bathroom mirror I saw that the raw redness of the bruises had deepened to yellow-brown-magenta splotches, and the least touch hurt like hell. I swallowed one more codeine tablet, then washed up. I was trying to button a fresh shirt when there came a knock at my door.

"Hang in there!" I called. I still couldn't get the hang of fastening a goddamn separate collar, and especially not with just one hand, so it was still dangling crookedly from the back collar button as I unlocked and opened the cabin door. Mabel Normand stood there. She was wearing something black and slinky, without frills, that set off her small, perfect figure and rounded bosom. Her dark eyes were huge, and seemed almost luminous as she looked at me.

"You can take me in to dinner, Willie," she said. "If you don't have other plans?"

"What would they be?"

"I have no idea."

"Allow me to give you one," I said, and drew her close and kissed her the way I meant it. She kissed me back for an instant, then gently pulled away.

"I'm beginning to think you are sex-crazed, Willie," she said, smiling.

"You'd better believe it," I returned. "At least as far as you're concerned."

"Me and a few others, Willie?" Mabel laughed as if it wouldn't have bothered her much if it were true, and I found myself recoiling, trying to curb my hurt feelings.

"Do you want the truth, Mabel?"

"No!" She made an imp's face at me. "And hurry up or we'll make a late entrance!"

"It's expected in Hollywood."

"Not here. Not tonight."

I struggled futilely with the collar for a moment, then Mabel came to my rescue. She fastened the collar, then knotted the tie with quick, overhand movements, and tugged it into place.

"There—you're almost as pretty as Wally Reid!"

She accepted the demure little thank-you kiss I gave her. She turned toward the door, then turned back as I touched her arm gently.

"Do you love me, Mabel?"

Her big, round, dark eyes were unreadable, but she smiled. "Damn right!" she said.

"Then, when I've got things worked out, will you marry me? I mean it."

"What things?" She smiled. "Little Baby Betty Blayne and her mama?"

"No. I'm serious, Mabel."

She studied my eyes for a long moment, her face settling into somber lines, making her look suddenly older. There was no lightness, no fun, in her voice. "Do you know how it would end for us, Willie?"

"Happily," I said. "It always does."

"Only in the movies," she said softly, and kissed me on the lips, very gently, without passion. "I'm not the way you see me, Willie—the way everybody sees me, up on that big screen, scatterbrained pratfalls and fun, even though I keep trying. But the images don't match, Willie, not really, not deep inside—and they haven't for a long, long time. . . ." She suddenly jerked free and shook her head. "Damn you, Willie, I don't like being serious! Now stop it or I'll have nothing more to do with you!"

For that brief second I saw the real Mabel, I'm sure of it, a woman who understood her own limitations, and the trap her life had become—the trap she no longer cared to try to break out of. It was sad, disillusioning, but it only made my feeling for her more intense. I wanted to help her, to make it work out for her, despite everything, to make it work out for the two of us. But I held it back, and made myself grin. I tapped her pert little nose with one finger.

"Just remember—I mean it, Mabel."

She moved into my arms and kissed me the way I had always wanted her to kiss me, without hesitation or reservation—and that was the moment the door was pushed open and Betty Blayne and her mother stood there. Betty frowned her little girl's petulant frown, which only made her seem younger.

"Are we breaking something up?" she asked, masking the anger in her voice only partly.

"Golly, no!" Mabel said, and laughed. "I wish you were! I was just tying Bill's tie."

"Which my sore shoulder appreciates," I put in. I picked up my coat, which Mabel helped me pull over my stiff shoulder.

"We heard about your accident," Mrs. Denker said stiffly. I could tell she wished it had been more serious. "Mabel was with you, wasn't she?"

"Yes," I replied, giving her a leer. "I conduct all my more passionate affairs on trolley cars—gives them zing, you know."

Some perverse notion made me add, "Mabel's old enough to be out with a man after curfew for the kiddies. . . ."

Betty Blayne openly glared at me, and whirled around and stomped away. In her frilly dress and low-heeled slippers she was the image of an angry child. Her mother looked pleased, and gave me a smirk, then followed after her "baby." Mabel gave me a look.

"Now you've done it, Willie!" She laughed. "Your harem has just shrunk by one."

Going out of the stateroom, a movement of the yacht caused me to wince as I bumped my shoulder against the door frame, and I was aware for the first time that we were under way. I could feel the very slight vibration of the powerful steam engines.

"We're on our merry way!" Mabel said. "I didn't think we'd sail until morning."

"The weather's calm. No reason to wait."

Dr. Jameson came down the corridor as we neared the stairs. "There you are! I was just coming after you, Mabel. We're passing Catalina Island—and the flying fish are jumping."

"Oh, I want to see!"

We climbed the stairs and went on deck. The yacht's powerful searchlights were on, angled low over the water, and we saw the silver flash of the fish as they leaped and sported in the bright beams. The water had a soft fluorescence to it, almost milky in places. A steward came out on deck and passed us, tapping his chimes.

"We mustn't keep the emperor waiting," Jameson said, and led the way into the main salon.

The big room was brightly lighted. It was lavishly furnished, including an ornate carved rosewood baby grand piano, which a young man with slicked-down hair was playing. His hair was so sleek and shiny, it looked like Japanese lacquer. *Valentino's really started something with his new image. I wish I owned some Vaseline stock. . . .*

Not to mention the condoms they still call "Sheiks."

The piano player's face was vaguely familiar, but I never did catch his name. A cruise was an informal event—or what passed for one—aboard the *Oneida*, and when the guest list was small, minor hangers-on would be called upon to fill in, doing their thing quietly, as nonpaid performers, hoping to be noticed by the VIPs. This jaunt there were four of them, two girls—both quite pretty—and two men, one the All-American Boy type, complete with freckles, the other the Valentino carbon copy at the piano, who lacked the animal appeal of the original Latin Lover. They would, I learned, be rewarded by Marion Davies and Hearst with small parts in her next picture. All four were overly casual, trying hard to give a carefree impression and not quite making it.

Stewards in white jackets carried trays of cocktail shakers and glasses about—no china teapots for His Majesty Hearst! The one-cocktail rule had apparently been waived—*two* were passed out. Mrs. Denker, with Betty close in tow, her little girl's face still sulky as she looked at me across the room, cornered Dr. Jameson. Mabel had wandered off by herself, leaving me alone. I stole a third cocktail when no one was looking.

The piano player struck a chord. We all fell silent. Our host and hostess entered the salon. Obviously the casual-clothes-on-the-first-night-out rule didn't apply to William Randolph Hearst and Marion Davies. He was wearing a tuxedo, looking a bit like an out-of-proportion penguin, his stiff wing collar setting off his horsey, ruddy-complexioned face. Marion Davies was beautiful in white organdy. She and her blond looks made a perfect pair of bookends with Mabel and her dark beauty. She was very petite, with enormous eyes bluer than cornflowers. She had a speech impediment, but it wasn't quite a stutter—at least not of the Roscoe Ates variety. They moved well together. Marion was completely self-possessed, the perfect hostess. But there was, underneath, a twinkling imp, perversely looking for any available mischief. She seized a cocktail and laughed as she raised it in toast and salute.

"Chin-chin, everybody!"

We finished our cocktails. Hearst lifted his glass for the toast, but didn't drink, just set it untasted on a steward's tray—where I managed to secure it as I deposited my empty. But I noticed he was big in the hors d'oeuvre department.

Marion made the rounds quickly, gracefully, speaking to each guest in her warm fashion. She grinned at me. "How ya doin',

Bill? And I *do* mean with the ladies!" She laughed merrily and winked one bright blue eye at me.

"Just fine," I replied. "Too bad I can't count you among them, Marion. . . ."

"Well, it's never too late!" Again she laughed. "Meet you at midnight in lifeboat number one!"

"Now, really, Marion!" Hearst had come up to us. He moved lightly and silently for so big a man. His thin, high-pitched voice seemed totally wrong for him.

"Jealous, W.R.?" She grinned and tucked her arm through his. "I like that!"

"You little minx!" His smile was broad. He looked at her indulgently, as a man might enjoy the antics of a well-loved child. "Pay her no mind, Bill."

"I'm glad she's joking," I answered. "It's pretty cold in lifeboats."

They both laughed. Hearst said, "We'll have a chance to talk later. Marion would like you to direct her next picture."

Smooth and direct. It would be hard to say no to a man like William Randolph Hearst. I nodded and they moved away.

There was a sudden uproar on the deck outside, shouts, pounding feet—then a man burst through the doors, stumbling and lurching. He was grubby, wore filthy clothes, and had a five-day beard. He was short, thin, and stood in the glare of the salon lights, blinking owlishly and swaying on his feet. Behind him, two sailors ran in and grabbed his arms. They were followed by a uniformed ship's officer. He looked quickly at Hearst.

"Sorry, sir," the officer said. "This man must have stowed away—"

"You can just bet your bleedin' ass I did!" the dirty, scroungy stranger shouted in a strident, broken voice. "They ain't puttin' yours truly on no fuckin' chain gang—beggin' the ladies' pardon—for vagrancy! Just drop me orff in Mexico, eh, guv'nor, like a good feller, huh?"

Hearst stood there very erect, obviously shocked and at a loss for words. Then, suddenly, Marion let out wild peals of laughter, ran forward, grabbed the dirty stowaway, hugged him, and then kissed him full on the lips.

"Jack, you crazy man—I love you!" she screamed.

The "stowaway" was John Barrymore. And nobody loved his joke more than Marion—and Hearst, too, for that matter. He quickly grinned and the crewmen let go of the dirty one. The officer looked confused.

"It's quite all right," Hearst said, waving them away. "I understood you couldn't make it, Jack. . . ."

" ' . . . I knew him, Horatio: a fellow of infinite jest, of most excellent fancy. . . .' Eh?" Barrymore chuckled in his booming actor's tones—and grabbed for a tray of cocktails. He downed two, one after the other, then bowed gracefully to Hearst and Marion, seized her hand in a gallant's fashion, and kissed it.

"Mine hosts! My obeisances, and love!" He took another cocktail—and Hearst still smiled; it seemed Barrymore worked his usual magic, even with him!—and sipped it. "One last drop of good cheer, and I'll hie myself aft and get cleaned up." He chortled through his nose, a snorting laugh I've never heard anyone else do. "How do you like 'Limehouse Louie'? A bit of a character assumed by my stout friend Sherlock Holmes in his relentless pursuit of his archenemy, Professor Moriarty." He chortled again. "Being most ably portrayed by Gustav von Seyffertitz. . . ."

The yachting party, I gathered, was now complete, except for Wallace Reid and his wife, Dorothy Davenport. Barrymore made a graceful exit, doing a priceless pratfall on a nonexistent banana peel that would have done credit to Chaplin himself, and threatening the guffawing Hearst with a zillion-dollar lawsuit for damages.

Dr. Jameson got free of Mrs. Denker for a moment and crossed to me. "Wally and Dorothy will join us after dinner. She's feeling a bit under the weather." He shook his head. "I wish to hell Mrs. Denker was!"

Dinner was served in the dining salon. The table was set with priceless damask and Irish linen, and eggshell china—with bottles of Heinz Catsup, beloved by Hearst, within easy reach. Barrymore reappeared, wearing a yachting outfit, and if not quite as tall as I expected him to be, he still dominated the room just by being in it. He spoke in a deep, beautiful baritone, using it like a musician would an instrument, cackling laughter discordantly, emitting hoarse, growly snarls, emphasizing every expressive change of mood. He was "on" every instant of his life, always playing a part. I had the feeling that there was no real John Barrymore, just an endless series of dramatic impressions, often deliberately satirical, virtual caricatures of himself. During the meal he ate very little, but seemed to become progressively more vibrant as time went by.

Jameson leaned closer to whisper to me, "He's bribed his waiter to keep his waterglass filled with gin."

We both laughed, but Mabel, beside me, didn't join in, which wasn't like her. She remained silent, almost withdrawn. Across the table, Betty Blayne frowned at us—and once, under the cover of her napkin, she stuck her tongue out at me. I grinned back at her; she had forgiven me, it seemed. I sensed that Taylor was pleased.

Don't get any ideas, Billy-boy. The old dragon will never let her out of her sight.

After dinner, Wallace Reid and Dorothy Davenport joined us back in the main salon. Reid's eyes met mine, but his handsome features retained a pleasant smile and his handshake was firm and strong.

"Good to see you, Bill," he said. "You know Dotty?"

Dorothy Davenport was a tiny beauty with bright-red hair and pale white skin that was almost transparent. Blue veins were plainly visible beneath it. "How are you, Bill?"

Marion had drifted close, and made a moue, looking disappointed. "The least you two could do is glare at each other ferociously, after all the stories I've heard!"

"Nothing to them," Reid replied, grinning widely. "Just a little publicity stunt. Bill and I are good friends!"

"Just a friendly disagreement, huh? Y-you liar, y-you!" Her slight stutter was suddenly noticeable, and I wondered if it was the effect of the cocktails. "B-both of y-you!"

The five-man jazz orchestra—all black—had quietly moved onto a rostrum at one end of the big main salon, and now began to play, holding it down, swinging the blues the way it was meant to be swung. Dorothy Davenport looked at her husband and frowned slightly.

"What's all this, Wally?"

"Nothing, really, honey," Reid said, and kissed her. "We almost didn't make it, Marion—Dorothy hated leaving little King Billy. . . ."

"I wish you'd brought him along," Marion said, a wistful note in her voice. "W.R. loves kids."

"Maybe when he's a little older," Dorothy Davenport said, smiling her understanding of the need inside Marion.

"Bertha's looking after him," Wally put in. "She's visiting us for a few months."

"Wally's mother," Dorothy said. Her voice was carefully modulated, but it didn't take a detective to figure out that her being "under the weather" was more emotional than physical. "How are Rose, Ethel, and Reine, Marion? We haven't seen them in so long!"

"My sisters are just fine. I asked Rosie to come along, but she had other things to do."

"Ah, the Douras female ménage," Barrymore said, over a glass half-filled with his 80-proof "water." "I have had the signal disappointment of being denied carnal knowledge of all four Douras beauties!" He moved away, dancing all by himself, in his graceful actor's movements.

"Do you mean somebody actually turned Jack Barrymore down?" Mrs. Denker had come up to join us. "From what I've been told about him, and certain other Hollywood men"—she gave me a hard look—"that's hard to believe."

Marion laughed. "You're so right! I'd be the first to give in—if I didn't *have* to behave." She shook her head. "And I suspect that Rosie might have a few regrets if she turned down his proposition."

Jameson came up to lead the quiet Mabel Normand to the dance floor. Wallace and Dorothy Reid joined them. Barrymore swung in, bowed most gallantly to Marion, and they danced off. A couple of the young extras joined in, too. The Valentino-type did his ballroom sheik bit.

Hearst came over and smiled. "Feel like a turn around the deck, Bill? Let the youngsters dance."

I followed Hearst out to the deck. The searchlights were off now, and Catalina far behind us, as the *Oneida* steamed south.

The ocean was calm, with broad, surging waves. It was a bit cold on deck, and to the west haze blurred the night.

"Smoke if you like," Hearst said quietly.

I felt Taylor's personality react to the suggestion; he liked cigars, and habit—his—had caused me to put a couple of perfectos in one inside breast-pocket from the leather case filled with them in his gladstone bag. The gold gadget on the keychain punctured the end, and Taylor rolled the end of the cigar in a match flame to warm it before lighting up. Hearst sniffed appreciatively.

"Good, clear Havana," he said. I remembered reading in a biography that he never smoked or drank, so it surprised me. "Had the cigarette habit myself, once. Broke it."

It's odd, but that statement somehow characterized William Randolph Hearst for me. He held absolute control of himself; he didn't need a crutch for anything.

We walked in silence for a few minutes. He paused near the bow and looked out over the phosphorescent sea. The mist was thickening, closing in.

"Would you accept a one-picture deal, Bill—for Marion's next? It will be *The Young Diana*—from Marie Corelli's fantasy—have you read it?"

Taylor had, so I relaxed, letting him carry the ball. "Yes, I have. A lovely story—very romantic. It will make an excellent change of pace for Marion. She'll love growing old in the story, and being made young and beautiful again. . . ."

"Then you'll do it?"

"There is a problem," Taylor replied carefully. "You see, Lasky has offered me an exclusive two-year deal. Good money—name above the title, which means a lot to me. I've worked hard for it." Taylor paused. "You'll be releasing the picture through Famous Players?"

"Zukor informs me it will all be Paramount Pictures, soon—but my own Cosmopolitan will produce it, of course, and I make my own commitments." He glanced at me. "The deal would be just between us."

"I see," Taylor said, noncommittally.

Hearst looked back at the ocean again, then turned and slowly walked on. He said nothing more. I gathered that the subject was closed for the moment. We completed three turns around the deck.

"We'd best be getting back to the others," Hearst said. "Marion raises ned if I'm gone too long." He paused. "We'll talk again later."

"Any time," Taylor replied. It had been a rough, long day, and suddenly I felt the strain of it pressing down on me. "I'm a bit bushed," I said. "Would you make my excuses to Marion and the others, please? I'd like to turn in."

"Of course," he said. "We've heard about your accident. Are you feeling all right? Perhaps Jameson could give you something . . ."

"I'm fine—just tired. Good night."

In my stateroom I undressed for bed, and the soft silk pajamas felt cold against my skin. My bed had already been turned down. I started to climb in, then thought of something. I went to the desk and opened the drawer. I'd left the bottle of scotch with the right-hand corner of the label at exactly one o'clock, but it was now turned slightly, and the corner was at three o'clock.

Whoever had doctored the bottle had been in to check up to see if I had opened it. I tried to remember who had left the group during the evening, but had no way of knowing, since I had spent the last hour with Hearst on deck.

I went to bed and snapped off the lights. I felt a little blurred, my thoughts unclear. What was in the bottle of scotch? Poison was unlikely; probably chloral hydrate—knockout drops. A dead man on Hearst's yacht would precipitate an inquiry, and most probably an autopsy would be held. I had the feeling that the person I was dealing with was ruthless enough to murder me, but not openly, not here. But an accident was another matter, and accidents do happen on boats. Somehow the idea didn't shake me up much; maybe I'd lived with the idea of somebody determined to kill Taylor for so long I was inured to it. . . .

My thoughts were jumbled, and I could come up with no final answers. But I had the feeling—the conviction—that I knew all the necessary facts, if I could just put them together in the proper order.

Which one of the people I knew was after my—Taylor's—scalp? Mrs. Denker? Doc Jameson? Wally Reid? Betty Blayne? The shadowy figure behind the drug racket? Mabel? Any or all of them? I pushed the weary thoughts away. I wished my door would open and Mabel would come in, and share my bed, and my life. I needed her.

You don't really think she'll come, do you? Taylor's thought was mocking.

She loves me. I know.

You—me—Mack—and how many others? You'll learn that you can always depend on Mabel—to let you down. . . .

I don't give a damn. It doesn't change a thing.

But, as usual, Taylor was wrong. I heard a noise, then the cabin door opened slightly, spilling in light from the corridor beyond. A woman's slim figure was silhouetted there. It was Mabel. She was wearing silk pajamas, a dark-blue flannel robe, and enormous fluffy sloppy-joe slippers. She closed the door behind her and I heard the lock click. She moved toward me where I lay on the bunk—bumped something.

"God damn it!" she cried. "Am I crossing no-man's-land? You strung barbed wire, Willie? Well, it'll do you no good—you're going to get laid just the same!"

I tugged on the lamp chain over the head of the bunk. The mirror at the foot of the bunk bounced the light back. Mabel blinked her enormous black eyes at me.

"Is that a promise?" I asked.

"You damn betcha!" She giggled. She was "up"—holding her high, vibrantly alive—for the moment. I forced the thought away. Not now! Not tonight!

She untied her robe, shrugged it off, unbuttoned her pajamas, stepped out of them. She came to me and helped me off with the coat of my pajamas. She blinked down at my bruised chest and shoulder.

"Oh, Willie—are you up to it?"

I reached for her and pulled her gently down. I guided her hand. "Does that answer your question, Miss Normand?"

"Indeed it does, Mr. Taylor, sir," she answered and giggled again. She jerked, and my pajama pants slid down around my

222

ankles. I kicked them off, then moved over and made room for her. She settled down beside me.

"You didn't have to ask me to marry you, Willie."

"It was my own idea."

"Why?"

"Because I love you. Because I'd like you to be with me—all the time, you know? Because—"

"Any other reason, Willie?"

"Isn't that enough?"

"Uhm, huhm . . ." She was kissing me, gently caressing my injured shoulder and side, exerting no pressure at all.

But with Mabel you never knew. She was pure quicksilver. Loving, gentle, one instant—the slapstick clown the next. We made love—it was good. Then, at a crucial moment, I felt her moving, slightly, beneath me. For an instant I thought she was displaying more passion than she had ever done before, even at the height of our previous lovemaking. But then I realized the truth—she was laughing! For an instant I couldn't believe it—but it was true. She was giggling out loud—then suddenly laughing wholeheartedly, breaking off to lift her head to kiss me.

"Oh, I'm so sorry, Willie—but do you realize just how ridiculous we look?"

For a moment it didn't make sense to me, then I realized that she had been watching our reflected images in the mirror at the foot of the built-in bunk! And, thinking of her watching Taylor's rather scrawny rear end in action sent me off, too! We lay there, locked in each other's arms, laughing helplessly. . . .

It was the kind of warm, crazy, wonderful, shared moment that can only happen once, and I would never forget it.

23

Saturday was clear, sun-bright, and warm. The *Oneida* steamed steadily southward. After breakfast—which I skipped—there was mild fun-and-games. Mabel had slipped away after I'd fallen asleep. It had been very late. We had made love again—after I'd turned the damned mirror to the wall! She wasn't up yet, and Mama Denker kept herself between Betty Blayne and me. I settled for a deck chair on the upper deck, out of the way, and enjoyed the sun.

After lunch, Hearst suggested another stroll, and again broached the subject of *The Young Diana*. He was both persuasive and persistent, mentioning how well Taylor had done with Mary Pickford, and that Marion should be given the same opportunity for public acceptance. It wasn't difficult for me to see that Hearst placed more importance upon her screen career than Marion did. I let Taylor take over and handle it, and he regretfully stated that a one-picture deal couldn't compare with the advantages of a term deal with a major studio. Again Hearst fell silent. He brought the subject up again in the midafternoon, over a game of shuffleboard—which I lost—and this time said that a two-picture contract might be more mutually satisfactory. Taylor said he would think about it, and there the matter stood.

Mabel made a late appearance with Marion, and the two of them started a game of hopscotch on the shuffleboard squares, like a couple of kids. After a while Betty Blayne joined them, and they giggled and laughed, enjoying themselves enormously.

I was back in my secluded deck chair spot when Dr. Jameson climbed up to join me, taking the next chair. He sank down into it, stretched out, and sighed heavily.

"Problems, Doc?" I asked.

"I just had a talk with Wally."

"And?"

"Bad. He blames you—Zukor—Lasky—everybody but himself. Even me. He's on the edge, I'm afraid. One little push . . ." He shook his head, looking off across the gleaming sea. "In a world as beautiful as this one, how can people mess up their lives like that?"

"The more you get . . ."

"I suppose so. But a man like Wallace Reid—I mean, how many men can ever hope to have all he's got? Fame, money, importance, love—he's got it all."

"He's also human."

"Meaning you pass no judgments, Bill?"

"I try," I said. "If I were in his place, I might do worse."

Jameson studied me for a minute, cupping his hands to get his bruyère pipe lighted in the sea breeze. "Then why are you so set on interfering—saving him from himself?"

"I told you before. Because he isn't the only one caught in that same damned trap."

"Meaning Mabel, of course? I didn't realize you were all that serious about her." I didn't answer, and after a moment he frowned, not looking at me, and said: "If you bust this thing wide open, the way you plan to do, Hollywood is going to take a hell of a shellacking. The newspapers will have a field day."

"Hearst will appreciate the rise in his circulation."

Jameson gave me a long hard look before he laughed. "Damned if I understand you, Bill." He shook his head, climbed out of the deck chair, and left me alone.

The sun was warm, and the deckhouse sheltered me from the

coolness of the ocean breeze. I dozed off. Something awakened me, a chill coolness. The shadow of someone across my face. I opened my eyes, but there was no one there. The deck was empty.

We pulled into Ensenada Bay just after noon. There were a few other boats, two or three smaller yachts, and some fishing boats, bobbing all together on the sparkling water. The town of Ensenada was smaller and dirtier than in my time, just adobe shacks and a couple of more imposing frame structures. No big hotels or fancy motels, no swank downtown shops and theaters. Just a tiny, sleepy, undisturbed Mexican fishing port.

We went ashore in the *Oneida*'s speedy launch, Mabel sitting beside me in the stern sheets, holding my hand. Betty Blayne was forward, with her mother, in the little cabin. Wallace Reid and his wife had stayed abroad ship. Jack Barrymore and Doc Jameson joined us aft. Marion Davies sat in the forward cockpit with Hearst.

We split up, once ashore, but Marion soon came after Mabel. Hearst, it seemed, had to return to the yacht—an emergency at one of his newspaper offices. They headed away, hand in hand, looking for shops to raid. Betty Blayne and Mama Denker had vanished, too. Which left Barrymore, Jameson, and Taylor to their own devices. Barrymore looked around conspiratorially.

"Shall we see what we can find, gentlemen?" And, without waiting for a reply, he set off. Barrymore had been here before.

Ensenada was a grubby mudhole set in one of the most beautiful natural settings in the world. There is no more scenically perfect harbor anywhere. The surrounding hills would someday be crowded with fine houses, but were now limited to a few shacks that seemed to have been built of driftwood and debris, and herds of scrawny goats. A cluster of shacks stood to one side at the water's edge. The pitiful hovels were worse than any *barrios bajos* of my own time; naked children begged for coins, their huge dark eyes staring hungrily. Small, dark girls— *putas* little more than children, themselves—stood silently in their stalls like sullen cattle, not even bothering to smile. One jerked her dirty blouse down to expose her small, round, brown-tipped breasts, and leered at me.

"Hey, meester—you want to fock young girl, heh?"

Jameson grinned at me. "Take her up on it, Bill!"

"Sorry—I never indulge in tortillas in the daytime," Taylor returned. Jameson laughed.

"A bit of spicy food never hurt anyone," Barrymore said, smacking his lips. "I'll catch up with you gringo bastards later."

He walked up to the girl in the stall and said something to her in Spanish. She stared at him, then giggled. She was about thirteen years old. Barrymore took her arm and they went into the stall. I heard the girl squealing laughter as we walked on.

Jameson led the way back toward the main settlement. A somewhat more imposing adobe building was set back from the dusty street. Jameson had evidently been there before, because he walked around to the rear of it. There was a tiled patio—and gambling tables. Considering the early hour, the place had quite a bit of action. Jameson headed for the crap table. I wandered around, tried a hand or two of blackjack, won three dollars, lost it—and ten more on top of it. At the crap table, Jameson was in command of the dice. He had dumped the contents of his wallet on the green beige cloth. He was an all-out gambler and followed no system as far as I could tell, just bet heavily, win or lose. He lost steadily, but it didn't seem to bother him. Losing that much dough would have bothered me. His medical practice must be highly profitable. Since he had settled in for the afternoon at the gaming table, I left, returning to the street.

I saw Marion Davies, by herself, at the far end of the pier. The *Oneida*'s launch was moving across the harbor toward the yacht. A tiny Mexican boy was with Marion, and she was holding his grubby little hand. They were both laughing. I paused to watch her for a moment. She was blond, slim, beautiful—and unhappy. I joined them. Her huge blue eyes smiled at me.

"No legal booze, no gambling—no Mexican girls, Bill?"

"Too early, too poor—and too tired, in that order," I replied.

She laughed merrily. She patted the little boy on the head and gave him a five-dollar gold piece, which he seized in dirty fingers before scampering off down the pier. Marion watched him go, her expression sad.

"What happened to Mabel?"

She gave me a sudden look. "She was tired—she's gone back aboard with most of our shopping for the party tonight." Marion knew. I could tell.

"I'm surprised to see you all by yourself, Marion."

"Oh, I'm let out of my cage now and then. W.R.'s on the boat—working on dispatches to his papers—or some other damn thing. . . . Did he proposition you about my next fillum?" Her stutter was not in evidence; the slight hesitation between words was attractive.

"Yes."

"Turn him down?"

"Afraid so."

The big blue eyes were filled with mischief. "Would you do it if I promised to go to bed with you, Bill?"

"If that's an offer, the answer's most definitely yes!"

She laughed. "You've made my whole day. Now, do you want me to get you off the hook?"

"I'd like to do your picture, Marion, believe me. But the new Paramount deal is for three years, and I'd lose it. Lasky made that clear. I gathered there is a power struggle between him and W.R. over the Cosmopolitan productions."

"I know. W.R. is shopping around for another distributor. I think he's talked to Sam Goldwyn. . . ." She shook her curly blond head. "That's enough movie talk. Now come on—you haven't bought your costume yet. We'll charge it to W.R.!"

It was dark when we all met on the wharf, where the launch was waiting to take us back to the yacht. The strings of colored lights between the *Oneida*'s masts were lighted, and their reflection in the still waters of the bay made a festive picture. Betty Blayne and Mrs. Denker had crudely wrapped souvenirs in their arms. Jameson was morose and silent; I gathered he had dropped a bundle. Barrymore was happy, slightly tipsy, and smiling.

"The little bitch stole my wallet—and after all I did for her!" he boomed in his actor's voice. "Ah, lechery and larceny are soulmates after all, Horatio. . . ." Then, winking broadly: "It was worth it—I have done my good deed for the day. The child's education has not been neglected—and I daresay I added to her curriculum this day. . . ."

"If you don't mind, Mr. Barrymore!" Mrs. Denker protested.

"Ah, ah—jealousy rears it ugly head," He chortled through his nose. "Patience, my dear woman—I'll get around to you in due time."

Marion stifled her laughter. Mrs. Denker glowered at everyone, then hurried Betty Blayne aboard the launch and into the little cabin.

There was no sign of Mabel—or of Wally Reid and Dorothy Davenport—aboard the *Oneida.* I went to my stateroom alone. The bottle of scotch hadn't been touched, as far as I could tell, and that worried me more than if it had. I rested on the bunk for an hour, then got into the Mexican vaquero outfit Marion had picked out for me. I hoped Mabel would show up, but she didn't.

The main salon had been decorated in fiesta style, with colorful serapes on the walls and multicolored paper lanterns strung overhead, with a huge *piñata*, highly decorated, and with colored paper streamers dangling, suspended from the center of the ceiling. Even the stewards had been got up in Mexican garb. Mabel waved to me as I entered; she was dancing with the Valentino-type, working out some intricate steps. At the little bar, I took tequila, a quartered lime, and salt, Mexican fashion, and downed it, South-of-the-Border style, letting the pleasant glow seep through me. Marion, wearing a skin-tight flamenco dress of white satin, with a frilled bottom, applauded my stylish gestures with the lime and salt, and imitated them—only to choke on the fiery tequila. Barrymore, in a perfect-fitting matador's ornate costume, pounded her on the back. She recovered and gave me a *muy doloroso* accusing look.

Mabel pranced out onto the little polished dance floor in front of the small mariachi band brought aboard just for tonight. She was wearing a black silk Spanish dancer's dress, high-heeled red slippers, a black lace mantilla flowing from a silver comb, and as the band played Mexican rhythms, she danced. She was light and graceful, and moved as deftly as the professional she was. Then she coaxed a smiling Wallace Reid onto the floor, and they danced, Reid, in his silver-laced grandee's outfit, giving an exaggerated, very funny imitation of Valentino's teeth-gnashing and head-tossing performances.

Only Barrymore worked at boozing, but the evening grew gayer, and the liquor seemed to have little effect upon him. Mrs. Denker had been picked out for his attentions. He seemed to enjoy her half-angry reaction when he felt her abundant rear end. But, oddly enough, the old harpy didn't react as strongly as I would have expected, even though he got progressively bolder. At one point he pinned her in a corner, and was feeling her up and kissing her sweaty red neck—and she wasn't resisting his advances at all. We're all human, they say, but in Mrs. Denker's case, I'd had my doubts. . . . Betty Blayne was staring at her mother, and took advantage of her preoccupation to join me at the bar.

"Would you believe it?" she asked, watching Barrymore whispering in her mother's ear, while squeezing one large breast with a busy hand. Mrs. Denker was flushed and flustered—but not a damned bit unhappy!

"Maybe I've used the wrong approach with your mother," Taylor said thoughtfully.

Betty Blayne giggled, and her mother's attention being diverted, snatched up a cocktail and drained it, then made away with a second. She giggled again, looking up into my face.

"If Jack keeps the old bitch busy tonight, maybe I can sneak away for a little while. . . . Would you like that?"

"I would indeed—but even the fabled Barrymore stamina has its limits—and after this afternoon ashore. . . ."

"I don't know." Betty Blayne's eyes were bright. "At least she wouldn't steal his wallet—and she might even add to *his* curriculum!"

The notion made us both laugh, and Mabel drifted past with her Latino dancing partner. "You two seem to be having fun—let us in on it, huh?"

Hearst didn't show up until just before dinner. He was wearing a ridiculous toreador costume, all spangles and brightly colored silk, and seemed to enjoy his awkward playacting of a bullfighter to Mabel's dashing—and shapely—bull. She pawed the floor, then charged him and his absurdly tiny red cape. He entered into the game enthusiastically, and when he spun lumberingly aside and his feet went out from under him on the slick dance floor, landing him on his massive butt, he laughed the hardest of anyone. Marion, laughing too, helped him to his feet.

"And now for the main event of the evening," she sang out, when she was the center of attention, her stammer was completely gone. She raised a gaily decorated *bastón* in her hand. It was time for the goodies, and everyone looked excited and pleased. Wallace Reid was blindfolded first, and Marion swung the fancy *piñata* away from him. He struck out, trying to hit it, but missed the target entirely and whomped the Valentino-type dude a good one alongside his ear. Everyone screamed with laughter except the dude.

Others took their turn, with no hits. Then Hearst was blindfolded. Marion spun him around and started the *piñata* swinging wildly. But W.R. balanced, light on his feet, timed it almost as well as if he could see, and slammed the paper-covered clay *olla* hard. It shattered to the force of the blow, and handsomely gift-wrapped packages cascaded to the floor. Everyone scampered for them, squealing and laughing, including Marion, who seemed to enjoy it most of all. Hearst tugged off the blindfold, grinning broadly, enjoying his moment of triumph.

The gifts were expensive, and greeted with oohs and ahs as they were opened. For the women, it was jewelry. For Mabel and Betty Blayne, identical diamond-studded heart-shaped lockets—a subtle joke on Marion's part, no doubt. An elaborate broach for Mrs. Denker, and fancy gold wristwatches for Wally Reid and me. Barrymore received a solid-gold cigarette case with his perfect profile engraved on it. Jameson got an expensive oral thermometer in a solid gold pocket case. Gold, too, were the Tiffany-made mesh purses, vanity cases, and cigarette lighters for the four young "extras."

It was nice to be rich in 1922.

Dinner was Mexican food, spicy, rich, and hot.

Afterward Marion and W.R. led the way into the main salon, where the decorations had been cleared away and a movie screen lowered, facing a group of comfortable chairs. The sheik who had played the piano seated himself at a small, theater-type organ console which slid from the paneled wall. The panels above it swung open, revealing an array of pipes of various lengths. The

Oneida had all the comforts of home, if your home happened to be a rich man's mansion. Everybody was seated, and the lights dimmed. Barrymore had squeezed in between Betty Blayne and her mother, and I heard Betty giggle. Barrymore played no favorites. The organ struck up a chord, and a picture flickered into life on the screen. Beside me, Mabel took my hand and held it tightly.

The movie was—what else?—a Cosmopolitan Production, starring Miss Marion Davies, *Buried Treasure*, adapted for the screen, and directed by George D. Baker, from *On the Borderland* by Frederick Britten Austin, with a cast featuring Norman Kerry, Anders Randolf, Edith Shayne, Earl Schenk, and John Charles. Just as the picture began, faintly above the throb of the organ, I heard the ship's bell dinging, and felt the vibration of the engines through the deck. We were under way again. Then I forgot everything but the film.

It was a fantasy. In the prologue, the soul of the heroine, Pauline Vandermuellin, was shown drifting through Eternity and being reincarnated in different bodies in different times. It shook me a bit. The main story dealt with the beautiful Marion going into trances and revealing forgotten knowledge. Her father shipped her off on a Caribbean cruise to get over a romance with handsomely mustached Norman Kerry, whom I remembered seeing in the Lon Chaney silent version of *Phantom of the Opera*, playing a society doctor. He reminded me of Jameson. Pauline went into a dream-trance and remembered a great treasure buried during some past incarnation. Her father, the greedy type, wanted it, but she sent him off on a wild-goose chase and led the heroic Kerry to the loot. Papa, the dog, was willing to accept the now fabulously rich young doctor as his son-in-law. Finis.

Everyone applauded. Marion took a little bow.

By the time the movie had ended, the *Oneida* was pitching a bit fore and aft. Hearst went out, then came back to announce that we were in for a bit of a storm. The *Oneida* would attempt to skirt the edge of it, which would delay our arrival back in Santa Monica by a few hours. Nobody objected. The screech of the wind grew louder, followed by a mutter of rain, coming down in torrents. The pitching of the yacht kept up, growing worse.

The party broke up soon after that, none of them being great seamen, it seemed. Mabel gripped my arm. "Let's go out on deck?" It suited me fine, for it was the first chance in hours that I'd had to really be alone with her. It was a struggle to hold the door open for her, for the wind almost slammed it out of my grasp. On deck, we were instantly deluged with rain. In the meager light from the deckhouse windows, Mabel's face was ecstatic, lifted to the stormy skies. I put my arm around her, to steady her, and she kissed me hard. Jameson broke it up, coming out on deck, looking for us.

"The captain says we'd all better get below decks—it's going to get pretty rough!"

Mabel kissed me again, then hurried inside. We followed her, the door slamming shut hard behind us before I could catch it. Mabel went on ahead. I passed on Jameson's offer of a nightcap, opting for my bunk. It had been another long day. I undressed, checked the bottle of scotch, which again hadn't been disturbed, and climbed into the bunk. I snapped off the light and relaxed. For an instant.

There was something in the bunk with me. Something that moved, crawling up my side, onto my chest.

24

The cabin was pitch dark. Things rattled and banged as the yacht jounced through the heavy waves. Rain clattered against the closed porthole glass, and wind howled faintly beyond the mahogany hull. And that damned thing crawled slowly to the center of my chest and stopped. I could feel it through the thin silk of my pajamas. A scratchy feeling as it moved. I lay stiff as a board, sweating profusely, my heart pounding heavily. Then I took a deep, slow breath and forced myself to think.

It was an insect. What, I couldn't tell—but awfully god-damned big! And I had the sinking conviction that it wasn't there by accident. Which made me only too damned sure that it was deadly, intended to finish the job for whoever was after Taylor.

Anger was my reaction. The dirty son of a bitch. Doctored scotch was bad enough, but this!

I tensed up, then forced myself to ease back, as the thing on my chest moved. Then I twisted, threw back the covers, and struck with my open hand, knocking the thing away from me, off the bunk. With a badly shaking hand I reached up and snapped on the bunk light. I saw the thing immediately, just righting itself on the rug. It was a pale, almost transparent brown—a four-inch-long scorpion, its stinger raised high, lashing angrily. I watched it for a moment, as it remained still. Then it started crawling toward the bunk—and I drew back. It took all my nerve to reach down and grab a shoe. I missed the first blow, and the deadly little bastard drew back, stinger ready to strike, darting forward over its back. The next blow did the job. The crunch was audible and gave me a feeling of satisfaction.

I was wet with sweat and shaking all over as I tore the bunk apart to make sure there was only one. I searched every piece of bedding, the mattress, and the floor. There was just the one—and it would have been enough, if my—Taylor's—luck hadn't held. If the damned thing hadn't crawled on me before I'd dropped off asleep, I would probably have rolled on it during the night—and Mexican scorpions were killers. I knew. I'd once covered a case dealing with the death of an airline stewardess who had brought one back from Mexico in her luggage.

I used a cardboard from a shirt to scoop up the remains. I placed it on top of the desk. Then the thought hit me. This was payoff time. Whoever had placed that damned bug in my bed would want to know if it had done it's work. So . . . I opened the desk drawer, pulled out the bottle of scotch. I opened it and carried it into the bathroom. I flushed a good jolt down the john, poured a little more into a glass. I left the bottle and glass on the desk. It told the whole story—the mashed scorpion, the opened bottle, and used glass. Then I sprawled across the bunk after turning out the light. I burrowed in, making myself as comfortable as possible, and then forced myself to relax, to portray the image of a man out cold, body totally lax.

The storm raged, growing worse. The yacht began to yaw as well as pitch, shuddering as it came through each trough. It was a hell of a night for a murder. And that was what was on my mind.

The man behind the attempts on Taylor's life played it safe, waiting two hours before making his move. The storm had grown steadily worse. I didn't hear him until the lock clicked and light from the corridor spilled into the cabin. He was just a figure, silhouetted for an instant, then he was inside the cabin. A thin flashlight beam lanced across me, but I didn't move a muscle. The flashlight, I saw through narrowed lids, went to the desk. I heard a man's soft, chuckling laugh. Then the light switch snapped, flooding the cabin.

Dr. Jameson stood there, looking down at me.

"Sorry about this, Bill," he said, softly. "I always liked you—but you're such a snoopy son of a bitch!"

The bastard! You're not surprised—you knew it was him!

It figured. "Mad dog"—1922 slang for MD.

Dr. Jameson came across the room, sniffed the whiskey glass, and frowned. He studied the remains of the scorpion for a moment, then picked up the shirt cardboard and carried it into the bathroom. I heard the commode flush. He had disposed of the crushed insect. He dumped the cardboard into the wastebasket beside the desk, then studied me again. He crossed to the bunk, grabbed me under the arms, and dragged me roughly to the floor. Despite the sudden pain in my shoulder, I continued to play dead. Give the son of a bitch enough rope and I'd hang him! He snapped off the light, opened the corridor door, and checked beyond it, then came back for me. He was strong enough to lift me, get me over one shoulder. He staggered as the yacht reeled through the rough seas, but balanced well enough to prove he was a pretty good seaman. He carried me up the stairs, moving carefully, making no noise, not that it would have been heard above the noise of the raging storm.

On deck it was mean as hell. The wind ripped at us, tore at our clothes, and he staggered, almost fell, caroming me against the deckhouse. Luckily it was my good shoulder that hit the wall. His intent was plain. He started for the rail, and if I didn't want a long, long soak in the briny sea, it was time to do something about it. I did. I grapped an upright post and jerked. It took him off balance and he dropped me. I was on my feet before he was. He stared at me, his face a pale blob in the light from a cabin porthole.

"You were faking, you son of a bitch!" he said.

"That's right, Doc. It paid off, too. I knew it was you, but I couldn't prove it. Now I won't have to."

"Now you know," he said, smiling tightly. He had no weapon I could see, but he was strong as a bull. Stronger than Taylor by far. "The stakes are too high, Bill, for me to let you put an end to the game."

"You've got yourself a good thing going, haven't you, Doc? Quite a setup. The kindly studio doctor—being the good samaritan—giving out his pills and shots so obligingly. . . ."

"Why did it matter so much to you? If you wanted a cut I'd have given it to you."

"No way, Doc. I told you that."

"You told me. Sands told me, too. If you wouldn't play ball with him, there was no way I could get to you."

"Except murder. Those goons worked for you."

"That's right—and something else I owe you for, Bill. You've played hell with my organization, I don't mind saying."

"That trolley-car 'accident'—you arranged that, too, even knowing Mabel was with me?"

"Why not?" His tone and face were coldly callous. "She's just another snowbird, too far gone to be worth bothering about. . . ."

"How did you know we were up on Mount Lowe?"

"Bribed Davis to phone me where you went. I sent Corbo up to take care of the matter for me, but you were lucky."

"You rigged the big studio lights to fall, too—then yelled at me, hoping I'd do just what I did—stop and turn around."

"If Barrymore hadn't interfered, it would have worked. But it doesn't matter much, now, Bill. It's all over. For you."

He held there, poised, then lunged suddenly, his powerful hands grabbing for me. I twisted, bent, and kicked. It caught him too high, in the upper chest, to do any real damage. He went back, surprised, balanced like a cat, then came in low. He seized me, his fingers biting into my injured shoulder, almost wrenching it from the socket. We swayed there for an instant, and I realized just how strong the bastard really was. He spun me around effortlessly, my back to the railing, and shoved. I almost went over. My feet left the deck, then the yacht keeled over in the opposite direction and we went down, hitting the deck. I knew better than to give him time to get set. I came up fast and moved in. He ducked low, but I'd timed it right. My karate chop caught him hard. He spun around and I brought the hard edge of my hand across his windpipe. It was a killing blow, and meant to be. He jerked back, his face twisting, both hands reaching for his crushed throat—then I bent and kicked with all the strength in my legs. He flew backward with the downward lurch of the yacht, clearing the railing and vanishing into the raging waters beyond.

Breathing hard, cold, wet, and sick, I held there. It took minutes to recover. There had been no outcry, no yelling. Not that it would have been heard, anyway. The wind was screaming too loudly for that. After a while I went below. I nearly fell down the stairs, my legs were so weak. Back in my cabin, I closed the door and locked it. I took off my wet pajamas, tossed them over a chair. The doped scotch bottle still stood on the desk. I picked it up, crossed to the bunk, opened the porthole over it, tossed out the bottle, then let the sea water spray in over the bunk, dousing the blankets. I swung the porthole closed, then punched the bell for the steward. It took a little time before a sleepy-eyed man showed up.

"Is there another cabin available?" I asked. "The damned porthole came unfastened and I nearly drowned."

He nodded sympathetically and led the way down the corridor to a smaller, empty cabin. Alone once more, reaction set in. I shook in the bunk for an hour before I finally warmed up.

It was over. Almost. But I had all the pieces sorted out, now, I was sure of it. I knew who would be calling on William Desmond Taylor next Wednesday night.

And I'd be ready.

25

Dr. Jameson wasn't discovered missing until late the next morning. The storm had driven the *Oneida* far off course, and the weather was still rough on the fringes of the front. The yacht was searched; Wallace Reid said that Jameson was probably playing some sort of trick, and the others seemed to go along with the idea. Realization that he was gone, really gone, came slowly, and hard. The storm had already put a damper on the high spirits, and this wiped them out. Marion remained in her quarters and Hearst stayed with her. Mrs. Denker followed Marion's example, keeping Betty Blayne with her. Barrymore seemed withdrawn, somehow, and kept close beside the little bar in the main salon.

Mabel was subdued, hollow-eyed, and stood by the railing with me, silently watching the sea. We spoke very little, but I welcomed just having her near me.

We docked in Santa Monica Tuesday morning, and it was almost noon when the Rolls dropped me off on Alvarado Street. We had gone to Mabel Normand's apartment first, and Betty Blayne managed to give me a pinch without her mother noticing. Otherwise very little was said. To her mother's surprise and frustrated annoyance, I gave Betty a kiss when I climbed out, but her only reaction was a frightened, worried glance toward her mother.

Wallace and Dorothy Reid had gone with John Barrymore in another car. Our leavetaking had been brief aboard the yacht. Hearst had muttered something about calling me later.

Peavey greeted me at the door with a wide grin, his gold teeth shining. I was to call Mistuh Lasky, soon as I got in. I did. He wasn't at the studio and his secretary didn't know where he was. We all have secrets. He would return my call.

On the long drive up from Santa Monica I'd done a lot of thinking and come to a lot of conclusions. There was one more important thing I had to do.

Taylor! Those guns in your bedroom—are they in firing condition?

Whom are you going to shoot?

Nobody, I hope. Now, answer me!

Yes, I suppose they are. Dirty, though. My favorite came up missing some time ago. Beautiful Webley.

Sands probably hocked it.

One of the keys on the chain unlocked the gun cabinet in Taylor's bedroom. There were two handguns, both old—a badly corroded Luger, probably a World War I souvenir, and a Colt's Pocket Model Revolver. The barrel of the Colt was splotched with reddish rust, but it was loaded. The barrel was dusty but clean; at least it wouldn't blow apart in my hand if I had to fire— which I hoped wouldn't happen. I took it downstairs to the study and placed it behind some books on a shelf. It would be there when I needed it.

I buzzed Howard Fellows on the little black phone-intercom. The Pierce-Arrow had been repaired and was waiting for me in the garage, all ready to go. The head hadn't been cracked after all. It had overheated because of a faulty radiator hose. It started easily, and handled as well as ever, as I drove down to Taylor's bank. In the bank lobby I picked up a pen and waited for Taylor to take over and write a check out to Cash for $2,500. I was recognized at the teller's window, and there was no trouble cashing it. It didn't leave much in Taylor's account, I remembered, from reading the files on the case. On impulse I asked for five twenty-dollar gold pieces, and dropped them into my pocket. The $2,400 I placed in Taylor's wallet. The bank was closing when I left.

On the way back to Alvarado Street I let myself relax a bit. If I was right—and I was certain that I was—I had it made. Nobody—especially not Taylor—would be bumped off tomorrow night. *What if you're wrong?* There was both fear and amusement in Taylor's thought. I pushed them both away.

I'm not—with no thanks to you. If you'd opened up, it would have been a hell of a lot easier.

You've had a chance to prove you're really a detective.

Thanks a lot.

I parked the Pierce-Arrow roadster in the garage, and before I got out I dropped the five twenty-dollar gold pieces into a slot in the leather-upholstered door panel. They slid snugly out of sight. They'd be there when I wanted them.

I ate dinner alone. Betty Blayne had called again while I was gone. It was most urgent that she speak to me. I rang her home number and the studio; got no answer at the first, and she wasn't at the second. Mabel Normand's maid answered her phone. Miss Normand had gone out. She had left word for me—she would drop by tomorrow evening to pick up the book she had asked me to read. It gave me a numb feeling. The records of the Taylor murder case indicated that Mabel Normand had been the last person except for his killer to see him alive. He had visited with her, had cocktails, then walked her back to her car, as her chauffeur, Davis, had attested. Then Taylor had returned to the bungalow apartment—and sudden, violent death. . . .

That isn't the way it's going to be, I promised myself and Taylor. No way!

I fixed myself a drink; straight gin over ice. It was pre-World War I Gordons, and had a label almost identical to that used in my own time except for a sticker that read "For Medicinal Use Only." There was a blurb, too, about the 18th Amendment, the Volstead Act, but my usual curiosity about such things didn't assert itself this time. To make matters worse, the gin didn't have much effect, medicinal or otherwise. So I prescribed myself a refill. I don't remember what I ate for supper, and I retired early. I was still shaken by what had happened on the yacht. Still, it had been worth it. I had decided that two different people had been determined to kill Taylor. Jameson was one, and I'd stymie the other tomorrow night. I felt confident. I had the answers now. But, somehow, the coldness in the pit of my stomach remained.

I undressed, got into my pajamas—white silk—and robe. I picked up the book that Mabel had asked me to buy for her. It had lain, unread, in my suitcase over the weekend. I skimmed through it. I'd never read an Ethel M. Dell novel before. It was slick and trite—even, I thought, by 1922 standards. *It will make a splendid picture!* Taylor disagreed with me. Personally, I wouldn't have watched it on TV for free, but Taylor knew his day and age better than I did.

If you are right—tomorrow evening—what happens then?

I don't know.

It was the thought I had been avoiding all day. But there was no way of escaping from it.

Will you—I mean—

Keep on being you? I think so. I'm not sure. Everything has pointed to that one moment in time—and when it occurs . . . I just don't know.

Perhaps things will—go back—to the way they were. . . .

I thought about it. The 1970s—my own life, what there was left of it. I'd probably eventually get married again. Maybe even have a couple of kids. But forty-five is pretty late to make a new beginning. And a retired cop doesn't drag down much of a pension, not with inflation the way it was, so I'd probably have to find something else to do. I don't know what. Something. I was aware of a vague yearning for something more than just that, but I couldn't put a name to it. One thing was for damned sure—I wouldn't stagnate, just let myself drift through the years.

But—if you don't—go back?

Damn it, Taylor, I don't know! Just keep on the way we are, I suppose. Your life—we'd have to share it somehow.

No! I'd rather die! I mean it!

I felt him withdraw. Did I really want to go back to Ernie Carter's life? I couldn't be sure. I missed a lot of things. I doubted if I could ever completely adjust to 1922. In time, it would happen, I supposed. And nobody could say it was happening for William Desmond Taylor. He lived the good life. Most important of all, there was Mabel. And what would happen to her, in the next few years, whether Taylor lived or died. Damn, damn, *damn!*

I drank more gin, but it didn't help, just made my thoughts blurry. I got back into bed, tossed fitfully, but finally dropped off. It was no good. I woke up in a cold sweat, thinking about the scorpion, feeling it crawling on my chest again. I got up, went into the bathroom, and rummaged around in the cabinet. I found a little box of powders marked "Sleeping Draughts"—prescribed by Dr. Jameson. He owed me a good night's sleep, so I dumped one into a glass of water and drank it off.

I slept what was left of the night.

Wednesday. The day William Desmond Taylor would be murdered. February 1, 1922. Sometime between 7:30 and 8:00 P.M., in this bungalow court apartment at 404-B South Alvarado Street. By person or persons unknown. Person—known.

I felt good. The day was bright and sunny. I even ate part of the monstrous breakfast that Peavey had fixed.

"Yo' won't need me today, suh? It's my day off."

Right with the facts in the case. Peavey would return tomorrow morning and find Taylor's dead body sprawled in the study. One .38 caliber bullet, entering his left side at the back, six inches beneath his armpit, traversing his chest, and exiting from his neck just below the right ear. That was the autopsy report. The bullet holes in his vest and coat wouldn't match the wounds in the body, indicating that his arms had been raised above his head at the moment he had been shot. But, strangely, his body had been found quietly laid out on his back, his arms carefully folded across his chest, in an attitude of repose. . . .

To hell with the facts—I intended changing them. When Peavey came home tomorrow morning, I'd fix *him* breakfast, by God—grits and eggs and an inch-thick ham steak.

Still, it was hard to put out of my mind. I remembered that damned report on the Taylor case, now, almost word for word. Dead of a single gunshot wound, caliber .38. . . .

I took the Pierce-Arrow roadster out for a spin. I drove easily, through the streets and out the boulevard toward the ocean. When I got back it was past lunch, but I wasn't hungry. Even during the drive, Taylor had not made his presence felt. I didn't blame him much; time was too short, but waiting seemed an eternity, a paradox I didn't even want to think about. I parked the roadster in the garage. Fellows wasn't there. It was either his day off, too, or he'd just left early. It didn't matter which. I stood beside the Pierce-Arrow for a long time, touching it, thinking about it. Saying good-bye? I forced the thought away.

I'm not sure how I passed the hours. I walked through the apartment, lay down, but couldn't stay put. I tried reading. Nothing worked. Peavey was gone most of the afternoon, but I heard him come back. He would be getting dressed for his night out. He would serve Mabel Normand and William Desmond Taylor cocktails and leave them drinking them as he went his way.

Then, suddenly, it was getting dark. My platinum watch said six. Peavey had said he would put out cold cuts, and he was as good as his word. The funny thing was, I felt great. I always did when things were finally coming to a conclusion. No more waiting, no more worrying. And suddenly I knew I would have the rest of Taylor's life to live—and Mabel. We'd make it, somehow, anyway we could. But we would make it.

It was seven o'clock when Mabel came, and I was just completing my phone call to Margie Berger, about my— Taylor's—income tax return. Mabel came in, eating the last of a small, striped, paper bag of peanuts, leaving the floor of her Leach limousine littered with the shells, as usual for Davis to clean out. They would be found in the street, tomorrow, by the police, after Taylor's murder—unless I prevented it from happening.

Mabel kissed me as I hung up the phone. The kiss was warm and tasted of fresh roasted peanuts. Peavey brought in a cocktail shaker filled with gin and orange juice, poured out drinks. Mabel chattered brightly; she was up, high. The Ethel M. Dell book—had I liked it? Would it do for her next picture? I said it would indeed.

Then, too quickly, she said: "I've got to run! Thanks, Willie. I'll tell Sam Goldwyn you liked it, too."

I wanted to hold her, make her stay, but I forced a smile and accepted her kiss. I gave her the book she had come for. Peavey was just leaving for the night, and said goodnight before hurrying off. The bungalow apartment court was dark and empty. Mabel and I walked slowly through the center garden to Alvarado Street and her car. I saw a movement in the shadows, close against the bungalow. Right on time, I thought.

Davis opened the car door for her. She got in, then leaned out to kiss me good-bye. Our last kiss? I closed the door.

"See you tomorrow," I said, hoping I was right.

"I'm game, kiddo!"

"I want you remember one thing, Mabel. I love you. For real. For always. Believe me."

She stared at me from her huge, dark, luminous eyes, then smiled. "I love you, too, Willie," she said, and leaned out the car window to kiss me again.

Then I was standing alone at the curb, watching the big, boxy shape of the Leach pull away, then speed off into the darkness. I hesitated. I could change fate by turning and walking away, down Alvarado Street, forgetting Taylor's date with destiny. But that wouldn't really solve anything. I returned to the bungalow apartment.

I went inside and closed the door behind me.

He was standing in the study, one hand in the side pocket of his wrinkled, dirty coat, obviously holding a gun clenched in his trembling fist. His face was worn and haggard. He needed a fix, and he needed it now. One cheek twitched slightly as he faced me.

"You've torn it now, you son of a bitch!" Edward F. Sands said, his voice grating. "You've really packed it in for me, you have! Busted things up for fair, haven't you, croakin' Doc? I know you did it, you bastard!"

"That's right," I answered slowly, watching him. The weight of the gun in his pocket made his coat sag and twist on his thin body. His hand, gripping the butt, trembled violently.

"I begged you, damned if I didn't," Sands whined. "But you couldn't leave it be. Little you care what happens to me—*me!* Your own brother!"

I walked over to the bookcase and leaned against it. I'd figured that out, too. Sands was Dennis Deane-Tanner, who had duplicated his brother's disappearing act of fourteen years before. Taylor's reticence about Sands, volunteering nothing, and then Doc Jameson's oddly phrased remarks about Sands, even saying that Taylor wasn't his brother's keeper. He hadn't been quoting anything, just stating fact. Sands—Dennis Deane-Tanner—was a part of Jameson's organization—and the murderer of William Desmond Taylor.

"You're wrong, Dennis," I said, and smiled. "I thought about you." I slowly pulled my wallet from my coat pocket. He licked his slack, cracked lips. His whole body was shaking in uncontrollable spasms, and he bent a trifle forward, his left arm pressing against his gaunt belly, fighting the pains of withdrawal. "This will take care of you." I took out the sheaf of gold certificates and tossed them toward him. They fell against his chest, scattered, and dropped to the floor. He stared at me, then the money—and took his hand, empty, from his coat pocket before kneeling to pick them up.

I flipped a book from the shelf and picked up the old Colt's Pocket Model Revolver. Dennis Deane-Tanner—Sands—looked up. I lined the sights on his forehead. He stared, suddenly frightened.

"Don't, Billy! Don't!"

"Just a precaution, Dennis," I said. "Now hand me your gun—easy—that's it!" I took the little .32 and laid it on a table behind me. I felt relaxed, in control now.

"What about the money?" he asked.

"It's yours, Dennis," I said. "All yours. Take it and go." I paused. "If you ever come back I'll kill you—just as I killed Doc and the hoods who worked for him. I mean it, Dennis. I'll kill you—make no mistake about that."

He stared up at me, licked his cracked, dry lips again, then nodded. He grabbed up the money, crumpling the bills, and thrust it into his coat pocket. It would buy him what he needed most, a fix. Nothing else mattered to him.

"Did you understand what I said?"

"That you'll kill me?" He squinted at me, trying to smile.

"That's right," I said harshly. Then I stepped close, brought up the big front sight of the Colt's revolver, and raked it savagely across his face. It cut deep and jaggedly. Blood welled. He grabbed at his face, cowered back, and screamed with fright. "Be sure I mean it, Dennis. If I ever lay eyes on you again you're a dead man."

"Oh, God," he whimpered. He stared at me, his eyes wide, terrified. Then he backed for the door. I laid the revolver beside the little .32 on the table and followed him out. He stumbled on the steps of the porch, fell; then, still holding his cheek, blood seeping from between his fingers, he turned and ran, staggering, between the buildings, toward Maryland Avenue, and was gone. I heard the sound of his feet, fading away.

It was over. I'd won. I held there, breathing deeply, savoring being alive. I looked at my platinum pocket watch. It was 7:47. And it was over.

I went out to Alvarado Street and stood there for a moment before walking back. It was good. Being alive was good. Nineteen twenty-two was a real vintage year, and there would be more, many more.

One thing remained in my cop's mind. Nagging. Worrying. One little fact that didn't square with what I knew about the Taylor case. Sands' gun. Caliber .32. .32! But to hell with it! Who cared how it might have happened before? This time I'd won!

Taylor! Do you hear that? You're alive—*we're* alive! I've won, damn your secretive eyes!

I went back inside the bungalow. I needed a drink. I felt jubilant. Time to celebrate. I didn't get a chance to pour it. I walked into the study, and a strident voice behind me said, "Raise your hands, you slimy bastard!"

I complied, slowly. I half-turned. Mrs. Denker was standing there, holding Taylor's old .38 caliber revolver in one fat fist.

"This will teach you!" she screamed at me—and pulled the trigger. "You'll goddamned well never take her away from me!"

The bullet hit me like a sledgehammer. I felt it tearing through me, and then everything spun, shattered, and fell into aching, empty blackness.

26

I opened my eyes and stared up at the pale green of a hospital ceiling.

"Hiya, Ernie!" Jacobs said, grinning down at me.

I was back where I—Ernie Carter—belonged.

Taylor! Where the hell are you? Taylor?

No answer. There would never be one. I was back for good.

I had been in a coma for a week, I learned. It seemed longer than that. A lifetime. Someone else's lifetime.

That was two years ago. It took me a little while to pick up the pieces. And it's funny, but *now* seems like the dream, and 1922 the reality. It's fading. Someday everything will be back to normal, and in a way I'll be sorry. The medicos say that trauma from a head wound can affect you that way, and last a long time, making you feel disoriented, a stranger in a very strange land. They don't know just how strange, because I've never told anyone about Taylor—and 1922.

What happened to me that night? I was shot. I've still got the scar in the center of my forehead, and the mashed .22 slug they dug out. A half inch to either side, or if it had been a heavier caliber gun, and it would have been curtains for Ernie Carter. So

I've reason to be thankful that the bastard was only carrying a Saturday night special, and that his aim was only too good. While I *was* William Desmond Taylor, I'd had a lump and a bruise where my scar now is. That January night was exceptionally cold, both in my time and in 1922. There the similarities end.

"Traumatic schizophrenia" is, of course, a catchall phrase, meaning that an accident causes the mind to withdraw from reality and substitute an imaginary world. The headshrinkers have long lists of patients who have, with complete logic, built a totally unreal psychic world and actually lived in it—sometimes forever, never recovering. The causes—and cures—are unknown. That's the medical side of it.

Is there another possibility? I'm not sure, but time travel—or temporal dislocation—is not unknown. It's happened to a lot of people. The most famous instance, I suppose, is the two middle-aged ladies on vacation in France, early in this century, visiting the gardens at Versailles. Walking down a path, they experienced a chill, a bit of mist, and found themselves somehow deposited in an unfamiliar part of the gardens, where they saw people in odd clothing, and speaking a strangely accented French. Only later did it become clear to them what had happened, that they had somehow stepped backward in time. Their description of those gardens match antique maps and plans exactly—and a beautiful woman they saw they later identified from a portrait as Marie Antoinette. . . .

Pretty hard to believe, huh? Unless it happens to you.

What about the man who walked around his horses, in plain sight of his family, and vanished into thin air?

And the hundreds of people, every year, who simply disappear and are never heard from again? Of course most of them are murdered or choose to drop out of their own accord, but some aren't that easily explained away. Dig into it the way I have, these past two years and you'll find yourself getting doubts. Big ones.

So, for the record, I was in a coma in a hospital bed for a week, after being shot in the head by a two-bit hoodlum. While I was out of it, my mind made up a fantasy world and I lived in it. Nothing strange, all well within the bounds of normality, as any doctor will assure you.

But not to me. I *was* William Desmond Taylor, and I *did* live the last week of his life, doing what he did, seeing what he saw, meeting the people he met, experiencing another man's life for that brief, long ago time, I'm sure of it. I've spent too much time checking it out not to know that it really happened, just the way I've told it here. After all, I'm a cop, a pro. I've never taken a half-baked theory on trust in my life. Only facts impress me—and let me tell you, they all—every damned one of them!—checked out, just as I remember it happening.

And, if I had any doubts, there is a clincher.

There are little questions that go unanswered, of course. I've read everything ever written about the Taylor case, reread the official file and every newspaper account written at the time it happened. Unsolved, they always conclude. I know better. I know who shot William Desmond Taylor. Betty Blayne's psychotic mother, protecting her "baby"—and her own vested interest—by removing the threat of Taylor and Betty marrying. Simple, ordinary motivation, and not much of a puzzle, actually; just the glamour of the time and place and people dazzled the eyes of police and public alike.

Who laid out Bill Taylor so neatly on the floor of his bungalow? That isn't hard to figure. Betty Blayne had been trying frantically to reach me—him—to warn that her mother was on the rampage. She had found Taylor first, and carefully straightened him out—probably even kissed his dead lips in farewell.

Betty Blayne. A tiny, naked, twelve-year-old body . . .

Mama Denker? After shooting Taylor she took both guns— Taylor's .38 and the .32 Dennis Deane-Tanner had carried—and probably dumped them in a hole somewhere. She lived into her seventies, and kept her "baby" unmarried until she was dead. Betty Blayne? She died a year ago, age eighty. The scandal that linked her to William Desmond Taylor's murder wrecked her movie career for good. She left films and founded a cosmetics firm that made her rich. Mama Denker must have enjoyed the money. Yes, I saw Betty once, before she died . . .

I trumped up a phony story about an investigation and talked to her for a few minutes. She was thin, arthritic, and mean-mannered. There was nothing left of the tiny, beautiful, girl I had known as Taylor. Nothing at all. When I got back to my car, I sat there a long time. And, when she died, I went to her funeral. There were only a few people there, and I knew none of them. I've put flowers on her grave both last weeks of January since then.

Peavey enjoyed the limelight, from what I read in old newspaper and magazine accounts of the Taylor case. He worked his life through and died a few years ago in Bakersfield. Edward F. Sands—Dennis Deane-Tanner—was never found, never heard from again, despite a nationwide manhunt for him. Sergeant Dan Cahill, the cop, never marked the Taylor murder closed, but worked at it for twenty-five years. I hope he had the satisfaction of finally figuring it out.

Mabel Normand.

William Desmond Taylor's mysterious killing ruined her starring career. It was all downhill for her. She died in Monrovia, California, on February 23, 1930, from what is officially recorded as tuberculosis. Her casket was carried by Charlie Chaplin, D. W. Griffith, Douglas Fairbanks, and Fatty Arbuckle. And Mary Pickford, Marion Davies, and Norma Talmadge walked beside it.

I've taken flowers to her grave, and stood there, and remembered her. And in every bunch of flowers I've placed a sprig of fresh mint.

There's one more thing. I checked the records and traced Taylor's yellow Pierce-Arrow roadster. It passed through several hands over the years, and was finally registered for the last time in Barstow. I found the place, a farm, now run-down. The farmer had removed the elegant boat-tailed body and replaced it with a homemade truckbed. When the car became too dilapidated to use, he put it on timbers and used the rear wheels with a belt to run a power-tool workshop. It hadn't been used in years, when I found it. And the old farmer, long dead, had been the saving type; he had stored the original body in the rafters of his barn. I bought the pieces for two hundred dollars.

Restoring the Pierce-Arrow roadster has taken most of my money, and much of my spare time, but it's exactly the way it was over fifty years ago, and you should see the eyes of people when I pass them in it. And, in restoring the upholstery, I removed the cracked, rotten old leather—and, here's the clincher—I found five bright, shining twenty-dollar gold pieces tucked inside, still there, waiting for me. Not William Desmond Taylor—*me*.

Where the bungalow courts on Alvarado Street stood, there is a shopping center, and it's already showing its years. The world of 1922 has vanished. Very little of it remains. Sometimes I pass an old building dating back half a century, and remember seeing it, back then. But not often.

All the streetcars are long gone. Even the tracks have been removed or paved over. The Big Red Cars of Pacific Electric are just memories, too. And Mount Lowe . . .

I drove up into the Pasadena foothills and found the old right-of-way. The tracks are gone. I walked up. The Alpine Inn burned many years ago—just rubble remains, forlorn and forgotten. I stood there, looking down on the brownish murk of smog over the L.A. Basin, and let my mind go back to that long ago night with Mabel Normand.

Laughter, peanut shells, and the taste of fresh mint.

Mabel!

It was dark when I walked back down the old trackway, to where I'd left the Pierce-Arrow, and my little miniature pinscher Kirby, scampered along at my heels, tired from the long, steep hike. It was cold, and the ocean was dumping mist inland. It closed around us, muffling my footsteps. Then Kirby stopped and turned to look back up the way we had just come. He perked his ears and whined a trifle, then barked. I picked him up and held him in my arms, and then I heard it, too. The faraway clanging of the old trolley-car bell, through the mists of time. I stood there, looking back up Mount Lowe, waiting for the yellowish shine of the old headlamp.

But the clanging faded, and the trolley car never came.

The dream was ended.